the SAFELIGHT series
volume 2
finding Reese.

Also by
IMY SANTIAGO

the SAFELIGHT series
volume 1
chasing Reese.

finding Reese.

a SAFELIGHT novel vol.2

IMY SANTIAGO

▲

RISC BOOKS, NEW YORK

Published by RISC BOOKS.

finding Reese. a SAFELIGHT novel vol.2

Editing by Kimberly Ito, Sakura Editing
Cover design by Marisa Shor, CoverMe, Darling, www.covermedarling.com
Cover image purchased at Shutterstock Royalty Free Stock Photography, #89275525
Formatting by Imy Santiago

PUBLISHING HISTORY
RISC BOOKS eBook Edition / May 2015 - RISC BOOKS Paperback First Edition / May 2015

ISBN-13: 978-0-9863580-5-0

Adult Fiction–Contemporary Romance

MATURE CONTENT WARNING:
This novel contains graphic language and sexually explicit content intended for individuals over the age of eighteen, and includes subject matter such as *Alcoholism, Depression, Anxiety and Panic Disorder*, and *Post-traumatic Stress Disorder*. Your discretion is advised.

For my Mom.

She taught me years beyond her death the meaning of sacrifice, and love. Sometimes you have to give up what you love the most, even if it breaks your heart. Thank you, Mom, for your loving sacrifice.

"I wouldn't even call snowboarding a sport. For me it's just a way of life. It's a chance to finally shut your brain off, and live within the moment. And for as long as I am able, **I will ride until the day I die."**

-Travis Rice, That's It, That's All

PROLOGUE

Jackson

The deafening sounds of the helicopter's rotors come to a stop once it lands on top of the Purcell Mountains. Kicking Horse to be exact. Grabbing my board and backpack from the cargo bins, I trek away from the helicopter. Chris and Rem are riding with me today. These guys are not only my buddies, they're also members of my snowboarding team. In the cockpit, the pilot lifts his thumb and I follow suit, letting him know we are good to go. The rotors roar back to life and the three of us crouch, shielding our faces from the snow that spirals as the chopper takes off.

God, I love the Canadian terrain. While Wyoming has some cool spots to snowboard, it's got nothing on British Columbia. The harsh weather conditions and roughness of the terrain, not to mention the threat of danger, beg me to shred the lines of this gorgeous mountain.

As the helicopter flies away, I survey the wintry landscape. Adjusting my polarized goggles, I look at the horizon, admiring the perfect azure sky. The sun glares blindingly against the icy mountaintops, and the howling wind lifts the powdery snow and blows it in all directions. Resting my gloved hands on my waist, I take in the incredible view. Kicking Horse has an elevation of 8,033 feet, and little old me is standing right on top of it. That's fucking awesome if you ask me.

The boys arranged this little expedition as a birthday present, and after spending a great weekend with my family in Casper, an outing like this is the icing on my cake. Fresh back from the press tour and winning first place at the world snowboarding championships in Port de Soleil, France my life is pretty darn good.

The walkie-talkie strapped to my chest chirps as home base makes contact. "How's it looking up there, Jax?" Robert asks, his voice cracking over the radio.

Robert Karlsson, the *Swedish Son* as he's known by folks in the industry, is a former Olympic champion and my coach. He was my childhood instructor when Dad enrolled me in snowboarding lessons when I was seven years old. I can thank Rob for my career in snowboarding. He saw something different in me, and from day one he believed in my potential. While we've struggled with my alcoholism, he's never turned his back on me. It saddens me that Rob is inching towards retirement. He won't be able to follow me around the world like he used to. I'm treasuring whatever time we have left together as athlete and coach.

"Oh, if you could see the view right now, Rob! It can't get any better than this."

"The weather conditions are passable, Jax, but I'm warning you, the snow is dry, and this mountain hasn't seen major ice movement for quite some time. There's an avalanche watch nearby, but the target team thinks if you stay away from the east side, it should be a decent ride. Just be careful with crevasses. We need you back in one piece, okay?" Rob cautions.

"Roger that," I reply nodding, eager to start our run. "I want to point out the visibility is low, and the wind is blowing something fierce. Base, let's get this party started. See you on the other side."

Strapping the radio back on my chest, I gather the guys for a safety brief.

"Did you guys hear the radio call?" I ask Chris and Rem. They nod, and await instructions. "Okay. Here's the plan. We need to go down in intervals just in case the ice patch is as loose as Base thinks it is. Rem, you go first and I'll go mid. Chris, stay close behind me and be careful. Got it, guys?"

Chris and Rem nod, then strap their boots onto their boards, and I follow. As I lock the last strap over the point of my boot, the winds shift direction, and then come to a complete stop. I feel a chill rising from the base of my spine, and working its way up to my scalp. There's an eerie feeling unfolding in my gut as I hear the howling wind in the distance.

The confidence I had this morning dissipates. A part of me wants to call Base and abort this run. I can't quite pinpoint what it is, but the bad feeling in my gut increases tenfold. It took a lot of convincing on my part to get the team to sign off on this run, especially Rob, so I can't pussy out. Let's just hope my lucky streak continues, and I'll be shaking off this bad feeling once we reach the bottom of Kicking Horse.

In the distance, I hear the rotors of the helicopter and I know that's Gabe, my videographer, ready to document the journey down. Looking to the guys, I call, "All right, guys, it's now or never. Let's have fun, and remember to stay away from the east side of the slope if possible. Let's do this."

Rem nods, and jumps down the steep ledge of the mountain. Watching him trek down unharmed builds my self-confidence. Seconds later, I hear Chris' characteristic whooping as he follows close behind.

It's such a peaceful feeling, trekking down the mountain hearing the sounds of your board scraping against the snow, the light spray of powder landing all over your goggles and going up your nose. These are the little things that mean so much to me when I'm riding. I enjoy the silence as I become one with nature. It fills my soul with feelings I can't even begin to describe.

But there's something off about this line in particular. There's an eerie feeling I simply can't shake off. Maybe I'm just over-thinking things, or Rob's resistance this morning somehow shook all of my confidence away, but a part of me feels this could be it.

A loud crack on the side of the mountain straightens my spine, followed by a shrill scream from Chris. Looking behind him, I see a cloud of snow and ice barreling down the mountain. The ground shakes as nature reclaims its territory. I let out a guttural roar to warn Rem, and he looks back at the monster behind us. I can't see his eyes, but I can tell he's scared by the way he's flailing his arms trying to figure out how to outrun it.

I journey over, trying to find a safe spot to land, and hopefully escape the avalanche. A garbled cry for help comes from behind me, and I turn my neck just in time to see Chris sucked into the claws of the avalanche. "NO!" I scream, horrified.

I've lost all sense of place and time, but my body seems to be taking me to safety as my board zigzags down to the west side of the mountain. I've been able to avoid avalanches in the past, but this time around, I'm not so lucky. It takes another second before the avalanche sucks me under.

My body is tossed around like a rag doll until I'm buried beneath the snow. It's packed in around me tightly; I can't move my legs or arms, and as the snow settles, it feels like I'm encased in a pool of hardened cement. It's becoming harder to breathe with each passing second, and I'm resigned to the fact that I will most likely die.

My mind replays memories of my life before me like a movie, and bitter, frustrated tears stream down my face, crystallizing quickly as the freezing cold sweeps over me. I've always feared dying like this, trapped in the place I love the most, in the snow. My thoughts are of my family, especially Mom and Jupiter. My tears quickly become painful sobs as the contractions of my cries tighten the snow pack around me. Catalina... My best friend and confidante. The news of my death will crush her.

I wrestle against the hardened blanket of snow and ice to move my arms, and after a few seconds of unwavering persistence, my arms come free. My hands desperately push the snow away from my chest, trying to get hold of the radio. With shaky fingers I press the call button.

"Base, this is Jax. Do you copy? I'm trapped, but I'm okay. Can anyone hear me?" Taking small, measured breaths, I wait for a reply, but all I get is static. "Base, this is Jax. I'm on the western quadrant of the mountain. I'm alive. Can anyone hear me?" Once again, static feedback rings in the small pocket of snow surrounding me.

No, no. This can't be happening. My body shakes violently as the freezing cold goes through all of my layers. I'm finding it hard to breathe, and if no one comes soon, I'll be dead from hypothermia.

I'm so cold I can't feel my limbs, and the more breaths I take, the more exhausted I become. My life as I know it hangs by a thread. Exhausted, I close my eyes and say a prayer. I ask God to have mercy on my soul. While I'm not the most spiritual of men, I think He's always had my back. All the stupid shit I've done, all the risks I've taken, I've always risen from them all.

The clock is ticking. I need to dig myself out somehow and go home. I refuse to let this be my end. *Catalina–the bracelet–look for me, please!*

"Base, please. This is Jackson Reese. I'm alive. Someone come and get me. Please," I cry into the radio, praying someone answers. I'll keep trying until my dying breath. This is not how I was destined to die. Not here and not like this.

Closing my eyes, I rest. What happens next is all in God's hands.

CHAPTER ONE

Stryder

"**S**tryder! Look! He's alive!" Catalina exclaims, her index finger shaking as she points at the screen of her laptop. There is a red dot blinking consistently on the screen at the foot of Kicking Horse Mountain in Golden, British Columbia–the site of a horrifying avalanche that sucked Jackson, Chris, and Rem under almost three days ago. I blink twice, completely in shock. I can't believe what I'm seeing. He's alive. My baby brother Jax is alive!

After returning home from a month-long press tour, we were in Casper celebrating Jackson's thirtieth birthday. Catalina, the woman I was assigned to work with during Jackson's press tour–and who I've fallen madly in love with–presented Jax with a friendship bracelet with a global positioning service tracking dot powered by pulse as a birthday gift. Catalina and Jackson share a bond I'll never understand, but I embrace it and encourage it.

I have to give it to my girl. That bracelet has proven to be the smartest gift I've ever heard of, and the fact that it continues to ping two days after the avalanche is a solid indicator that Jax is alive and kicking somewhere underneath a pile of snow. This newfound knowledge makes us aware each passing second is a frantic race to find him alive.

Yesterday evening, the Canadian officials announced their plans to abandon their search and rescue efforts after recovering the bodies of Jax's companions, former members of the National Snowboarding team Chris James and Rem Highleigh. As I look at the incessant red dot flashing on the screen, I know this news changes everything, and don't think twice before dialing Kaelan's number. As I wait for her to answer, my body shakes with a confusing combination of nervous energy and elation.

"Jupiter," Kaelan greets me, her voice gravelly and sad.

"Kaelan, Jackson is alive!" I scream over the headset. "Our boy is alive!"

I hear her sharp exhale over the line. "Jupiter, it's impossible, honey. I know this news is difficult to accept, but we need to grasp the reality that Jax is gone, baby. The sooner–"

"No, Kaelan," I yell, interrupting her mid-sentence. "We tracked him down. We know the exact coordinates of where he is! Jax is alive. I know this sounds crazy and all, but trust me when I say he's alive!"

"Stryder, slow down there... I don't understand. How did you find him?" Kaelan asks, her gentle voice denoting utter confusion.

"Catalina got Jax a friendship bracelet for his birthday. On the tag, there's a GPS tracking dot embedded in it, and it's not powered by battery, but by pulse. With everything going on, she forgot about it until several minutes ago. She looked up the tracker identification key," I ramble excitedly. "Kaelan, the bracelet is emitting pings. That could only mean one thing! Jax is alive!" I practically scream.

"What?! Oh my God! Thank heavens! Okay. Can you send me his coordinates and any information you have about this bracelet? I need to pass it on to the Canadian search officials. This changes everything, Jupiter!" Kaelan sings.

I ask Catalina to forward all the information to Kaelan via email, and Kaelan offers to get both Catalina and me on the first flight out of John F. Kennedy Airport towards Calgary. Without a moment's hesitation I accept her offer, and quickly disconnect the call.

We need to get out of here, and there's no time to waste. I'll be damned if the Canadian officials give up on finding my best friend and brother–the one I always wanted but never had–alive. Jax is a fighter and always has been. Call it intuition or providence, but deep down I know it will only be a matter of hours before he is found.

Tossing the phone aside I walk towards Catalina, and embrace her. My lips quickly find the silken skin of her tanned neck, and pepper it with adoring kisses. I know this is the least opportune time to be affectionate, or start something I can't see through, but at the same time she needs to know how I feel. If Jackson is found alive and in one piece it will be all thanks to her. Hope floats in my chest at the mere thought of kissing the agony of the past few days away.

"Cat, I love you so much. This news gives us hope. Jax is alive and we need to get to him as soon as possible. Kaelan is getting us a flight. We need to get out of here quick. I'm not packing anything. We can buy what we need when we get there, but right now that's the least of my worries."

Her teary eyes connect with mine. The vision before me breaks my heart, and judging by the non-stop quivering of her lips, I know she has her doubts. "What if the bracelet is broken, Stryder? What if it's just a glitch and Jax is really gone?" Catalina whispers, her voice cracking with each word.

Her words unsettle me. In a fit of desperation I shake my head repeatedly, and one of my hands cups the back of her neck while the other covers her heart-shaped lips. "Shh. The last thing we lose is hope, Catalina. If we lose it, then what's the point of living and dreaming? Stop. He's alive. I feel it in my gut. Don't be negative, because right now our friend is trapped in the snow in the middle of nowhere probably freezing. We can't give up. Do you understand me?"

Catalina nods, and when I remove my hand from her lips she smiles softly, bringing to surface the dimple on her right cheek. Her dainty palm tucks a wayward lock of raven-colored hair behind her ear. "Okay," she whispers, nodding and trying to sound convincing, but deep down I know she's anything but.

Catalina has experienced a world of crippling loss, and seeing her saddened upsets me. Given her past this was the last thing she needed, most especially when she bonded the way she did with Jax during his press tour. That's how Catalina Pardo and I met. Assigned to work as her photojournalist, touring the world and chronicling Jackson's career; it was a twist of fate that brought us together. The truth is I knew I wanted Catalina the moment I laid eyes on her, and it was only a matter of time before she became mine.

The first moment I saw Catalina, I was drawn to her like a moth to a flame. The more time we spent together, the more I felt I needed to be with her. At first it wasn't easy. There were these push and pull situations between us; the duty to perform a job and the realization that there was more to us than just a professional relationship. Jackson's press tour has been one of the highlights of my life. I was fortunate to be able to spend time with my childhood friend, and it was during that time I met the woman of my dreams.

I never knew I'd be so deeply in love with her, so yes, that simple fact still shocks the heck out of me. The more I get to know her, the more I vow to spare her pain. Catalina experienced a rough start in life starting with the unexpected passing of her parents when she was a mere child, culminating with the death of her fiancé and unborn child in a fatal car accident four years ago.

The press tour gave us a fresh breath of life. It inspired friendship and hope, but more importantly love, so it hurts me immensely to see the shadow of the woman I met almost two months ago consumed with grief.

Don't get me wrong; Catalina is a tough cookie, but to see her stripped of that fierce persona I met and fell in love with is jarring. I pray we find Jax alive, because I worry she won't be able to cope with–let alone recover from–another devastating loss. She once told me, *'Everyone I ever love leaves me,'* and her words, while eerie, ring true, especially now. I need to prove to Catalina her tragic past ended with Blake. Us meeting was fate, and I doubt destiny is cruel enough to continue with the heartbreak she's already endured.

Catalina tries to break from my hold, but my hands hold her tightly in place. Looking into her dark chocolate eyes, I feel the urge to reassure her. "We're going to get on a plane and get our boy back, and next time we see him, you can slap him hard across the face for putting us through this agony. He's always been dramatic. Well, this stunt takes the cake," I declare with a small smile, yet feel the sting of tears forming in my corner of my eyes.

Catalina leans in for a kiss. "Thank you for being strong for me, for us, but it's okay to break down every once in a while, Stud," Catalina murmurs, and for a second there I swear I can hear a part of my heart breaking. Catalina knows me better than I give her credit for, and can read me like a goddamn book.

My hands move to cup her cheeks, and I bend forward to kiss her forehead. As soon as my lips make contact with the warmth of her skin, the tears that had been forming fall freely from my eyes and wet my cheeks. "I know, baby, I know. I just can't stand to see you worried or sad. I promised I would make you smile and make you happy, and right now I'm breaking those promises," I whisper trying to bite back a sob and failing miserably.

Since the moment I found out about the avalanche and the possibility of losing Jax forever, I've felt the need to rein in my true feelings. All this time I've kept my composure, trying to be strong for both of us. I guess finding out Jax could very well be alive floods me with relief, and all the worry and anger I've been holding in makes its way out. I've had nightmares of getting that life-altering phone call in the middle of the night where I'm told Jackson is dead, and his body has been recovered, mangled and frozen in the snow. The thought alone makes me shudder, and my muted crying morphs into full-blown sobs.

I nestle my head in the crook of her neck finding comfort in her warmth, and take in her unique scent that reminds me of candy. As my crying evens out, I don't care if I reveal moments of weakness and despair to Catalina, and to be honest I don't think she'll see me as less of a man if I cry. That's why I'm so goddamn lucky to have her in my life. Ever felt like you met the woman of your dreams? Yeah, that's me all right.

"Stud, let it all out," Catalina croons while her fingers gently brush away strands of my hair which skim against the collar of my shirt. My chest heaves less and less with each calming breath I take, and when my tears subside Catalina squeezes my shoulders. "Let's pack some clothes so we can get the hell out of here and find Jax."

Her sudden strength is infectious. I nod and kiss her neck softly, agreeing with her. As soon as I let go of Catalina, my phone rings. In the blink of an eye there's a moment of absolute panic going on inside my head as I try to think who might be calling and why. Without taking a glance at the caller ID, I answer on the third ring. I sigh in relief when I hear Kaelan's soft-spoken voice flooding the line.

"Jupiter, can you make it to JFK in an hour, tops? There's a flight in an hour and a half. Just say the word and it's yours."

"Yeah, Kaelan. Go ahead and book it, and email me the flight info. We're gathering some things and we'll be right out the door. Any news on the coordinates we gave you?" I ask, hoping she delivers us some much needed good news.

"Yes. Right now the search and rescue officials are keeping mum to the press which is good. The last thing we want is to bring the public's hopes up, in case it's not a happy ending. The folks here are moving all of their resources to find our boy. The bracelet is still giving out pings, so all in all it's great news." Kaelan replies confidently, which eases my anxiety a bit.

"This is great news! We'll be there in a few hours. I hope by the time we arrive in Calgary, we'll have news worth celebrating. Thanks, Kaelan."

"Okay, son, have a safe flight," Kaelan says and promptly hangs up.

Catalina is busying herself trying to get the essentials packed, but the steady shaking of her hands and her constant pacing back and forth in the room isn't getting anything accomplished. Our nerves are frazzled, and time is against us. We need to get out of here, and fast.

"Come on, baby. Let's just wash up and leave," I breathe encouragingly, taking the sweater away from Catalina's trembling hands and throwing it on the bed.

After some coaxing, I guide her into the shower and we bathe together, making sure to be in and out in less than five minutes. With small overnight bags in our hands and equally tired and weary faces, we emerge from Catalina's loft in SoHo twenty minutes after Kaelan's call. I hail a cab, and we begin the trek to JFK. Good fortune is on our side when we arrive at the airport; we're checked in and through security in under fifteen minutes. Feeling mentally and physically exhausted, we sit in the First Class lounge watching cable news. Every so often the flashing news ticker pops up with the top world headlines, among them, Jackson Reese remains unaccounted for, and the chances of being found alive are slim.

News channels continue to play the footage of the avalanche on a constant loop; analysts are interviewed and prominent members of the sports community are seen offering their condolences to the families of Chris and Rem as well as Jackson. The more I watch the news, the more my stomach churns. I hate the fact that the world press is practically declaring Jax dead when those closest to him haven't lost hope. I find it to be exploitive reporting and quite frankly it disgusts me. As we're being called to board, the red block letters of BREAKING NEWS pop up on the screen followed by a reporter standing at the foot of Kicking Horse ready for a live-shot. We both halt in our steps, and Catalina squeezes my hand painfully hard as we look at the TV—both of us holding our breaths.

"We have seen increased activity today at the base of Kicking Horse. It would appear the recovery efforts that were suspended yesterday evening have resumed. Search and rescue teams are now actively searching for Olympic gold medalist snowboarder Jackson Reese. Sources say he may be alive, but our experts indicate the probability of survival is less than ten percent. Experts further indicate the average length of time

a person can survive in these frigid conditions is at best twelve hours. Given it has been close to forty hours since the avalanche struck, the odds of finding Reese alive are extremely low. However, our sources indicate rescuers know the exact location where he is trapped, and it is too early to speculate the condition in which he is in. Folks at home who are watching, if Reese is recovered alive, it would be the bit of good news his camp and family desperately need. We will be here as long as it takes, and will break the news as soon as we get more information from the Canadian officials. Reporting live from the Purcell Mountains, this is Troy Evans for CBC, back to the studio."

Ungluing our eyes from the flat screen TV we exchange glances, and while none of us say a word I'm pretty sure we're sharing the same thoughts. *Please let them find Jackson alive.*

"Good afternoon, passengers. This is the first boarding announcement for flight 1701 with non-stop service to Calgary. We are now inviting those Business and First Class passengers to begin boarding at this time. Please have your boarding pass and identification ready. Welcome aboard."

"Come on, baby. That's us," I say to Catalina, holding her hand and whisking her away from the TV set.

Walking down the jet way my mind whirls back to the day Catalina and I first met. We reach the threshold of the cabin door, and I turn Catalina around for a quick hug, not caring if we are blocking anyone else from entering the plane. Her arms snake around my neck, and her erratic breathing speaks volumes, she's afraid and understandably so. The fact that we'll be thirty thousand feet up in the air for several hours means we'll be incommunicado. The news could go either way during that time; Jax could be found alive, or dead.

"He's going to be okay. Trust me on this, Cat. Jax will be okay."

Catalina exhales deeply and breaks our hold. Walking into the cabin, she plops herself against the leather seat, and as soon as she's buckled in, she takes hold of my hand and ever so sweetly kisses the skin above my knuckles.

"Deep down I know he's fine, but when stuff like this happens, I go into self-preservation mode. I can't help but prepare myself for the worst so if I get bad news, I'm sort of mentally ready for it," she confesses with sad eyes.

"You need to stop that, Catalina. You're only making yourself sick with worry. You have to be positive. Listen, we're both tired. Let's take the next few hours to get some rest. This-no-longer-random-stranger's-shoulder needs girl-who-sleeps-better-on-a-random-stranger's-shoulder to rest, okay?" I wink as I call her by the moniker she introduced herself with on the day we met.

Catalina smiles softly and after leaning over for a chaste kiss, she nestles against the crook of my neck. Not even twenty minutes after takeoff, she is sound asleep against my shoulder with a tiny grin on her face.

God, if you're listening, please spare my kid brother's life. Keep him safe and well until we get there. I don't think Catalina could handle another loss in her life. Please. I know I sound like a hypocrite praying to you when I never do, but desperate times call for desperate measures. Guide those rescuers to wherever he is. Please.

I fervently pray until my eyelids feel heavy, and what seems like a New York minute later I'm awakened by the rattling sounds of the cabin as the plane lands at Calgary International. Glancing to my side, I see Catalina looking out the window with a worried expression on her face, which takes me back to the day we landed in Vancouver on the day we first met.

"Hey, how'd you sleep?" I ask her in between yawns.

Turning her head to face me, she replies with a small grin, "Oh you know, incredibly well. That shoulder of yours is miraculous. I'm feeling much better."

I remove my seatbelt and stretch my long legs and arms. "Good, so did I."

Reaching into my pocket, I grab my cell phone and power it on. As soon as it buzzes to life it begins to ring loudly in my hands. Catalina looks at me with hopeful eyes, her teeth grazing her plump lower lip with a look that screams she's desperate to hear good news.

I'll admit my finger is shaking as I swipe the screen to unlock my phone and exhaling a huff I read the text messages. There are some from Jax's mom, Kathy, some from Kaelan, some from Jax's coach, Rob, and even a few from Olivia my ex-fiancé and Jax's youngest sister. Holding my breath, I decide to start with Kaelan.

<KP: Good news, he's alive. Call me as soon as you land. K.>

<KP: He only had a few hours left. He's in the ICU being treated for chronic hypothermia. He's in a coma, but he's breathing on his own. Our boy is alive!>

I take the deepest breath and my eyes instantly wet with tears. Crouching over in my seat, I clutch my phone with a closed fist with my eyes closed, and hands locked tightly in prayer. Exhaling shakily, I open my eyes and see Catalina. She must've misinterpreted my reactions to the texts because she breaks down in tears in the middle of the cabin.

"No, God, please, no," she wails loudly, garnering the attention of our fellow passengers. I kneel in the small space in front of her. My hands squeezing her shoulders soothingly.

"They found him, baby. He's in a coma, but he is alive." I declare, my voice cracking with emotion. My hands move to cradle her face, my eyes full of elated tears as hers weep inconsolably.

"He's alive?" Catalina asks, her soft voice cracking. As I nod, a small smile emerges on her gorgeous face and it's in that moment I know everything is going to be fine.

"Yes," I reply, returning her smile. "We are going to meet Kaelan at the hospital. He's there now being treated for chronic hypothermia. If we're lucky, we'll get to see him. See, baby? You saved his life. Thanks to you, he's alive."

Catalina's hands cover her mouth, and a look of wonder takes over her features. "I saved his life," she whispers looking at me square in the eye.

"Yes. You did."

Catalina removes her buckle and pulls me up to stand. Joyful giggles leave her chest as we hug in the middle of the people exiting the aircraft. I don't care if other passengers think our actions are over the top. Just as long as my Raven Girl is happy, that's all that matters to me.

We are the last ones to get off the plane, and a polite flight attendant hands us cocktail napkins on our way out. I impulsively kiss the nice woman's cheek shocking her in the process. "He's alive!" I exclaim to her. The pilot and co-pilot standing in the galley look at each other with a puzzled expression and shrug their shoulders. The flight attendant, meanwhile, stands there with flushed cheeks, and her hand touches the cheek I kissed her on.

Taking hold of Catalina's precious hand, I run up the jet-way with our carry-on bags searching for the customs desk with the shortest wait, and then bolting towards the nearest exit towards ground level in search for a cab. While Jackson isn't out of danger, the fact that he's in the hospital and in the capable hands of medical professionals makes me hopeful. Tossing our carry-on bags into the trunk, we climb into the cab and make the less than three hour journey to the Golden & District Hospital. Every so often Catalina sighs loudly and I can relate because I'm dealing with some anxieties of my own.

From time to time our phones chirp with incoming messages, and while Catalina ignores hers, I'm periodically checking mine. Jackson remains in a coma but his vital signs continue to improve. Just as the cab pulls up to the hospital drop-off area, my phone rings. It's Kaelan.

"We're here," I answer before she has an opportunity to even say hello.

"Wonderful. He's in room 1023. You are both on the list of authorized visitors. He is isolated right now, but in a few hours he will be allowed visitors. See you in the waiting room. We'll chat further. Oh"–Kaelan pauses, taking a deep breath–"heads up. Olivia is here."

Groaning, I hang up and pay the cabbie. In the parking lot I see countless news vans and reporters standing around. Some are doing live shots, while others stalk the entrance of the hospital waiting for news on Jackson's condition. Holding our bags, I follow Catalina into the hospital and check-in at the desk. After receiving our visitor badges, we enter the elevator. Catalina's breathing becomes uneven, it appears she's fighting back tears. Whisking her to my side, I whisper reassurances, trying my damnedest to pacify her.

"I hate hospitals, Stryder. They bring back bad memories," Catalina mutters with her arms wrapped tightly against her chest. I nod, knowing Catalina must've spent some time hospitalized after that fatal car accident she was in. Not to mention her black-out episode at *Xsports* which landed her in the hospital after she saw the coverage of the avalanche on network TV.

"I get it, babe. Hopefully, we won't be here for long. Jax is pretty resilient, and if he was able to survive an avalanche, this should be a walk in the park for him," I tell her softly as the elevator doors open.

Waiting for us are Kaelan and Kathy. I wrap my arms around both women who mean so much to me as Catalina stands close by smiling. Kathy breaks free from my hold and hugs Catalina fiercely, and holding back sobs, she speaks.

"You saved my boy's life, Catalina. How could I ever repay you?" Kathy cries, holding onto Catalina's cheeks with her palms. "If not for you, we wouldn't be here right now. Thank you, my dear. Thank you."

My heart swells to watch my second mom embracing Catalina like that. It's not hard to see how much my family loves her. Looking over my shoulder I notice Olivia standing nearby with her arms crossed, watching us. Raising my hand, I wave at her but don't get close. After the way she treated Jax at his birthday party, it's needless to say she's no longer in my good graces.

Oli waves back, lowering her gaze in embarrassment. I'd bet money she's regretting her bitchtastic ways, especially now that Jax is in critical condition. Oli approaches Catalina reluctantly, and whispers, "Hey."

Catalina looks at Olivia with sympathetic eyes and while women can be evil with each other, especially when there's a man in the middle, I have to remind myself Cat isn't like most women. Extending her arms, she embraces my ex-fiancé lovingly.

"Hey. How are you holding up?" Catalina whispers to Olivia.

I guess being held by Catalina is too much for Olivia because she breaks down in tears. "I'm so sorry. You saved him. Thank you," Olivia mumbles in between breaths.

Catalina looks at me tenderly, and I blow her a kiss all while her hands rub soothing circles against Oli's back. "There's no need to thank me, Olivia. I'm just happy that bracelet exists, and Jax never took it off. He promised not to, but you know guys..." Catalina giggles softly, trying to put Oli at peace.

Nearby, Kaelan and Kathy hug each other and look at me with appraising eyes. I offer them the widest of smiles knowing that in Catalina, I have found the noblest of women. Catalina removes a small packet of tissues from her purse and helps clean Oli's tear-stricken face. I swear Catalina must be an angel because her kindness and compassion blow my mind.

"Better?" Catalina whispers, and Oli nods silently, excusing herself and entering the restroom in the intensive care unit waiting room. Catalina waves goodbye and takes out her cell phone to make a phone call.

I walk over to Kaelan, and ask her about Jax's prognosis. She replies by telling me the doctors are trying to stabilize his body temperature, and are running tests to make sure there isn't permanent damage to his vital organs.

"You should've seen him, Jupiter," Kaelan whispers squeezing her eyes shut, and quirking her head to the side. "He was purplish-blue when they brought him here. He almost didn't make it," Kaelan cries softly into her hands. "I almost had to bury my baby boy."

This situation is tough on all of us. Pulling Kaelan into my shoulder I let her cry freely. She was Jax's nanny when he was a kid and also his godmother. Kaelan has never been far away from Jax, even during his days in rehab. If anyone knows Jax in every way, it's

Kaelan–from the most intimate stuff to the most outrageous details. It's no secret she loves Jax like her own flesh and blood, and I know Jax feels the same way about Kaelan. A doctor approaches Kathy. My whole body stiffens as we walk slowly towards them, and Kaelan reaches out for Kathy's hand and squeezes it tightly.

"Mrs. Reese, the condition in which your son was found was completely unexpected. The sole reason Jackson is alive is because he was wearing a survival suit underneath his snowboarding gear. He is severely dehydrated and we are having a tough time stabilizing his heart rate and body temperature, not to mention frostbite which is more visible on his fingers and hands. We are hoping he won't require skin grafts, but that is not an immediate threat.

"Now to the good news... Brain wave activity is normal, and rules out any brain damage concerns we had when he was first brought in. Apart from two broken ankles, probably due to the fact his board was still attached to his boots when he was brought in, your son is in wonderful shape. While we stabilize his vitals, we're keeping him in a medically induced coma. Jackson is very lucky to be alive," He declares happily, patting Kathy reassuringly on the shoulder.

"I have to give you this," the doctor says, placing Jackson's bracelet in her hand, "it was causing interference with the MRI machine, but it's also what saved his life. I'm going to do some rounds and I will be back to update you. Right now, we don't recommend visitation as we need to allow him to rest. If his condition changes, I will let you know."

I place a kiss on both Kathy and Kaelan's foreheads, and step back searching for Catalina. As I'm walking away Kaelan stops me.

"I made arrangements for the two of you to stay at Kicking Horse Lodge. Why don't you guys head over the hotel and get some rest?" Kaelan asks kindly. "I'll buzz you if we hear anything."

Nodding, I walk down the hallway in search for Catalina. As I turn around the corner of the long hallway, Catalina stands in front of the glass divider that separates Jackson from us. Halting in my tracks, I hear Catalina mumbling into the glass.

"Please, Jax. I need you to wake up. If you can hear me, I know it's nice wherever you are, but it's not your time yet. You got me? I need you."

Catalina cries into her hands, repeating herself over and over. My heart breaks just watching her pleading, and praying for Jax in front of his door. I walk towards her and wrap my arms around her waist, and bring my head to rest on her shoulder.

"He's stubborn. He'll come around whenever he wants," I whisper, kissing her neck softly. "Come on. The doc says they aren't allowing visitors. Kaelan said she'll call us if anything changes. Let's go to the lodge and get some rest, okay?"

"But what if he wakes up and we're not here?" Catalina whispers amid sniffles, her palm caressing my scruffy cheek.

"If he does, Kathy and Kaelan will tell him we're close by. I promise I will bring you back here as soon as we get the word that he's awake, but for now you and me need to get some rest. Come on, Catalina. He is in the best hands."

Catalina reluctantly leaves the window, and we take the elevator down to the lobby so we can leave the hospital. As soon as we walk out of the glass doors of the hospital entrance, we are bombarded by flashing light bulbs, and questions being yelled at us by reporters demanding an update. Lifting my elbows, I push past them as they continue to scream questions at us. Thankfully there is a cab at the rotunda so we throw our bags in and slide inside quickly, and the driver doesn't hesitate to drive away before he asks us for our destination.

Once at the lodge and in the safety of our suite, I draw us a bath, and strip Catalina down to her bare skin. Her hand continues to fiddle with the bracelet she bought for herself the same day she bought Jax's. Her eyes wander the room, and I know better than anyone she's anywhere but here. Catalina won't be able to rest until she sees Jackson awake and cracking jokes with her. Until that happens, I will have to do whatever I can to make her feel safe and wanted, and man, I miss my Raven Girl. Call me selfish but I need to feel her skin against mine, and I miss hearing her say my name when she falls apart in my arms. She has her ways of coping with distress—well, so do I.

I hate that she's barely talking and it's like she's in a daze, moving along, just going through the motions. I'm so used to having Catalina speak her mind, and using her sass and wit against me. Seeing her so quiet and withdrawn—reserved even—makes me insecure. I don't know what to do to make it better.

In quiet silence, I undo the buttons of her blouse. My eyes widen when I see her tanned, silken skin. It rouses my dick, but I know all too well now is not the time. I'm relieved knowing Jackson is recovering. It gives me a sense of normalcy, and the realization I am no longer skirting on the edge of disaster, holding in my breath, and waiting for bad news to arrive helps my mind relax a bit. Without haste, I remove the rest of her clothing and throw it on the floor, doing my best to avoid looking at her lips which beg me to kiss them. Foregoing her needs in favor of my own would only prove I'm a selfish asshole. My heart tightens in my chest when I see Catalina's eyes closed, her forehead scrunched with deep worry. I miss her, and desperately need her to come back to me. *God, this is driving me insane!*

With hesitant steps, I lead her into the bath, making sure she's settled in before I give her the privacy she needs. Kissing her forehead, I exit the bathroom, closing the door softly behind me. Resting my head against the wall, I battle the urge to go back in, disrobe myself and make love to her. But she's worlds away, and I don't know how to bring her back. She is my heart and my home and until her universe is righted mine will be royally fucked-up, and I have no other choice but to deal with it.

Walking over to the bed, I lie down and rest my arm over my forehead. All the flurry of activity and days of sleeplessness over Jackson's disappearance finally catch up with me. As soon as my head hits the pillow I fall asleep, grateful to shut up all the noise of my stressed-out mind. Hopefully when I wake up, I'll feel better, more rested, and less frustrated.

CHAPTER TWO

Stryder

Feathery light kisses disrupt my peaceful slumber, and warm fingertips trace the outline of my jaw and lips. I smile inwardly, grateful I'm still wanted despite all the craziness of the past couple of days. I open my eyes and it takes a second for them to adjust, and when they do I see before me the most precious sight. Catalina's long raven hair cascades past her shoulders covering her large and perfectly round breasts, and her almond-shaped dark chocolate eyes are looking down at me. My hands reach for her cheeks to touch the softest of skin, and when she cradles into my touch I sigh with happiness.

"Hey," Catalina whispers, her cheeks slightly flushed.

Clearing my throat, I smile. "Hey, how was your bath?"

Inhaling and exhaling deeply, she replies with a wistful smile, "It was lonely... I missed you. Why did you leave?"

My heart tightens in my chest when her eyes search mine for answers. Perhaps I was over-thinking things when I decided to leave her alone in the bathroom. Maybe she wanted me there, but in fear of being rejected I hauled ass out of there in the blink of an eye.

Running my fingers through my hair, I reply, "I wasn't sure what you wanted, but I knew if I stayed my need for your closeness would've trumped all reason." Taking hold of her palm, I lace our fingers together. "I'm trying my damndest to do the right thing here, Catalina."

She quirks her head and an amused smile curls her lips. With a raised eyebrow she asks, "And that would be?"

My eyes close in relief when she grins wide. Right now I want to do back-flips because, my sassy girl is back. Thank God. The grin she's put on my face mirrors hers. Winking, I reply, "Keeping my dick in my pants. But like I've told you once before, I can control myself but I can't control him." My dick twitches in response against her hip, and her shocked face tells me she felt it all right. Shrugging my shoulders, I concede, "It's inevitable when I'm around you."

Catalina doesn't break my gaze. Her eyes look into mine intently almost apologetically. "Stryder, I know I haven't been quite myself since Jackson's disappearance. I'm sorry. I'm so used to losing people my go-to defense mechanism is to shut down. I'm sorry if I shut you out, but thank you for not giving up on me. I love you, Stud."

Letting go of Catalina's hand, I wrap my arms around her and engulf her in a fierce hug. "Shh... You don't need to explain yourself. I get it. I'm just happy you're back. I missed you."

Her heart-shaped lips collide with mine. Her kiss is urgent and my hunger for her mouth knows no limits. I'm instantly consumed by the addictive taste of her tongue, and with my hands holding her face I reciprocate her affections and then some. It doesn't take long to feel her delicate hands roam freely underneath my layers of clothing an unmistakable sign that she wants me.

I know it's my job as a man to keep it together when she's feeling low, but right now Catalina is showing me how much she wants me, and damn me when I say I want her just as much. My hands abandon her face in search for her breasts, her hardened nipples pressing sexily against my chest. Her hurried palms sneak underneath the hem of my shirt as she gently clutches my hips.

Taking hold of her waist, I roll us over so I'm laying flush against the softness of her curves and reluctantly break our kiss. With more than eager hands, I remove my shirt, and her warm hands waste no time grasping my chest staking her claim.

"Mmm, I missed this so much," I whisper as my lips nip at the curve of her neck.

My tongue trails the length of her neck, bringing her skin to a flush, and in no time she's covered in goose bumps. Her skin is so soft and her sweet scent invades my nostrils, urging me further as I lose all of my self-control. Her sighs and gentle moans fuel my need to taste the flavor of her body.

I trail kisses on her; starting at the base of her neck where her pulse beats lively. Catalina unmans me with her affections, and that doesn't bother me one bit. My mouth finds the roundness of her breasts and while my hand gently squeezes one, my mouth worships the other. Her nipple elongates under my tongue and I latch on like the greedy son of a bitch that I am, suckling, tasting, and teasing.

Catalina moans and writhes beneath me as her hands squeeze my ass cheeks and tuck underneath the waistband of my jeans and boxers, her fingernails scratching my skin.

"Fuck," I mumble, as lust gets the better of me. "I need to taste you. Right now."

My words are Catalina's undoing as her hands abandon my ass cheeks in favor of my head. Her palms gently tug at my hair and push me down lower to where her pussy is. Smiling against the skin of her navel, I take her lead and trail my tongue down, painstakingly slow until I reach her slit.

I blow softly against it, and Catalina tilts her hips up; her body begging for me to taste her wetness. I chuckle softly and look up to her. Our gazes meet. Watching her lust-filled eyes and unabashed need for me never ceases to amaze.

"Feeling needy, are we?" I ask softly, taking hold of her leg, and raising it so my lips can kiss the inside of her thigh. When I do, Catalina trembles and throws her head back, laughing softly.

"Yes," she says amid giggles. "Just shut up and get busy, Stud."

And shut up I do. My lips kiss the bareness of her pussy, my tongue licking her hardened clit slowly, and when she tries to tilt her hips upwards again, my hands pin them back down against the bed. Her frustrated breaths and fingernails scraping my scalp have me on cloud-fucking-nine.

We've been together a handful of times and I'm learning with each encounter how to read her body and gauge her reactions so I can please her like no other man has before. My mouth clamps over Catalina's hardened clit and her breath quickens. I free one of my hands and gently caress her plump pussy lips and inwardly smile at her dripping arousal.

My eager fingers touch Catalina's sweet spot and she lets out a long, drawn-out moan of contentment. I lavish her with my fingers as my tongue focuses on her clit, and when her body begins to quiver, I quicken the pace. Pleasuring my Raven Girl puts me in a state of euphoria, and my thick dick presses painfully against my fly in response. I need some relief, and while I'm all about giving Catalina hers before I get mine, the truth is I want to be buried deep inside of her.

I withdraw my fingers, and Catalina's whimper of disapproval is a clear sign she's not thrilled with the loss of friction. My mouth unlatches from her clit, and I stand to take off my jeans and boxer shorts. Walking towards the closet, I search for my duffel bag to retrieve a box of condoms.

We have never used protection since we started having sex, and while I've been mindful of not coming inside her, I desperately want to. I loathe using condoms with the woman I love, but I'm not a selfish bastard either. Our relationship is fresh, and it would be inexcusable of me to not exercise reasonable precaution for her sake. Grabbing one, I bring it over to the bed, and lay over her.

Catalina's eyes follow me with an amused expression. I'm curious to know what brought that on, but I'll save it for later because right now I want to lose myself inside her. My lips meet hers; I kiss her hungrily, our tongues slow-dancing. Catalina's warm, soft hands hold my face, and being held like that makes me feel like the luckiest man on the planet. When her hands abandon my face in favor of my dick, I'm not embarrassed to growl my appreciation, all while her deft palm strokes my shaft, my balls tingling in response as I enjoy every second of it.

"God, I've missed you so much," I mumble, as her thumb rubs the bead of moisture on the tip of my dick. I close my eyes and surrender to her touch. I feel Catalina's free hand rustling around, so I open my eyes. That's when I notice she's reaching for the condom. I quickly snatch it away, and with a devilish grin I dangle it over her face. "Allow me."

Using my teeth, I rip the packet open and begrudgingly roll the condom down my shaft already hating its obstructive properties. Catalina observes my every move, enthralled with parted lips.

"I'm sorry for stopping when I did, but I desperately want to be inside you and can't wait another second," I confess sheepishly, loving that sharp breath she takes in with my words.

"Well, then get to it, Stud." Catalina taunts.

And so I do. Aligning my dick to the entrance of her pussy, I slide in slowly and whisper, "I love you."

She lets out soft mewls of pleasure as I settle deep into her, and as I pause to place a kiss on the warmth of her chest, her clenching pussy squeezes my dick nice and tight. "I love you too, Stryder," she murmurs, her eyes connecting with mine.

Taking hold of her hands, I weave our fingers together and thrust myself in and out of her. At first my movements are gentle, but with each thrust I lose myself in her body, riding her like my life depends on it. Catalina meets me thrust for thrust, her dainty fingers gripping mine fiercely. I close my eyes for the briefest of seconds, and each moan and growl that leaves us rights my tilted existence. The walls of her pussy tighten, and her once-soft moans intensify. I'm right there with her as my own lust-fueled growls echo against the skin of her neck.

"Cat, you feel so fucking good. I can feel all of you. I love you," I declare, not caring if I sound like a love-sick fool. I've never felt this way with anyone, including my ex. What I have with Catalina exceeds anything I've ever experienced in my entire life, and I'm never, *ever* going to let go of her. I know she's close to coming, so I swivel my hips, offering that perfect friction that makes her buck wildly.

"Stryder, baby, please don't stop. Just like that," she pants as she squeezes my hands. "Oh, yes, yes."

I unlace our hands and take hold of her beautiful face, my eyes locked on hers. I'm giving her what she asks for; I don't stop moving. In fact, I quicken the pace. And just like that, my sexy Raven Girl comes gloriously, calling my name like a prayer. Two more thrusts and I follow, her greedy pussy milking me of all that I have.

Completely out of breath, I kiss her lips softly. Her gentle fingers run over my scalp, prickling my skin. Could our sex get any better than this? I'm having a tough time wrapping my mind around that. Despite having had her a second ago; I want her again and again.

Breaking our kiss, Catalina mumbles almost unintelligibly. "Feel better?"

Our eyes meet, and I nod. "I guess you could say that. And you?" I ask with a smile, my hands removing the hair covering one of her eyes.

Catalina nods. "I have no complaints. I needed that, thank you. Nothing lifts one's spirits better than some bump and grinding," she answers wickedly.

I laugh at her words, feeling the happiest I have in days. Getting up from the bed, I take the condom off and throw it in the trash bin by the nightstand. I walk to her side and, extending my arm, I beckon. "Shower with me."

Catalina wraps her hand around mine and replies, with a mischievous glint in her eyes, "Why? So I can wash the scent of us off? Nah... I'd rather keep this on if you don't mind."

My jaw drops at her words, but I challenge her nevertheless. "Have it your way, minx." Looking down at my hardening erection, I speak. "Okay, I guess it's just you and me in the shower, buddy."

Catalina's scandalized reaction makes me chuckle. She flies off the bed, landing into my arms quicker than a snap of fingers. "You don't play fair," she laughs.

Holding back a snicker, I taunt, "Neither do you."

Smiling and sneaking quick kisses, we walk into the bathroom to shower and continue our little rendezvous until we are both left breathless and satisfied. After a nice rejuvenating bath, we climb back in bed, falling asleep as soon as we pull the covers over our naked bodies.

My phone chirps in the distance, and I toss in bed, trying to ignore the constant sound coming from it. After the seventh chirp, I reach out for the damn thing. Rubbing my eyes and sighing loudly, I look to my side to ensure I haven't woken Catalina up. With her raven hair fanned against the stark white pillow I see her breasts peeking out from under the covers, making me hard again. Covering her with the thick blanket and ignoring the swell below, I check my notifications.

> **<KP: Jax is coming around. He hasn't woken up, but he keeps mumbling.>**

> **<KP: He squeezed my hand!>**

> **<KP: Jax called for Catalina. Over and over again.>**

> **<KP: Are you asleep?>**

> **<KP: He woke up!>**

> **<OR: Jax woke up! He's up!>**

<JR: It's Jaxsicle. I'm back from the dead.>

<KP: Can you guys swing by the hospital? Jax is eager to see you two.>

The excitement buzzing within me has me flying off the bed, and rummaging through my duffle bag in search of clothes. Once dressed and freshened up, I approach the bed and kiss Catalina's shoulder, happy with the fact the universe has righted itself once again.

"Go away, you fiend. Beauty sleep," she murmurs in her sleep.

I chuckle at her grumpy ass, and drape my arm over her shoulder, squeezing it softly. Mumbling, Catalina reaches for my chest, and when her eyes open they meet mine.

"Why are you dressed? Going somewhere?" she asks amid yawns.

"Jax woke up. Look," I whisper with a smile, and place my cell phone into her expectant hands. Catalina breathes in and out in relief, and without a moment's hesitation she closes her eyes and prays in Spanish. I don't know her exact words, but the gist I get is that she is thanking the angels above for their mercy. Opening her eyes she eagerly reads Jax's text messages and flies off the bed in search of her phone. She reads her messages and falls to her knees laughing. I watch her completely amused.

"Um, what did he say?" I ask, intrigued, but she shakes her head and continues laughing.

"No, I don't think you want to read that, babe. It might make your eyes burn," she replies, unable to control her laughter. "Let me get dressed so we can visit him. I'm so excited!"

I walk towards Catalina and hug her fiercely. After placing the briefest of kisses on her lips, I leave her alone to get ready, and call the front desk to get us a taxi. As I hold the line, I walk towards the window and draw the curtains. The panoramic view of the Purcell Mountains surrounding the lodge appears peaceful as snowflakes gently fall from the sky, but when I look closely at the fierceness of the terrain it makes me shudder. It almost took the life of my best friend and baby brother.

Catalina's hands wrap around my waist, and a contented sigh escapes from my mouth. "Ready?" I ask, my hands stroking hers.

"Yes, I can't wait to see the other man in my life," Catalina chirps. I turn around and smile. She's dressed in dark blue jeans with a red blouse, her trademark skulls emblazoned all over it. Her make-up is minimal, yet that sexy-as-fuck black eyeliner and cherry red lipstick enhances her natural beauty.

Since we met, Catalina has lost weight, but not enough to lose the curves that drive me insane. To me, she is perfection; I take all that comes with her: the good, the bad, and the ugly. I know I'm jumping the gun here, but I find myself dreaming of a future with her. If that makes me a fucking softie, then so be it.

Chuckling, I kiss the tip of her nose. "Careful, I don't share well with others..."

To my complete surprise, Catalina grabs my crotch and squeezes softly. "I don't either," she declares confidently with a smile on her face. Once she lets go, she winks, making me chuckle, and after grabbing our winter gear we head out the door.

At the hospital, there's a massive amount of reporters doing live shots. Someone must have recognized us, because they begin to shout questions at us.

"Is it true Reese has been given his last rites?"

"Can you confirm Jackson Reese is out of a coma?"

Ducking my head and sheltering Catalina from the blinding lights, we rush through the automatic glass doors of the hospital and step into the elevator. As soon as the lift doors close, I let out a breath of relief. "Jesus, can you believe these assholes? What kind of fucked-up questions were those?" I exclaim, completely rattled by the bullshit queries our colleagues threw our way.

Catalina shakes her head, her facial features bearing a mixture of disgust and rage. "I agree, Stryder. Those sons of bitches need to get their facts straight. Lately, journalism has taken a deep shit. The days of factual reporting are long gone. Scandal boosts ratings, and tragedy even more."

She's holding tightly onto the metal rails of the elevator and judging by the color of her knuckles, Catalina is angry. She needs to calm down before Jax sees us. As the elevator doors open, I weave my hand into hers, and we walk down the hallway towards Jackson's room. We are met by Kaelan. Her usual prim appearance is long gone; her face is free of make-up and the dark circles and bags underneath her eyes prove she hasn't slept in days. Her short blonde hair is tied up with a rubber band, and her usual professional attire has been replaced with baggy sweats and a wrinkled t-shirt with the hospital logo, courtesy of the gift shop downstairs. I wrap her in a warm hug, gently kissing her hairline.

"Oh my sweet boy, being tamed I see?"

I scoff at her words but deep down I know she's right.

"How are you holding up, Kaelan? You look tired," I say empathetically, rubbing her back.

Kaelan puts me at arm's length and holds my cheeks affectionately. "I am, but knowing my boy is safe and sound makes all this exhaustion worth it." Turning to her side, she greets Catalina by giving her a hug and a kiss on her cheek. "Catalina, dear, he's been asking for you... irritatingly so." When Kaelan rolls her eyes in mock annoyance, we all burst into laughter.

"Okay, let's go see him then!" Catalina beams happily.

Approaching the glass door leading to Jax's room, Kaelan gives us the thumbs up first and then we enter. Jax is watching something on his tablet and when he hears the door close behind us, his head snaps up in attention. I take a moment to process the image before me.

Jackson's face is painted in different shades of purple and red, and both of his ankles are covered in a plaster cast; one of them elevated by a sling. His head is bandaged and his arms are covered with scratches and bruises. I can't imagine what his chest and legs look like underneath his hospital gown. At first glance you'd think little brother took a beating in a street brawl. Not many have survived an avalanche, and seeing Jackson alive on the hospital bed makes me want to jump for joy.

"Look what the cat finally dragged in," Jackson jokes while wiggling his eyebrows. "How are the lovebirds?"

Catalina rushes to his side, her lips kissing his cheeks repeatedly. With tears leaking from her eyes she breathes, "If you ever pull a stunt like that again, I will kill you with my bare hands, you son of a bitch."

He wraps his arms around her neck to give her a quick peck on the lips like long-time friends would. His bandaged hand softly wipes the tears away from Catalina's cheeks, and upon closer inspection, Jax's cheeks are wet with tears of his own.

"I'm sorry," Jax whispers. "I'm so, so sorry, Catalina. As I was struggling to breathe, I thought of you and how the news of my death would crush you. Thinking of you kept me alive, Cat."

Standing there, watching my best friend and the woman I love share a moment of pure love doesn't make me jealous like it used to. I don't fully understand the dynamics of their relationship, but it's probably one of the most beautiful friendships I've ever seen. They are like two kids who love each other deeply, and the vision of them warms my heart. Catalina takes hold of Jax's wrist and smiles when she sees her friendship bracelet back in its rightful place. She kisses it, and when her eyes connect with mine she smiles.

"Who knew having me on a Lo-Jack would save my life, huh, Catalina?" Jackson jokes, his body broken but his humor completely intact. I snicker from across the room and shake my head. Catalina giggles and nods.

"When I gave you the bracelet, you didn't have to prove its reliability by playing hide and seek in the snow, and testing it out, Jax," Catalina admonishes, but deep down I know she's using humor to deflect her concern. To ease her wavering emotions, I scoot her to the side.

"Can I say hi now?" I ask, rolling my eyes and feigning irritation. Catalina sticks out her tongue at me, but moves aside. Jax struggles to sit up, so I place my palm on his chest to stop his movements. It makes him wince.

"Easy there, brother," Jackson mumbles.

I don't care. I need to feel his warmth to reassure myself this mangled body before me is in fact my little brother. Wrapping my arms around him, tears fall from my eyes unrestrained. "You son of a bitch," I cry softly, "I thought I'd lost you, Jaxy boy." As I cry, Jackson sobs in my arms and nods.

I know this kid through and through. The thought of him being dead makes me cry harder and I know he's thinking the same thing. We sit there in silence with Catalina's arms around us both. As our tears subside, Jackson goes on to tell us about the avalanche, and at the mere mention of Chris's and Rem's names, he breaks down in tears again.

If anyone knows about survivor guilt, it's Catalina. I'm sure she will be by his side to help him work through it. She's helped him work his issues with alcohol out since they bonded in Whistler, and now more than ever he needs her. Jax has a long recovery ahead of him, and while his body will recover, I'm more concerned about his mental state. Somewhere in the world, two mothers and two fathers, not to mention sisters and brothers, are making preparations to bury those who died the same day Jax survived. A part of me feels heartbroken, yet another part feels immense relief the same fate isn't rested on our families.

Breaking away from the pack, I take a seat near Jax's bed and watch the two people that matter most to me lose themselves in conversation. My thoughts drift back to a few months ago when Catalina arrived into my life. Everything has changed for the better I smile more often, fret less and look forward to many happy days ahead of us.

A nurse walks into the room, interrupting my thoughts. In a stern voice, she announces, "All right, family. Visitation ends in ten minutes. Mr. Reese needs his rest."

She assesses the room and frowns when she sees Catalina is curled right beside her patient on the bed. Catalina places a kiss on Jax's forehead and gets down from the bed to gently squeeze his hand.

"See you tomorrow?" she asks.

Jax nods and smiles longingly. I move to stand and pat him shoulder, giving him a reassuring squeeze. He looks sad and that breaks my heart.

"We'll be back in the morning for breakfast, got it? What are you going to do tonight?" I ask.

Jax lifts his tablet and with a wicked grin he goes on, "Thank goodness for cellular signals. I'll be falling asleep to the soothing sounds of moaning and grunts."

Catalina looks at me puzzled, and I shake my head while chuckling. "What?" Catalina asks confused.

"Porn, Cat. He's going to watch porn," I explain, slightly amused at her shocked expression.

"Jeez, Jax. Make sure you remove your heart monitor then. The nurses will think you're having a coronary. They'll be rushing into the room with a defibrillator," Catalina quips amid laughter.

The nurse who is standing near the door huffs and, turning on her heel, walks out of the room with red cheeks. We all look at each other and laugh even harder.

Jackson points towards the door and asks, "That one... Do you think she'll offer a helping hand? She's a little old for my taste, but hey, a man has needs."

Catalina laughs until tears stream down her face. She bends down and kisses his cheek and whispers as best as she can. "Be a good boy, Jax."

"Me? Good? Never!" he replies with a grin.

Taking hold of Catalina's hand we bid Jackson farewell, and leave the hospital in high spirits. As we are walking out, I notice a freshly dressed and impeccable-looking Kaelan standing beside a hospital official. Both are briefing the press. With everyone's eyes focused on the press conference, we hop into a cab and return to the lodge with grumbling stomachs.

As soon as we arrive at the room, I place a call for room service and order a movie for us to watch while we wait for our dinner. Leaning into each other on the suite's sofa gives us an opportunity to unwind after the past few long, stressful days. When the food arrives, we waste no time devouring our meal, taking the liberty of drinking beer and enjoying each other's company. With full bellies, we lay against each other, and Catalina dozes off on my shoulder far before the movie ends with a soft smile on her face.

Picking up my Raven Girl, I lay her on the bed and peel all of her clothes off. I take mine off as well, and then curl beside her. Wrapping my arm around her waist, I feel content with how my life has changed for the better ever since this amazing woman walked onto that plane and into my life.

"I love you, Catalina. So damn much," I whisper into the silence of the room. Catalina curls into me in her sleep, sighing softly. I close my eyes and quickly surrender to my exhaustion, feeling happier than I have for as long as I can remember.

CHAPTER THREE

Catalina

A soft ray of sunlight shines through the slightly drawn curtains of our suite. Stryder is fast asleep with his strong arm wrapped around my wrist. The soft whistle of his even breathing makes me giggle. He must be catching up on sleep. It has been a long week.

I gently remove his hand from my wrist and go to the bathroom to settle into my morning routine. We promised Jax we'd go visit him during breakfast, and I want to make sure we don't break that vow. After taking a nice hot shower, I emerge from the bathroom bundled in a fluffy white towel.

I rummage through the contents of my duffle bag only to discover I have one outfit left. In our rush to get here, we only grabbed a couple of things. At some point today we will need to get more clothes. I'm not heartbroken over it. After the press tour, half the contents in my closet are no longer useful. I've lost close to thirty pounds in the past two months. After living with a curvaceous body for most of my life, I've learned to embrace its beauty, and so far Stryder hasn't complained.

Without haste I put my sort of baggy clothes on: a combination of grey leggings and a long black blouse with patent leather grey riding boots. Stryder is still fast asleep, so I take the opportunity to finish getting ready. My phone rings and I smile when I see it's Faith.

"Hey, you!" Faith chirps happily, making me grin from the inside out.

"Hi!"

"I saw the news last night... That Jackson Reese is one lucky son of a bitch. I mean, who gets sucked into an avalanche and lives to tell the tale? That's amazing. Where are you?" Faith asks, and I find it difficult to hear her because of the loud background noise.

"I'm in B.C. with Stryder. We got on the first flight out yesterday when we found out he might be alive."

"That's awesome. Oh my God, Catalina! We need to talk about that hunky man of yours. Seriously, we haven't had quality time since you bumped into him at Velvet Box. What is going on there?"

I giggle at her breathy, almost whispered question. "Faith, I told you I needed time to figure my shit out, you know? I guess shit figured itself on its own. The moment I met Stryder I knew there was something there, but I don't want to share the details over the phone. As soon as I get back, we'll talk over dinner and drinks. All you need to know is that I'm very happy. This is the happiest I've been in a very long time."

Faith lets out a howl, and the unmistakable sound of her excited clapping comes through the line. "Catalina and Stryder sitting in a tree K-I-S-S-I-N-G," she sings. "I'm so happy for you, Cat! I've only been waiting for this moment, like, forever?" she pipes, in that valley-girl voice she uses to make fun of me.

I roll my eyes, yet chuckle in the same breath. "I know, I know. Listen, I'm about to leave the lodge for the hospital. As soon as I'm back in town, I'll call you and we'll make plans to meet up."

"Yes! Absolutely! Oh... before you go, I wanted to ask you how you're feeling after your little episode. Are you taking the meds?" Faith inquires her voice stern all of a sudden.

"You mean the shit anti-depressants I was prescribed? Hell no. I threw those out. I'm feeling fine," I explain. "I don't need them. Jax is alive and well, and watching the coverage of the avalanche was life-altering. I hate when doctors see someone sad and think the solution is to write a prescription when it's not. I'm feeling great. Thanks for asking."

"Hey, don't get defensive. It's the doctor in me asking. You may not want to realize it, but dealing with PTSD the way you do is admirable. I'm just watching out for you, that's all," Faith counters reassuringly. "Okay, my coffee is ready. I have to go. Love you!"

"I love you too!" I hum and end the call. I rest the phone against the counter and brush my hair, then style it in a bun. As I'm about to apply my lipstick, a sleepy and very tousle-haired Stryder walks in. Placing a kiss on my cheek and smiling softly, he walks over to the toilet, and I quietly slip out to let him get ready for the day.

I dangle a paper sack with a toasty-hot bacon egg and cheese sandwich over Jackson's head. He looks so peaceful asleep, and I'm so happy we will be the first people he'll see as soon as he wakes up. After a few complaining grunts and groans, he finally opens his eyes.

"Good morning, Jackson." I whisper, placing a kiss on his scruffy cheek.

Jackson smiles lazily, those remarkably crisp blue eyes looking tenderly into mine. The truth is, they remind me so much of Blake's in a sweet, nostalgic kind of way. Jackson's nose twitches as he sniffs the air in the room.

"Good morning, Cat," Jackson mumbles, looking eagerly at the paper sack in my hands. "Please tell me there's bacon in there 'cause damn, I smell it," he says.

I nod repeatedly as I retrieve the rollaway tray table and bring it to his bed. Jackson eagerly sits up and rubs his hands together with a smile on his face. Removing the breakfast sandwich from the parchment paper, I place it in his hand. Jackson uses his free hand to hold my chin, and regards me sweetly.

"I think Jupiter is one lucky son of a bitch. He gets to see that sweet, adorable face of yours every day. You're a good girl, Pardo."

My mind struggles with the idea of responding with banter, but for some reason, I simply accept the compliment. Oddly enough, my cheeks feel hot and it makes me smirk that Jackson Reese is genuinely trying to be sweet.

"Well, look at you and your virginal blush, Catalina." Jackson quips, bringing to surface the banter we are accustomed to. I giggle at his assessment and pat his shoulder.

"Shut the hell up. Eat your sandwich before I take it away, smartass." I reply, laughing, and place my palms over my cheeks.

"Touché, Catalina. Touché."

As Jackson enjoys his breakfast, I sit on the chair beside his bed and watch the news. Minutes later, Stryder walks into the room with a paper bag in his hands, and Jackson eyes it suspiciously.

"You look like a hobo, Jax." Stryder smirks as he opens the bag and rests its contents on the tray table. "I got you shaving cream and a nice sharp razor."

"Well good morning to you, Sunshine," Jackson says rather sarcastically. "Um, I don't know if you noticed, asshole, but I can't stand, let alone shave."

Without saying a word to either of us, Stryder walks into the bathroom and fills a bowl with warm water, dunking a washcloth into it. He brings the bowl over and wrings the excess water from the washcloth, then places it over Jackson's face. That is when I realize what he's about to do.

Jackson sighs contentedly as a small cloud of steam lifts from the washcloth. Stryder looks at me and winks. I'm putty on that chair as I watch an act of supreme tenderness between the guys I absolutely adore. I blow a loving kiss to Stryder and he catches it, placing it over his heart.

Removing the warm washcloth from Jackson's face, Stryder sprays shaving foam into his hands and rubs them together to warm the lather. Then he dabs the cream all over Jax's cheeks, upper lip, and chin. Once done, Stryder rinses his hands and, picking up the razor, he slowly shaves Jackson's face.

"I should get injured more often. I could totally get used to this." Jackson smirks, crossing his hands behind his head.

"Blow me, Jackson. Now shut up before I cut you. This is a new blade," Stryder jokes, biting his lip and concentrating on the task at hand.

I'm watching in rapt attention, looking at Stryder's deft fingers remove Jackson's scruffy beard. I've never seen Jackson without it, and now I'm dying to see what he looks like clean-shaven. It takes about fifteen minutes and a few changes of water before Stryder finishes. Tilting Jackson's chin, Stryder inspects it with a smile. "Better?"

Jackson touches his face and replies happily, "Yes, no more itchy beard. Thanks, bro."

Stryder pats him on the shoulder affectionately. "No problem, man." Stryder says, but as I look closely I can tell there is softness in his stare like that of an older brother and a younger sibling. I swear my heart has turned into mush at the sight of them.

Standing, I walk towards them and instinctively touch Jackson's bare face with my palms. He looks so different young and very, *very* attractive. One of his pin-straight strands of blonde hair falls on his forehead and hovers over his eyebrow. Smiling, I whisper into Jackson's ear, "You are so handsome."

Stryder clears his throat and frowns. Jackson winks and turns his face to look at me, and kisses the tip of my nose. "I know, but let's continue our affair away from the old man here." Looking at Stryder he raises his palms and says, "Shave it and they will *come*."

The three of us break into peals of laughter. A pretty young nurse comes into the room to replace Jax's IV bag and notices his freshly shaven face. "Very nice, Mr. Reese."

I raise my thumb at Jackson in approval of the nurse's comment, but Jax doesn't react. *Hmm. She must not be his cup of tea.* Nevertheless he replies, "Thanks, doll." The nurse smiles and leaves the room with a nice shade of pink all over her face.

Jackson yawns and smiles drowsily. "Sleepy medicine," he mumbles, and minutes later he's fast asleep.

"He'll be out for a while. Why don't we head out to the stores and get some clothes. I think we'll be here for a few days. Sound good?" Stryder asks with a small smile.

Nodding, I stand and walk over to Jax, place a kiss on his cheek and wish him sweet dreams. As we walk out of his room, I pause at the doorway and take a last glance at Jackson's sleeping form. I can't help but think he has a long recovery ahead of him, and while he's been in good spirits, he has yet to talk about losing Chris and Rem. I've coped with survivor's guilt for the past four years, and I know more than anyone if he needs to talk to someone about it.

Stryder places a kiss on my hair, interrupting my thoughts. "Are you okay?"

"Yeah, I'm just worried about him."

Stryder takes hold of my hand and kisses my knuckles. "I know."

After spending the afternoon at the small shops in downtown Golden, we return to the hotel exhausted with several bags with clothes and toiletries. While at the drug store, I distracted Stryder for a moment to pick up lady products before he could see what I was buying. I've been feeling yucky and it's only a matter of days before that dreaded cycle shows up. With my purchases in hand, he surprises me with a bag of chocolate and a knowing smile.

Lying on the sofa of our suite, I rest my head on his shoulder and it isn't long before we're both naked and in bed loving each other. Sated and completely exhausted I fall asleep curled up to his side.

I am the first to wake up from our nap, and sure enough the dreaded cycle is here. Feeling less than enthused, I begrudgingly shower then dress in the loosest, most comfortable clothes I have. As I lay on the sofa I curl into myself, trying to mitigate the pain brought on by the evil troll kicking the shit out of my uterus, and after tossing and turning I abandon the sofa and return to bed irritated.

Stryder's arm reaches out for my waist and the urge to swat it away is great, but I know it's only the hormones talking and not how I really feel. I hate getting my period because it is god-awful. After the miscarriage my cycle worsened and after losing one of my ovaries post accident, my body rebels with out-of-this-world pain.

Raising his head from the pillow, Stryder places his head against my belly and kisses it. "What's wrong, baby?" he asks adoringly.

I'm mortified at the thought of sharing with him such personal information. Surely he's acquainted with periods given he's a son and brother, not to mention he lived with his now-ex-fiancée... He grew up dancing around countless women, so I'm confident he has an understanding of what's going on, but for some reason I feel shy and highly embarrassed to talk about it.

"Is there anything I can get you? Heating pad, medicine? Chocolate?" he asks, and smiles wickedly at the last option. His thoughtfulness makes me want to kiss him long and hard; nevertheless my hot cheeks reflect my embarrassment.

"You realize I was expecting this to happen, Cat. A part of me is relieved given our first encounters, and we've been together for a month now. Don't feel embarrassed about it, baby," he whispers, his lips kissing my belly again. As they do, my fingers run through his obsidian hair in wonder and appreciation.

Exhaling a sharp breath, I speak. "Can I see you in a week? I'm a moody and unstable bitch when it's that time of the month. I hate myself and the world even more."

Stryder chuckles loudly and sits up to hug me. "I'll just need to over-emphasize how beautiful you are and stock up on chocolate just in case you take that inner bitch out for a stroll."

I smack his shoulder playfully and kiss him, happy at how normal this awkward topic gets carried out between us. He leaves the bed gorgeously naked and walks gracefully into the closet to retrieve an electric blanket. My eyes devour him hungrily, and it pisses me off that I can't do anything about it for the next few days. It's not until you can't have something that it becomes the one thing you crave the most. The more I think about it, the more it pisses me off. *Fuck.*

"Tsk, tsk, Catalina," Stryder scolds with a smirk on his face. He moves his hands to cover himself and winks. "I *suppose* I should put some clothes on."

Feeling incredibly frustrated, I exhale loudly and throw my head back against the pillow. My thoughts go astray as I stare at the ceiling, trying to figure out creative ways to fast-forward time, and I come to the conclusion that I'm absolutely ludicrous. Stryder lets out a breath as he crawls back onto the bed and lays over me. The hardness of his sculpted body presses against my soft curves prompting me to close my eyes and sigh loudly.

"I'll try my best to stay away, but if you miss me too much there's always the shower," Stryder murmurs, and my eyes open wide with surprise.

My hands reach for his and I lace our hands together tightly; he kisses the crook of my neck and whispers sweet nothings that make me look forward to the end my cycle.

"I love you, Stryder."

"And I love you, Catalina."

After sharing kisses and copping a feel like teenagers, Stryder leaves our bed and showers before our evening visit to the hospital. Freshly showered, he looks amazing with his damp, straight obsidian hair skimming over his cheeks. Wearing grey jeans, a black undershirt, and a grey and black flannel shirt with his well worn Doc Marten boots, he looks so hot. I look down at myself and feel really blah. Nevertheless, I make an extra effort to look presentable and a final glance in the mirror confirms I look better than I feel. Exiting the bathroom, Stryder smiles, his eyes surveying my body hungrily; his arms wrap around my waist, pressing me flush against him, and he rests his forehead against mine.

"Could you at least try to look less appealing, Catalina? I don't want to look like some junkie jonesing," Stryder whispers against my lips.

His words make me feel wanted–something he has done since the very beginning. I trail my tongue over his lips, and then gently tug his lower lip with my teeth. From the back of his throat emerges a sexy growl which makes my belly flutter.

Stryder takes my hand and cups his erection with it. "If we didn't have plans already, I'd say I'd pick you up and fuck you standing in that shower, Catalina. Cramps will be the least of your worries."

The way he is looking at me makes me want to say screw the hospital visit and have him fuck me instead, but at the same time, it's rather odd for me to consider being intimate during that time of the month. I never have, but the fact that Stryder apparently doesn't mind it one bit makes me love him a tad more. There are some things I've never done with anyone before and this is one of them. A part of me looks forward to exploring many firsts, and at my age, with my experience, that's a rare thing. Avoiding temptation, we trek towards the lobby holding hands en route to the hospital.

Our visit with Jackson is pleasant. Kaelan brought in a few things for him, including a video game console. I sit next to him and we play a virtual snowboarding game, Stryder leaving us alone to play like two kids. Time passes by too quickly, and the young cute nurse kicks us out again. This time, she shares a knowing look with Jackson. I smile inwardly, but keep my assumptions to myself because at the end of the day there's nothing that would make me happier than to see Jackson find happiness just as I have with Stryder.

All those years of ranting from Faith make total sense now. She simply wanted me to experience the same excitement and happiness she found when she met Matt, her now-fiancé. Closing Jackson's door behind me, I see Stryder looking at his phone with a forlorn expression on his face. As I walk towards him, he looks up and smiles, but it doesn't reach his eyes. In such a short amount of time, I have learned to decipher all of his mannerisms and right now I'm certain something is bugging him and I think he's afraid to tell me. While I'm itching to know the cause of his discomfort, I'll let him come to it on his own terms.

Arriving back at the lodge, Stryder makes good on his promise to make love to me no matter what. At first, the thought of us being intimate during that time of the month makes me cringe, but with his tender kisses and affectionate embrace I give, and I'm pleased that I did. Running water is key, and call me crazy, but my cramps ease up after our little shower rendezvous. Sated and sleepy, we call it a night and fall asleep; our bodies cocooned next to each other's.

"I'm going to need a few days, Simon. With the family emergency, my priorities have shifted a bit. If you want, start looking for someone else just in case. I can't leave my family until I'm certain they're okay." Stryder sighs into the line, and pauses. "Simon, my family comes first, and if the client doesn't understand that, then I'm not the right guy for the job. I can't even think about going halfway around the world when I have two funerals to attend this week. Please understand, Simon. Surely you'd know this isn't an easy time."

I roll onto my side as the morning rays of sun creep into the room. Stretching in bed, I look towards the window, where Stryder stands wearing nothing but a pair of flannel pajama pants that hang low on his hips. I can appreciate all of his delectable male form; those chiseled abs and broad shoulders, his Mediterranean skin making a wondrous contrast against his obsidian hair.

Pressing a button, he throws his cell phone angrily against the sofa, and brings his fingertips to rake his scalp. "Fuck," he mutters under his breath. He paces in front of the window for a moment, then sits on the sofa, completely unaware I'm awake and watching him. I rise from the bed and wrap the blanket around me and tip toe towards the sofa, where he sits with his forearm over his eyes. Sitting beside him in silence, I bring my hand to his hair and caress it, which makes him hum in response.

"Sorry to have woken you up," Stryder mumbles.

"No need to apologize, Stryder. Is there anything I can do to help?" I whisper. He removes his arm from his face, and curls up next to me to rest his head on my shoulder.

"It's work. I have a queue of clients wanting to work exclusively with me, and I'm trying to find replacements. I'm overwhelmed, Catalina," Stryder replies softly. Leaving my shoulder, he sits forward on the sofa and rests his head against his knees. "I wanted to take time off, and now it seems impossible."

"I understand, baby, but these opportunities may not present themselves again, you know? If you're worried about Jax, don't. I'm on vacation and have the next three months to help out with his rehab. I'm sure Kaelan and Kathy would appreciate the help. I'll be home waiting for you..." I say reassuringly, but there's this pain in his eyes and I want to get to the bottom of it.

"I just want to spend time with you, Catalina. I just found you. I can't find it in my heart to take a month-long assignment and not be with you. Just the thought of it makes me sick," Stryder confesses, as he clears his throat.

I understand where he's coming from. I've enjoyed our company from the first moment we met on the plane on our way to Vancouver. Just thinking about not being together for a month makes my heart ache, but at the same time, Stryder has a career and he can't walk away from it because of our relationship.

"What worries you, baby? Being apart, or is it something else?" I ask, my eyes searching his. Judging by the way he's looking at me, tells me this has everything to do with his past and not with me.

Stryder kneels in front of me and brings his hands to rest on top of my thighs. He talks to my belly as if unable to make eye contact. "An assignment like this could make or break our relationship. I've seen it happen before, and my thoughts are a jumbled mess over it," Stryder confesses, raising his chin to meet my expectant gaze. "Olivia..."

My heart sinks to the pit of my stomach at the mere mention of Stryder's ex-fiancé. I know she cheated and broke his heart badly. I don't think Stryder is capable of hating anyone, but Olivia comes close. I can't say I blame him, especially after the exchange I witnessed between her and Jackson on his birthday. Olivia Reese is not a nice person, and despite her apology at the hospital, I'm extremely cautious when it comes to her.

"I took a three month job once. It happened a few weeks after I proposed. I hated leaving her behind in New York while I went overseas for my assignment, but it was a good opportunity with great pay and I knew that job could help with the cost of the wedding, so I didn't think about it twice. I left, but felt like half of my heart was left behind in the city. Not a day went by where I didn't consider quitting and going home back to her. She was everything to me at the time, you know?

I nod and smile softly, allowing him to get his fears off his chest. The more he speaks, the less enthused I am about Olivia Reese.

"Time zones were a bitch to manage, but somehow we made it work. As the weeks progressed, I kept hearing less and less from her, and I knew something was off. A part of me wanted to believe I was being an insecure asshole, that my brain was fucking with me, but deep down I knew something was up. I got a weekend off and got on a red-eye to surprise her. Imagine me, a bouquet of flowers in hand and the shocked look on my face when I saw the woman I loved being fucked in the ass on *our* bed by someone who wasn't me."

"You're scared something like that might happen again," I acknowledge, trying to keep my voice even. If I said his doubt didn't hurt me a little it would be a far cry from the truth. A look of embarrassment claims Stryder's features and it makes him appear more vulnerable to me than ever before.

"Feel free to slap me, Catalina. I deserve it," Stryder whispers, resting his head on top of my thighs. "I know I shouldn't doubt us, especially after all that's happened..."

Placing my hand on the back of his neck, I caress it. "Shh, I get it," I say, trying to stifle a smile. Without trying, Stryder is telling me how much I mean to him, and if I had any doubts about his affections and the depth of his love, I can throw those out the window right now. Stryder Martynus *loves* me.

Exhaling loudly, I continue. "I won't sit here and make promises to you. Anyone can do that, Stryder. What I will do is show you with every breath and every action how much you mean to me. Only time will tell where this thing between us goes, but know this: I will miss you with each beat of my heart and will cross out the days on my calendar until you're in my arms again.

"I will video call you and write you love letters, because that's what two people in love do. I'm so fucking in love with you that I'd write you corny poems and even doodle your name in the margins of my journal, but more importantly, I'll wait for you because you're worth it, Stud. Ease your troubled mind."

Stryder's hands take hold of my neck, and he kisses me with an intensity I haven't quite felt before: love, affection, trust, and desire sealed into one amazingly perfect kiss.

"I love you, Catalina. I will think about you every day, dream of you at night, and look forward to having your body wrapped around mine. I hope you understand, no matter what happens I will love you unconditionally. I'm just scared of losing you.

"Sometimes I feel so unworthy of you because your soul is so heart-crushingly beautiful and I'm just... *me*. A part of me feels I went through that shit with Olivia because you were meant to walk into my life. It was because fate had you in store for me."

His sincerity moves my soul, and now more than ever I understand why he's been out of sorts. My hands rise to his face to cup his jaw, and my eyes gaze into his, which look greener than usual with the morning light filtering through the windowpane.

"Why do you say such beautiful things, Stryder? Like you, I feel undeserving of this love, but I guess that's why God brought us together. I used to roll my eyes at those scenes in movies where the protagonists go over the top with their love declarations, but now I totally get it. It's not cheesy when your heart knits feelings into words. I had it *so* wrong."

Stryder kisses the tip of my nose and rises to stand. Extending his hand, he helps me up, brings me close to his chest, and declares, "You are everything to me."

The way he says those words–full of conviction and unmistakable confidence–rattles me down to my soul. It's as if those words have the ability to travel down to the deepest confines of my soul and knock down that final ice wall he's been chipping at since the moment we met. I still can't believe that, of all people, it would be the random stranger I met on a flight who would break down all of my walls, steal my heart, and make it his.

CHAPTER FOUR

Stryder

I stand in front of the window, holding onto my girl and feeling like the luckiest son of a bitch in the world. Wishful thoughts of growing old and grey beside Catalina take over my mind, and a sly smile creeps over my lips. There is no doubt in my mind I have found the woman I want to call my wife. This may sound crazy, and maybe my heart is moving faster than my feet, but I don't care. This love makes me sick with happiness, and damn me if I don't want to be cured.

The conversation between Cat and me could've gone in a different direction. She could've gotten pissed off at my trust issues and moreover hurt at the mere mention of Oli, but that's what separates Catalina from all the women I've ever been with before. She gets me and it is so odd, yet gratifying, to know she can put her feelings aside and listen to what I have to say with an open heart.

I'm relieved knowing Catalina will be waiting for me when I return from my assignment. I dismiss the urge to decline all incoming job offers to stay here with her; the reason behind it was wrong and brought on by my insecurities rather than necessity. Catalina doesn't deserve that. I desperately need to get my head back in the game, and make a mental note to call Mom and chat with her about this. If anyone gives me spectacular advice in my life, that's my Mom. In a weird way, Catalina reminds me of her. I smile, remembering Jackson's party where she was teaching Catalina the basic steps of the Cha-cha.

Then there is Catalina's vacation... It's good to know she'll be surrounded by my family and helping Jackson during his recovery. Between her, Kaelan, and Kathy, Jax should be up and snowboarding in no time. We just need to get through the next few days, attend Chris's and Rem's funerals, and try to move on with all of our lives. The thought that it could have been Jackson's funeral we're attending makes me shiver.

Breaking our hold, I bring Catalina back to the bed and tuck her in. Her eyes search mine and, kissing her lips chastely, I say, "I'm going to get us some breakfast at the main building. I need to get some fresh air. I'll be back soon, okay?"

Catalina pouts her lips and nods her head slowly. God, she's so adorable. It takes all of my willpower to break away from her, but I also know she understands why I need some time to think. I brush my teeth and put on sweats and trainers. By the time I return to kiss her goodbye, she's fast asleep with a smile on her face. I kiss her hair, taking in its sweet scent, and leave the suite.

Instead of heading straight to the lodge restaurant like I originally intended, I stop by the lodge's gym and run on the treadmill at a threatening pace. As I race, my mind goes amok with thoughts of the past and how I need to let it go. I can't let my past control my future with Catalina. The more I run, the more I feel liberated from Olivia's ghost. No matter how much she hurt me, a part of me still held onto her. Even when I lost myself in bed with lots of women, I always had Olivia in my head.

And now, I feel no love for her, and while that much is true I worry that not all people share my ideals of fidelity. All the depth of my feeling belongs to Catalina. I have to shake off the devil's seed of doubt planted in my brain because of my past. Drenched in sweat, I get off the treadmill and pick up the courtesy phone to make arrangements for a nice brunch to be delivered to our room. Olivia was my past, but Catalina is my future, and I'll be damned if I fuck this up with my insecurities.

Picking up a towel, I wipe the sweat from my brow. Through the mirrored walls I see two women eyeballing me, and I groan inwardly. *Look away, ladies, because looking is all you'll be able to do.* Throwing the towel into the bin, I leave the gym and return to our room. Luckily,

Catalina is still fast asleep, so I duck in the shower and make it quick since I want to greet room service without waking her up. Wrapping a towel around my hips, I walk to the closet and dress for the day. The sound of my phone chirping in the bathroom redirects my attention. As I pick up my phone, my heart clenches in my chest.

<KP: Jax is having a bad day. Docs aren't allowing visitors today. Sorry if you made plans.>

I reply quickly.

<SM: Define bad day. Please keep me posted.>

<KP: The docs want to release him but when we told him we were expected at Chris's and Rem's services in WY he broke down. They gave him sedatives to calm him.>

<SM: Shit. Okay. I'll make flight arrangements for us. Keep us posted.>

<KP: We are all flying together. I already made the reservations. And I will.>

<SM: Thanks, K. I'm worried. This is going to be hard... on all of us.>

<KP: I know, but we're a family and we stick together. Let me know when you get the flight info.>

I check my email inbox and see Kaelan's itinerary. We leave tomorrow afternoon for Casper, Wyoming. Closing the application, I reply back.

<SM: Got it. Thank you. Tough times ahead, Kaelan.>

The raps against the door of the suite prompt me to place my cell in my pocket and run to the door. I collect the trays from the room service cart and place them on the small table in the suite. The smell of waffles and bacon wafts into the room, waking Catalina up. There's my girl, her raven hair messy, and a smile on her heart-shaped lips. Her alluring beauty takes my breath away.

"Good morning again, baby," I whisper as she yawns and stretches in bed.

Yawning, Catalina says, "Good morning to you too." Coming over to the bed, I kiss her lips softly. She sighs happily."You smell so good."

I tilt my neck until her nose and lips touch my skin. "There. Better?" Once again, Catalina inhales deeply, but this time she licks me, and my dick quickly takes notice of her affections. I chuckle inwardly, thinking no woman but Catalina has the ability to get me going with the simplest of actions, and I love that about us.

"Stop teasing me, Catalina," I groan, and after putting a considerable distance between us, I stand to help her up. "Come on, baby. Brunch is here."

Catalina scoots out of bed in her oversized t-shirt and pajama pants, and we eat at the table in comfortable silence. Perhaps now is the time to break the news about Jax. I explain the text messages Kaelan sent me, and the look on Catalina's face reflects worry and sadness. I can tell her mind is racing but she only says, "That sucks."

After brunch, I propose we do some sightseeing, but one glance out the window at the snow shower quickly cancels my plan. So we settle for watching movies, reading, and simply enjoying each other's company. I can't believe how exhausted she is as she naps in intervals curled up in my lap. The only time she gets up is to use the bathroom. My Raven Girl looks a little pale and judging by her pained expression, her time of the month is kicking her ass, and then some.

I just can't wait for her to get past it so that we can resume the closeness I can't get enough of. I'm dying to taste her, lose myself in her skin and go into reckless abandon. We need to talk about contraception, because I really don't like using condoms and I have yet to share that with her. I don't want to sound like a rueful jerk, though, and I know this topic needs to be brought on gently. Clearing my throat, I speak my mind because there isn't a delicate way to talk about it.

"I think we need to talk about something important," I begin a little awkwardly.

"What's up?" Catalina asks, her eyes searching mine.

"We've been together for some time now, and I was wondering how you feel about condoms."

Catalina's face flushes, but she answers. "I hate them, and I know you do too. Am I wrong?" As I nod in agreement, I'm pretty sure my face is the same shade of red as hers.

"No, you're not. It's restricting, but at the same time they're a necessary evil."

Catalina nods, and says, "Tell you what. Now is the perfect time to start birth control. We'll still have to be careful, but I'll do it if that's what you want. Though..." she trails off. "After the accident, the doctor had to remove one of my ovaries. It's not to say I can't bear children, but I was advised getting pregnant again wouldn't be easy. I have a lot of issues with my plumbing, but it's not unwise to be safe. Thank you for being considerate in our encounters. It says a lot about you," Catalina asserts with luminous eyes.

Whoa. I didn't expect to be saddened by her words, but I am. It hurts to know she has endured so much pain and suffering over the years, and the aftermath of the fatal accident still haunts her to this very day. I want to say something that will comfort her, but the right words don't surface. Sighing, I kiss her forehead and the dreamer in me takes the conversation one step further.

"How do you feel about kids, Catalina?" I ask earnestly. I don't really know why I'm even asking that, but I'm curious to know her response.

"To tell you the truth, after losing the baby, my womb felt empty... like someone stole something precious from me, but my baby wasn't the only person I was robbed of. Blake was too, and after his death, I gave up on the idea of love, and on my dreams of becoming a mom. I decided I could help those in need, so I have charities for single moms I donate to on a monthly basis and I've volunteered at a woman's shelter in the city. But to answer your question, motherhood was a dream I always had, but now in my thirties I'm afraid that ship has sailed."

"Why do you say that, Cat? Women are having kids in their forties nowadays," I whisper, feeling disheartened. "Why give up so easily?"

Catalina sniffles and raises her head up from my lap. Crossing her arms against her chest, I notice her chin and lips quiver as dew droplets form in the corner of her eyes. Placing my hand over her heart, I feel it drumming furiously.

"Because you don't know what it's like to want something so bad and see it ripped from you in the blink of an eye. I wouldn't call it giving up, Stryder. I call it self-preservation. I can't bear the loss of another child. Not in this lifetime," Catalina whispers shakily, wiping the corner of her eyes with the hem of her t-shirt. Standing up, she returns to the bed and buries herself underneath the covers.

Her unmistakable sniffles tell me she's crying, and I hate that I'm the cause of them. I scramble towards her, not knowing what to say that will ease her sadness. I need to say something, but a repeated "I'm sorry," is all that comes out.

"I'm sorry, baby. I didn't mean to bring this up. I just... I just wanted to know. Cat?" I ramble, rubbing her back over the layers of blankets covering her. When she doesn't respond, tears of my own slip out at the realization that I, too, want something I've never wanted before.

A part of me realized it the day I met Catalina. I helped a woman carry her sleeping toddler into the flight cabin, and when that half-asleep child called me 'Dada', something in me clicked. Somehow I knew at that moment life is too short and being a father is something I'd aspire to be in the not so distant future, and now that my heart belongs to Catalina, I want it all the more.

Listening to Catalina's experience makes my chest tight. The woman I love has been through so much, and there's nothing I'd like more than to wipe away those horrible memories and replace them all with happier ones. I won't give up on showing her with every waking moment how much she means to me, and how much I want her to have hope and dream of things she once deemed impossible. And she *will* bear a child. I won't give up on that dream until *I* make it a reality.

I undress, and lifting the thick blankets, I curl in bed beside her. At first Catalina tries to push me away, but after I trail small kisses against the soft curve of her neck, she concedes. Words aren't needed, but I know my lady well enough to know she's okay, and that helps me breathe easier. I'll let this conversation go for now and wait until our lives return to normal. With all the recent events, perhaps I'm jumping the gun here and sprinting towards the finish line, when the truth of the matter is I need to slow down for her sake.

"Are we good?" I whisper into the silence of the room.

"Yeah," she replies quietly, but says nothing further.

I exhale a shaky breath, trying to get past the awkwardness of our conversation. Her delicate hand touches the bare skin of my back, and scratches it gently and affectionately. I groan, and in a matter of minutes all the stress of the past week seems to fade away under her touch.

"I love you, Stryder. Just don't give up on me, promise?" Catalina's words are firm and full of promise.

I raise my head, and look deeply into her eyes, which are slightly bloodshot by tears. My hands find the curve of her jaw, and I say, "I love you too, Catalina. I'd never give up on you, or us for that matter. Never."

My eyes zone in on those heart-shaped lips of hers, wanting nothing more than to kiss them, but I hesitate. Not because I don't want to, but because I love her so much, and I'm overwhelmed with our kind of love. You know the kind that makes you a lunatic, have out-of-body experiences, and do stupid shit. I love Catalina with every fiber of my being and want her to love me with the same fire and intensity. I'm not saying she doesn't, because I know she loves me. There's no doubt about that, but I'm a guy who needs his reassurances too. I close my eyes and breathe heavily, trying to dispel my insecurities and doubts. Catalina doesn't deserve an ounce of my idiotic thoughts right now.

As if sensing my hesitation, Catalina raises her head, and her lips meet mine. She kisses me softly, and all of my negative thoughts are replaced with the reassurance that she loves me, and that alone is enough to make my blood travel south in a heartbeat.

My whole body shakes with anxiety as we step into the First Methodist Church in Casper. I'm flanked by Catalina as I push Jax in his wheelchair while Catalina holds his hand. Unlike Catalina, Jax and I knew Chris and Rem for many years, and seeing their closed caskets with red roses atop of them brings to the surface many beautiful memories that are now painful. My heart feels contrite, and a part of me just wants to break down and cry.

Crying is part of the grieving process, and if anyone knows about loss it's Catalina. She has experienced so much death in her life. I have cried in the shower since the avalanche, because I, too, lost friends that day. And standing here in this church makes me teary-eyed, but I bite my lip and try my damndest to keep my shit together. One glance at Jax, and I can tell he's trying to rein in his emotions, but the non-stop quivering of his lower lip gives him away. Placing a kiss on Catalina's forehead, I excuse myself to pay my respects to Chris and Rem's parents, and ask her not to leave Jax alone.

It was difficult leaving his place this morning. He was a mess, and I thank God Cat is here to help him through this terrible process. He refused to attend the wake last night because he didn't want to see their open caskets. He said it would mean the finality of their once adventurous lives, so he took sleep medication instead, taking the easy way out and not coping with his losses head-on. I understand, though. Who am I to criticize him?

After greeting Chris's and Rem's folks and paying my respects, I see Jax and Catalina approaching the caskets on the base of the altar. I walk over and place a hand over Jax's shoulder in solidarity and the other on Rem's casket while Catalina kneels before the caskets and says a prayer in Spanish. As she prays, she clutches Jackson's hand firmly while his free elbow rests against the wheelchair armrest. He lays his head into his hand and rubs his forehead with trembling fingers, his breathing becoming erratic as small sobs leave his chest.

Catalina ends her prayer and whispers something into his ear. Her arm wraps around his shoulder reassuringly, and he whispers back in between sobs.

"I should've aborted the run. I knew something was off. I was too embarrassed to admit to Rob I was wrong, and he was right. This is my fault." His words break at the last word, and the sobs he was desperately trying to hold back come out full force. "I'm so sorry, guys. This is *my* fault. This is *my* fault! I'm sorry!" Jackson repeats endlessly until his cries turn into screams the kind that give you nightmares echoing against the walls of the church.

"*This is my fault, and I can't do anything to bring you guys back! I'm sorry! Please forgive me, guys, because I fucking can't!*" Jackson cries, his entire body shaking with grief. "*Please!*"

Catalina looks at me with tears streaming past her cheeks, and I bite my lip as tears of my own threaten to fall. Using hand gestures, we silently agree to back away from the caskets and find our seats, but as we try to move Jax's wheelchair his hands reach out to the shiny casket housing Chris's body.

"No! I need to beg for forgiveness. It was me who needed to die out there that day, not them, Jupiter! It was me who didn't deserve to live. They need to hear me out, they need to forgive me!"

I kneel before him and place my hands over his knees. "Listen to me, brother. You can't do this to yourself," I command, using my shoulders to dry the tears that fall from my eyes. "You are *alive* for a reason, Jax. You can't torture yourself because you lived and they didn't. You survived and you are *here* for a reason, and I will *not* let you do this to yourself. You can cry, get upset, and even be mad at me, but *none* of this was *your* fault, do you understand me?"

Jax tries to brush me away, but I raise my hands from his knees to cup his cheeks and look into his bloodshot eyes. "You are *alive*, and we *love* you, and we *will* get through this, understood? Please stop beating yourself up over it," I desperately plead.

Jax nods slowly as tears continue to trickle down his face, landing on his shirt and tie. Catalina slowly pushes the chair away from where the guys rest. As we work our way back to our seats, Chris's and Rem's parents come over to Jax, and crouch to hug him. In the silence of the church all I can hear are his never-ending cries for forgiveness, and while he bears no fault I couldn't possibly fathom reacting differently if I were the one in Jax's shoes.

Jackson was supposed to read a eulogy in honor of his dearly departed friends, but given his fragile state Catalina rises to stand in his place and walks towards the pulpit with purposeful strides. She grabs a guitar from the choir bench and brings it with her to the pulpit. After adjusting the microphone to her height, she fiddles with the guitar tuning the strings. Once satisfied, she speaks into the microphone.

"I didn't know Chris and Rem like Jackson Reese and Stryder Martynus did, but I met them once in Port De Soleil when Jackson won the World Snowboarding Championship. While our encounter was short-lived, I knew the moment I met them they were special men. Friends of my best friend, and while their bodies are no longer with us, their spirit remains within each of us. We'll feel them on the slopes riding alongside us, and when the time is right, we will all meet again. I'm not a woman of many words so I will let this song do all the talking. On behalf of Jackson Reese, Chris and Rem, this one is for you both," she says as her fingers begin playing the opening chords of Skylar Grey's "I Will Return."

I touch Jackson's shoulder and pull him close, as Catalina's voice echoes through the walls of the church leaving everyone a teary mess. When she returns to our pew I hear Jax whisper his appreciation and commend her for words and song.

As we sit there during the rest of the funeral service and later at the burial, I can't help but feel gratitude to God for sparing Jackson's life. Through the emotional events of the day, Catalina focuses all of her attention on Jax and I couldn't be more thankful. She was brought into our lives for a special purpose, and she is a prime example of the fact that life indeed moves on, even after loss, and if I've learned anything from her, it's that hope is something you can achieve if you only believe.

The few weeks that follow the funeral are the hardest on Jax, and I'm glad we've spent every waking moment with him, but it's almost time for me to leave the love of my life and my best friend behind. Catalina has been working endlessly with Jax, taking him to his physical therapy and psychologist appointments. So far he's shown some improvement in his mobility; however his mind is taking a lot longer to recover than his limbs.

Back at Jackson's ranch, we try to move on from the pain of the accident. All of our moods are affected mainly because Jax is sunken in a depression that is messing with all of our moods. Catalina and I are trying to be patient, and we're working with him to get his life back on track. Despite having two broken ankles, Jax is determined to move around, and his mood while hostile, is a reflection of how he feels on the inside.

Leaving Catalina asleep upstairs after a long and exhausting day at the medical center with Jax, I run downstairs to work from his office. As I'm walking through the kitchen, I see him drinking vodka straight from the bottle with a pill bottle in front of him. I halt in my steps horrified.

"What the fuck do you think you're doing?" I roar, in complete disbelief. "I can't believe you're doing this shit again!"

"Don't just stand there and patronize me, asshole. You don't know how much it fucking hurts, Jupiter. You don't know what it's like to wake up each day and have the death of two of your friends over your motherfucking head. Do not judge me, you son of a bitch!" Jackson screams, as tears roll down his face. "Don't you fucking dare!" he cries, slamming his hands flat against the countertop.

My heart aches for Jax. A part of me wants to punch him in the face because clinging to a bottle hasn't done him any favors in the past. And while I understand his pain, I can't look the other way. I storm towards him, and rip the bottle away from his hands, and empty its contents in the sink.

"I will *not* let you do this to yourself. I will *not* sit idle and let you grieve like this. You want to cry? Cry! You want to scream? Then fucking scream! But this bullshit drinking will not happen again. I don't give three shits if this pisses you off, but I will *not* let you fall again!" I yell, as tears blotch my face. "You're not the only one who lost friends that day! I lost them too, but you don't see me hitting the goddamn bottle and drowning my sorrow with fucking vodka. This is your life and you're wasting it!"

Catalina runs into the kitchen barefoot in just her nightgown. "Guys, what's going on?!"

I lift the bottle from the sink and wave it in the air. "This shithead thinks it's okay to mix pills and booze!" I answer absolutely enraged.

Catalina inhales loudly and walks towards the counter where Jackson is sitting. Crouching down, she looks into his eyes. "Babe, you can't do this," she whispers. "Death is a traitorous bitch, and you've done so well with your sobriety. Now is not the time to seek comfort with booze, and you *know* it."

Jackson reaches for Catalina's face, and brings his head to rest against hers. "I'm sorry, Cat.," he cries. "It just fucking hurts. I can't breathe."

"I know, baby. I know," she says holding onto him.

I watch them in silence. My anger-fueled state dissipates and is quickly replaced with sorrow. Jackson is grieving, and drinking booze is only way he knows how to cope with Chris's and Rem's deaths. Catalina coaxes him back into his room so I take advantage of this opportunity to raid the entire house, searching for liquor bottles, and disposing of them. After my clean-up, I fill two black, lawn bags with almost three cases of liquor and beer combined. As I walk towards the trash bins, I shake my head in disbelief, and pray I got every single drop of alcohol out of the house.

At this point I have no choice. I have to tell Kathy. I dial her number, and she answers on the second ring.

"Jupiter?" she says alarmed.

"Kathy... The death of our friends has caused a major setback in Jackson's sobriety. I did a sweep of the house after I found him drinking his meds with vodka."

Kathy sighs. "Oh, this child is going to be the end of me. You don't suppose he's abusing his medicines too?"

"I don't know, but I think you need to alert his medical team. He might be trying to substitute one fix for another."

"Okay," she sighs, resigned. "Thank you for alerting me. I don't know what else to do. I've never understood his need for drinking. Let me give them a call, and talk to the doctors about it."

"No problem. I'm sorry. We'll keep an eye on him." I end the call.

A part of me wants to stay because belligerent Jax is back, and while Cat and Kaelan seem to be managing him well despite his anger-fueled state, I know my presence soothes them all.

Catalina has urged me not to turn down work, and I'd be lying if I didn't admit I miss working despite finding love with her. I've agreed to photograph a string of surfing competitions in Australia, and it will be a month-long tour. My chest tightens at the thought that I won't be by Catalina's side.

It's late, and while Catalina is sleeping in our warm bed, I'm catching up on emails in Jax's office. I sit, pensive, in front of my laptop looking at the inbox full of unanswered emails with different job offers which could easily keep me busy for the next six months. I've struggled with thoughts of declining all work. I mean, that's all I've done for the past seven years... travel, come home, and do it all over again, and again.

And for the first time in years, I have something to fight for, and someone waiting for me to come home. A part of me wants to give myself an opportunity to live life differently–to love like I've never known how. And then there's the pressing urge to take our relationship to the next level. The pessimistic side of me thinks she'll freak out with a proposal and run, so maybe diving back into work will dull that urge. It's better that, than to sit here and wonder if she's content with what little we have, and whether or not she's ready to trust me with the rest of her heart.

I slam the cover of my laptop shut. It's half past midnight and regardless of the time, I need to speak with the only woman who knows exactly what to say when I feel lost. I forego the worries of time zones and manners, and dial her number. On the third ring, a very groggy voice answers.

"Jupiter? Baby, are you okay?"

"Mom. Hi. Sorry for calling so late. I didn't mean to wake you..." I reply sheepishly, my free hand squeezing the back of my neck.

Mom yawns over the line and replies, "Don't worry, Tesoro. What's troubling you so late at night?"

I take a deep breath and pray Mom withholds all teasing until we end this chat. "How did you know Dad was, you know... the one?"

Mom answers with a giggle. "Oh, sweetheart, I didn't. I just let time knock some sense into me until I realized your father was the man for me." She exhales loudly and asks, "Why are you in such deep thought at this time of night?"

"I don't know, 'ma. I'm just scared of fucking up my chances with Catalina," I admit as I rise from the chair and pace aimlessly in Jackson's office. "I mean, the press tour is over, and we've dealt with some adversity since Jax's accident, but eventually we'll get back to our lives, and she has her job and I have mine... I have a lot of job offers to work abroad, and I'm scared of history repeating itself. Look what happened the last time I was in a relationship... Olivia cheated because I was never here."

"Stryder Martynus, I'm going to stop you right there. I don't know Catalina all that well, but she's not fickle, and she's not anything remotely similar to your ex. Trust me when I tell you I felt immense relief when you broke off that engagement. I love Oli like a daughter, but it's the truth. On the other hand, Catalina is a sweet girl who I know for a *fact* loves you very much."

"How would you know that, Mom?" I ask, with a smile.

Mom giggles, and decrees, "A mother knows these things. All it takes is one good look at the two of you to know you belong together. Your father would agree with me on this, you know..." Mom pauses to clear her throat. "Sweetheart, do you love her?"

"Yes, Mom, I do. With all of my heart, but it's too soon, isn't it?" I answer, cringing.

"No, my son, it isn't. We can't choose a specific time and place to fall in love. It would make life terribly boring and predictable, don't you think? I always knew your time would come, and I have to say, as your mother, it makes me happy you're finally having this conversation with me," she sniffles.

"Catalina's the one, Mom," I reply without thinking twice.

"Have you told her that, Tesoro?"

"From the moment we met, I've felt like my heart has been taken from me and started beating inside of her. So yes, I told her recently I love her. It took her some time to say it back. I know when she said it she meant it, but I want so much more," I confess, the last few words coming out a little strangled as the knot in my throat starts to loosen up.

"You don't tell her, Jupiter. You show her with actions that you are worthy of her. Think of it as a Paso Doble. She is your bull and you are the *Matador*. At first she will be feisty and try to fight you, but you can't give into your fears or insecurities. You need to remain firm, well-grounded with your feelings towards her. Us women... we like to test our men. We want our guys to fight for us, because it shows us how much they love us. Why we do this, I'll never know, but with time she'll realize she won't have any excuses to throw at you and she'll give into you. As your mother, I ask you to trust me on this," Mom explains, with a click of her tongue.

I chuckle at Mom's never-ending supply of dancing analogies. "Mom, what do I do about my assignments? I don't want to be away from her."

Mom sighs and replies, "Only you can make that decision, Jupiter. I can't tell you what to do because this is your career, but if I could give you a piece of advice, it would be to take a short assignment. Put some space between you and Catalina. It will give you both time to think about your feelings for each other, and it will give her the opportunity to miss you. Remember, absence makes the heart grow fonder, or so the saying goes."

I stop pacing and stand still for a minute, considering Mom's words. As they sink in, I can't help but come to terms with the fact that she is right on all accounts.

"Stryder, are you still there?"

"I'm here, Mom. I was thinking, and you know what? You're right. I need to sort out the mess in my heart before I can move forward. Distance isn't such a bad thing... This will be our first test," I say with smile. "Mom, you always know the right thing to say."

Mom laughs again. "That's why I'm your mother, Stryder. Take your time with Catalina and don't rush things. Treat her like the princess she is. Love her without restraint, and offer your heart without fear. It will all work out in the end. She is the arrow to your bow, remember that."

I nod and choke back tears. Exhaling raggedly, I whisper into the line, "Mom, I love you. You're the best. I'm sorry for calling so late. You must be tired. Talk to you soon."

"That's what mammas are for. Ti amo, Jupiter. Now fight for her!"

I nod once again, and this time I'm feeling good about taking an assignment and letting time do its thing. Yeah, I'll miss Catalina terribly, but given we've been joined at the hip since Whistler this could be healthy for our relationship.

Turning off the lamp in Jackson's office, I return to our room. Catalina is fast asleep on the bed, her gorgeous hair fanned against the pillow, with her arm stretched out on my side of the bed. I lean against the doorjamb and take the vision in. I can't believe after living carelessly for so long, I've been rewarded with Catalina's love. I want more, but for now I need to be patient. If Catalina has taught me anything, it's this.

Walking towards the bed, I undress, leaving a trail of clothes in my wake. Fully undressed, I slip under the covers and reach for my girl. God, she's so warm to the touch, and her soft silken skin begs to be kissed. Catalina's soft breathing makes me smile. Although I want to wake her up and make love to her, I just lie on my back and stare at the ceiling, enjoying this perfect moment. When the timing is right, I will make this woman my wife.

CHAPTER FIVE

Catalina

"Hello, Jackson. My name is Dr. Badcocke, and I will be your physical therapist. How are you feeling today?" the doctor asks, as he looks over Jackson's chart.

"Not as bad as your last name, Doc," he replies irritated with his eyes closed.

I place a hand over my mouth stifling laughter. Jackson's mood has been flip-flopping over the past weeks, and while his humor is somewhat there, his remarks can be off the cuff and quite offensive.

Dr. Badcocke chuckles heartily. "I get that a lot, Jackson. Now, today we will be working with your gluteus maximus and gluteus medius, and see if we can regain range of motion in those regions of your body." Dr. Badcocke lowers his eyeglasses and looks at Jackson square in the eye. "In case you were wondering those are your butt muscles."

"You'll be working on my ass? Joy," Jackson replies sarcastically while tapping his fingers impatiently against his knees.

I look at Dr. Badcocke and give him an empathetic smile, which he returns two-fold. Surely it's not his first rodeo with a wild bull patient like Jackson Reese. I'm just happy he's not taking Jackson's actions personal. To be honest, it's been hard not to over the past two weeks.

"I need you to lie on your side," the doctor points at the blue, padded mat on the floor, "and lift your leg and keep it elevated for fifteen seconds, okay?"

Jackson begrudgingly moves towards the mat and positions himself as the doctor asks. As he's raising his leg, pain is etched across his features. "I can't do this, Doc," and lets his right leg rest against the other.

"Sure you can, Jackson. I'm going to help you raise it. Work through the pain."

Doctor Badcocke kneels beside him and raises Jackson's leg. "Now I'm going to count to fifteen. One, two, three–"

"Fuck! That hurts!" Jackson mutters but keeps his leg elevated and pushes through his pain thanks to the encouragement of the good doctor.

"Okay. Now the left," the doctor exacts.

They repeat the process until they get through the therapy session. "See, Jackson? We'll get you back in shape in no time," Dr. Badcocke declares with a smile. "You got this."

I sit back and watch Jackson closely. While there is fury in his eyes, I also notice there's a spark of determination behind them. To say the weeks since Chris's and Rem's funeral have been challenging would be an understatement. Jackson is struggling with his recovery and between his bouts of depression and frustration over the physical therapy process, to say I'm running on fumes is an understatement.

I'll be staying with him in Casper while Stryder goes to Australia on a month-long assignment. My heart tightens in my chest at the thought of being separated from the man I've grown to know and love. The selfish side of me wants him to cancel the trip and stay by my side. The other wants to encourage him to go out there and further his career. If I'm perfectly honest, I think a little space would do us a world of good.

To think we only have two days left together before he leaves makes me weary. I know Stryder has noticed, and being the sweetest and most understanding of men he says nothing. There are moments I feel the urge to slap myself in hopes of getting my emotions in check.

I want Stryder to stay.

No. Stop being so selfish, Catalina. He has to work.

No, no! I want him to stay.

Ugh. I know I'm sending Stryder mixed signals by being sad one minute over his impending departure, and the next acting like it doesn't bother me. I need to get a grip on my feelings before he runs out the door scared. I imagine Stryder boarding his flight, falling asleep on someone else's shoulder, falling in love with someone else, and forgetting me altogether. These things can happen, right? I mean, look at how we met. I realize I'm being pessimistic here, and I hate this insecure side of me. I totally get it... He had a life and career before I came along, and like he's told me before, the Earth hasn't stopped turning... *Pfft. Isn't that the truth.*

As I sit on a barstool in Jax's kitchen with my elbow propped against the granite countertop, I think about how this assignment could make or break the beautiful relationship we've built over the recent months. I know we've said *I love you*, but the more I think about our relationship the more I know my love for Stryder is greater than anything I ever imagined possible. And words fail me when I try to describe the depth of my love for him.

When I'm not with him I miss him, and when he's away, I feel crippled by his absence. I'm really worried how this trip will affect me emotionally, because I've become co-dependent on him, losing a part of my inner strength along the way.

Your heart is open.

Every single hair on my body stands on edge, and I shiver as a cold chill overcomes me. I straighten myself on the barstool, wondering if I've really lost my marbles. Call me crazy, but I swear I heard someone whisper those words. They didn't pop up in my mind uninvited.

My breath catches as I look around for the source completely sure I've lost my damn mind. A deep chuckle I know and remember all too well rings in the air.

Your heart is open. Don't be afraid.

"Catalina?" I startle at the sound of my name.

I raise my head from the counter, disoriented. My hands reach for my cheeks which tingle and are surprisingly tender to the touch. I worry my jaw from side to side and it's only then I realize I fell asleep at the kitchen counter in the middle of the afternoon.

"Cat?" Jackson's voice rings into the vast kitchen space, his deep timbres echoing softly. "Are you okay, girl?"

I straighten my spine against the leather back of the barstool and stretch my arms over my head. A few yawns escape me, and I see

Jackson standing on the opposite end of the counter looking at me with his brows furrowed.

"My back is killing me," I answer, amid yawns which make him laugh.

"I thought you were dead, woman. I walked in to get something to eat, and the first thing I saw was you slumped over that damn chair," Jackson jokes.

"I'm just tired, and I haven't been sleeping well," I clarify as I stand. I place my hands on the counter. They're trembling.

Jackson chuckles, and wiggles his eyebrows devilishly. "Just stop fucking like bunnies and you may just get a good nights' sleep. Not judging, just saying..."

If I wasn't so rattled I'd laugh along, but right now I feel contrite and unable to enjoy Jackson's crack at our healthy sexual appetite. I look into Jackson's eyes and sigh which in turn makes him hobble over to me. Placing his gruff hands on my shoulders, he keeps me at an arm's length, his crisp, azure eyes regarding mine.

"What's the matter, Pardo?" Jackson asks, sounding incredibly serious as his eyes blink rapidly.

I exhale loudly and hang my head low, my eyes focused on the seams of the hardwood flooring. "I just–I'm physically tired, and I'm freaking out over Stryder leaving. I don't want him to go."

Jackson's hands move to embrace me, pulling me close to his chest. My arms instinctively wrap around his waist, and when he winces, I loosen my hold.

"So you're scared of losing Jupiter, aren't you?" Jackson mumbles against my hair, and I nod in response. "Girl, you don't need to worry about a damn thing. You have that man wrapped around your pinkie and you don't even know it," he asserts with a chuckle.

Despite this reassurance I don't feel any more secure. When you love someone as much as I love Stryder, it's easy to come up with a million reasons to be frightened. My heart is open, as the voice said, and the walls that once protected it are gone. I'm left vulnerable and it scares me to no end.

I know you can't die from a broken heart, but thinking how long it took me to breathe again, to live again after losing Blake makes me want to never endure that kind of pain again.

"Hey, where'd you go?" Jackson asks, interrupting my thoughts.

"I'm here," I cough, forcing a smile. I hope he doesn't notice it's not a genuine one. Jackson Reese has so much going on in his life right now, the last thing he needs is to worry about me. "Are you hungry?" I ask, desperate to change the subject.

"Famished, actually." He brings his head to rest on the kitchen counter. He's so cute when he's having a good day, and by the looks of it today is one of those days.

I busy myself making us cold-cut sandwiches with mustard and mayonnaise, then rummage through the cabinets looking for a cutting board. In my search I come across a juicing machine, and take some carrots, an apple, and some kale from the refrigerator. At first, Jackson gives me a disgusted look when I place the brownish-green concoction in front of him; he even crosses his arms over his chest and shakes his head like a petulant child. But when his lips meet the frothy goodness, he chugs it down and asks for more.

"Is this juicing-crap healthy? I've gained weight since the accident," Jackson complains, as he gestures at his body. When I nod, he smiles in relief. "Good, because I need to lose fifteen pounds, and fast! I'm not a narcissist, but this body isn't me."

I smile from behind the counter, and place my sandwich back on the plate. Looking at him square in the eye, I speak. "Being fifteen pounds heavier is better than being dead six feet under."

Jackson looks at me and blinks twice. I can tell by the look on his face my words are sobering. For a man filled with humor, he was yet to come up with a witty comeback to my solemn words. To dispel the sudden silence between us, I continue.

"Juicing will be a great way to keep you healthy and it will definitely help you lose some of the weight. Before you know it, you'll be back in shape and cleared by the medical team to resume snowboarding."

Jackson looks at me and smiles. "I sure hope so. Another juice please," he says, as he gestures at the machine on the counter. I laugh at his eagerness and spoil him by making him another.

We eat our lunch at the counter in comfortable silence. My mind is filled with worry for the man sitting beside me. I've seen him sit by the large windowpane for hours at a time staring at the Wyoming Mountains that form part of the view of his backyard. I may not know Jackson Reese like Stryder does, but I know him well enough to know he misses snowboarding. I mean, he's used to being in the great outdoors and being confined to four walls and a ceiling is definitely playing a huge role in his depression. Hell, being indoors makes me feel confined too, ever since the press tour ended.

And then there's the part of the puzzle that worries me the most. Despite accompanying Jackson to his sports medicine and psychologist appointments, it's like his body is there, but his heart and mind are elsewhere. It breaks my heart to see him sitting on the damn family room couch with a lost and defeated expression. He refuses to talk about the accident. I've sat beside him on that very couch holding his hand and praying he opens up, but I can't force him. He has to come to terms on his own. I know because I've gone through the same thing, and now more than ever I understand Faith's constant nagging over the years, and make a mental note to apologize to her next time I see her.

"Where's Jupiter?" Jackson asks in between chews.

I exhale a little louder than intended and reply, "He's out getting supplies for his trip."

Jackson drops the sandwich on his plate and reaches for my hand. "Girl, don't be sad. He'll be back before you know it, and hopefully by then we can all go snowboarding... and find some normalcy. You're staying with me while he's away, right?"

I squeeze his hand tightly, and looking into his eyes I answer. "Sadness is inevitable, but having you by my side will make the wait easier. My focus is to get you better," I confirm as I let go of his hand. I place one hand over his heart and the other on top of his messy hair. "Your mind will take some time to catch up with what's happened, but your heart will never heal unless you allow it to. Please talk, if not to me then at least say something to the therapist tomorrow. *Please.*"

Jackson nods, and a stray tear escapes from the corner of his eye. I catch it with my thumb and smudge it across the top of his cheek, and that makes him swallow hard. I rise from the stool, and wrap my arms around him, bringing his head to rest against my chest. One of my hands cradles his scruffy face while the other rubs his back in wide, soothing circles.

"It's my fault, Catalina. I killed Chris and Rem," Jackson concedes in between sobs. "I knew in my gut something was off, and for a second I thought about calling Base and letting Rob know I wanted to abort the run. I always listen to my gut, and I don't fucking understand why I didn't make the call." His last words come out choked, and bitter sobs leave his chest.

"Jackson, it wasn't your fault, you hear me? We can't accept responsibility for an act of nature. Trust me, it took me a long time to understand that, because Mother Nature ripped away my fiancé and baby, and for a very long time I blamed myself for something I had no control over. This wasn't your fault, and please, for the love of God, stop blaming yourself," I beg, as tears of my own stain my cheeks.

"Oh, Cat. I'd be in a lot worse shape if not for you. I'm sorry if I've been such an asshole. I've never lost anyone in my life before, and I don't know how to cope without alcohol. Right now, all I want to do is drink, lose myself, and find temporary happiness to replace the pain in my fucking chest."

Jackson lifts his head from my chest and looks into my eyes. "How'd you do it, Cat? How'd you live after losing everyone who's meant something to you? Tell me how to get rid of this pain that makes it so fucking hard to breathe because right now, I feel like giving up. It was me who should've died that day, not them!"

I move my hands to cup his cheeks, and when our eyes connect I see a raw vulnerability in his eyes a look I've seen in the mirror for years.

"You are *not* giving up. You *deserve* to live, to breathe and sigh, to laugh and cry because you are *worthy* of that and more! You have to look back at these moments and face adversity with a smile because that is who you are. You *are* Jackson Reese, and champs *never* give up. You *will* get through this, and together we will heal like we have before, got it? No more '*I feel like giving up*' shit-talk. That's not you–that's grief feeding your mind with bullshit."

Jackson looks shocked at the bluntness of my words, then rests his head against my chest as hearty chuckles leave his throat. This inspires me to laugh as well, and when our laughter subsides he raises his head.

"I can see why Jupiter likes these. They're soft and shit," he mumbles, with that mischievous glint in his eyes I haven't seen in weeks.

Laughing hysterically I push him off my breasts, and smack him softly on the arm. "Jackson Reese, get off my tits before you get a swift kick in the balls," I warn playfully.

Shielding his junk he shakes his head, and a goofy smile spreads across his lips, but the smile quickly fades and a determined and thoughtful Jackson looks back at me. Clearing his throat, he speaks softly. "Thank you for listening, Cat. I think it's time to talk with the shrink. I owe it to Chris and Rem, but more importantly, I owe it to myself."

I exhale loudly, thrilled with his epiphany. It's tough coping without the right kind of support, and I will be by his side every step of the way. Sometimes destiny and fate have a weird way of reminding us of our inescapable vulnerability, but more importantly our inexorable humanity. Life is fleeting; and what little time we have left in this world, we must make do with what we have and cherish those whom we love by our side.

"Jax, you don't need to thank me. I love being here with you, and I hope we can look back at this moment and see it as a first step in the right direction. The weeks to come will suck because you'll go back and forth with your memories of the accident, but the most important thing to keep in mind is *you survived*, and you're still here for a reason and you're most definitely not alone. Remember that. Now finish your sandwich."

Jackson nods and carries on with his lunch while I tidy up the kitchen. Shortly afterwards, the front door opens and closes, and I smile. *He's back.* Drying my hands with the dish towel, I walk towards the foyer to greet Stryder.

Stryder drops his shopping bags next to the console by the front door, and walks towards me with determined strides. One glance at me and his brow furrows with concern. I give him a reassuring smile and point my chin towards the kitchen. He sighs.

"Hi, baby," Stryder whispers, as he places a chaste kiss on the tender spot behind my ear. His touch is innocent, yet my skin prickles and my nipples harden underneath my sweater. A knowing smile turns his lips up, and he wraps his arms around my waist to pull me closer. "I've missed you."

"Me too," I confess, my knees wobbling. I bring my hands up to hold his face, and bring my forehead to rest against his.

My mind swirls with thoughts that are tender and bittersweet. Being held like this by the man I love has the ability to make me *and* break me, and I know I don't want him to leave. As my thoughts go into total disarray, Stryder kisses my forehead and breathes, "You've been crying, Cat. Please tell me it isn't about me leaving."

With his lips still pressed against my forehead, I shake my head. "No. Jax started talking."

Stryder breaks our hold and quirks his head towards the kitchen. A small smile graces his face. Looking down at me, he whispers, "That's good, Cat. You're the only one who can make a breakthrough with him. What did he say?"

Not wanting to make Jax uncomfortable, I take hold of Stryder's hand and lead him upstairs. Once in the privacy of our room, I give him a recount of the conversation Jax and I had downstairs. He drags his fingers through his hair and sits on the edge of our bed. I walk over and sit beside him, giving him a minute to process whatever he's feeling. But the silence is unbearable, so I gently squeeze his thigh, reassuring him I'm there if he needs and wants to unload. Stryder smiles softly, and places his hand over mine, his long fingers caressing my wrist.

While nothing can be heard in the quiet of the room, I know there is a riot going on in both of our heads. The more I think, the harder I squeeze Stryder's thigh.

"What's going in that beautiful mind of yours, Catalina?" Stryder asks, raising his free arm and draping it over my shoulder. When I don't answer immediately, he exhales loudly and pulls me in closer.

"I'm just worried about a lot of things, Stryder. Your trip... Jackson... us..."

Stryder kisses my temple and says, "I'm worried too, Catalina. I have the same concerns, but you need to know that while I'm away I'll think of you every waking second, and I'll be counting the days until I can return home. I love you, babe."

I sigh happily because I know I will be doing the same thing; missing and thinking about him every minute. Rising, I wrap my fingers around the hem of my sweater and pull it over my head. Stryder straightens his posture, his eyes darkening with need. Unhooking the clasp of my bra, I let the straps slip from my shoulders as I bare my breasts to the man I adore.

Stryder's strong hands take hold of my waist, pulling me forward, his mouth kissing the skin of my abdomen. At first his kisses are measured, but when my hands clutch his hair, urging him lower, the more hurried they become.

"I love you, Catalina," Stryder declares against my heated skin.

Swallowing hard, I reply, "And I you. Make love to me. *Please*."

His deft fingers trace the skin above the waistband of my jeans, and with each touch my body trembles. My breasts feel heavy, and both nipples harden as every square inch of my body flushes with heat. I'm covered with goose bumps under his tender touch. One of his hands undoes the button of my jeans while the other slowly lowers my zipper.

Nuzzling his head into my belly button, he breathes, "I will have so many memories of you to hold me over while I'm gone, but your soft, silken skin is one of the many things I'll miss the most." He slowly pulls my jeans past my ankles and throws them on the floor. Stryder rises, his large hands framing my face, and our gazes meet for the briefest of moments. I know what he sees in mine, but it shocks me to see the same fears, worries, and insecurities reflecting in his.

I rise on tippy toes, and kiss him with all that I have. I push past the opening of his mouth, tangling my tongue with his, and he responds with equal fervor; he commands the kiss, every so often giving a sexy growl. Both of his hands slip under the waistband of my panties to gently squeeze my ass, all while pulling me closer to him.

I let out a whimper of my own, delighted with his affections and majorly turned-on at the same time. I feel the shapeliness of his well-defined body through his clothing, and my hands waste no time tucking underneath his shirt to feel the definition of his sweltering skin. As soon as I touch his abs, I gently trace my fingernails up and down, side to side over them, and let out a moan which reflects the desire blossoming in my belly. Mimicking his movements, I let my hands roam underneath the waistband of his jeans, making sure to tuck them underneath the fabric of his boxer shorts, and squeeze his glutes which are hard and oh-so-very-shapely. Kneading and squeezing them, I let my fingernails scratch them slightly. With each affection, Stryder groans into my mouth, and I reciprocate with a moan—or two—of my own.

Removing my hands from his pants, I unbuckle his belt, pulling it sharply from the belt loops, and throwing it on the floor. The clunk against the hardwood floor is an unequivocal symbol of our need for each other. My fingers undo the button of his jeans, and before I lower the zipper, I make it a point to gently cup and squeeze his cock, feeling its unmistakable hardness and thickness.

Stryder lets out a ragged sigh, and I'm not so far behind. I break our kiss, and then lower my heels to stand at my normal height. His hands find their way through my ponytail, and he tugs on the elastic, freeing my long black waves to tickle the dimples at the small of my back. His fingers scratch my scalp softly, and his deep chuckle elicits a smile.

"Mmm," I mumble, unable to formulate a coherent thought.

Stryder looks down at me, his teeth worrying his lip. I can see so much in those eyes of his, and gosh, I'm at a loss here. How am I going to wake up each morning for the next month and not have Stryder beside me? How am I going to go to bed each night without feeling his loving embrace, his tender kisses heating my skin? Who am I kidding here? It blows my mind how I could have survived for four years without a single kiss or touch. The past few months, I've been spoiled rotten with love and affection, so badly that I can't imagine my life without them.

My chest fills with sorrow, and I know if I don't distract myself soon, Stryder will end up mopping my tears instead of making love to me. I can't let him know his upcoming departure has me tied up in knots, and I hate myself for being so weak and needy after being independent and strong for all these years.

Determined not to ruin our remaining time together, I focus on us, on our bodies, and lose myself in his gaze. I pull on the hem of his shirt and bring it over his head, tossing it across the room. His jeans and boxer shorts quickly follow, joining the remainder of our clothes on the floor. Standing before him in nothing but my panties, I push him onto the bed.

Like climbing a tree, I hover over him, and with both of my knees cemented to the bed, I plant my throbbing pussy over his face. I look down to him with pleading eyes. Without breaking my gaze, Stryder hooks his deft fingers underneath the elastic of my panties, pulling the fabric aside to reveal my pussy, while the other takes possessive hold of my waist.

Stryder cranes his head forward, and his warm, wet tongue licks my throbbing clit. He latches on, sucking and nibbling the tender spot of my center. I moan in pleasure, throwing my head back and closing my eyes in ecstasy as I ride his face without shame or restraint. His hand leaves my waist and gently tugs on my hair, making me moan. I extend my arms behind me, and my fingernails scratch his abdomen and chest as my frenzy grows. *God, this is Heaven and I don't want him to stop.*

His tongue laps my pussy and he tongue-fucks me until I unravel like a spool of thread over him, calling his name, and sagging against his face in sweet surrender. Coming down from my high, I bring my head forward and meet his loving gaze. As our eyes connect, I'm greeted with a smug, satisfied smile while his strong hands push me down his sculpted torso and washboard abs until I'm straddling his mid-section.

Stryder rolls his hips and that movement alone makes us moan with satisfaction. He hooks one of his hands on the elastic band of my panties while the other pulls against the fabric tightly. The sound of ripped cloth shatters the tranquility in the room, and when he brings the tattered panties to his face to smell them, my eyes meet his scandalized. That unexpected gesture makes me kiss him feverishly, a kiss that could start a fire with its intensity alone. My quivering hand grabs his throbbing length and positions it towards my entrance. I slide myself slowly onto his cock, loving how every delicious inch of him fills the most intimate parts of me.

Once he is completely sheathed in me, Stryder hisses. Deep within my core, I feel his cock twitch repeatedly. I roll my hips in circles, and the pleasured groans he releases delight me. Reaching for one of his legs, I bend it slightly to tilt his body towards mine until we are scissored against each other. The penetration is exquisite; we couldn't be closer if we wanted to. Lost in my blatant need for Stryder, I ride him hard, the sounds of our wet flesh and panting breaths echoing loudly in the room.

Stryder's groans and grunts grow louder with each of my thrusts. Neither of us says a single word; our bodies are doing all the talking for us. Need and love mix together as we lose ourselves in this moment. His hands hold me in place, squeezing, grabbing, kneading, scratching, and his eyes connect with mine in awe and wonder.

His cheeks are reddened, and our movements bring us to a blissful sweat. I'm lost in his arms, sheltered by his love, and oh my God, I never want to let go of him. Laying my head in the crook of his neck, I can taste the salty sweetness of his skin mixed with his cologne. One of his fingers traces the outline of my lips, and I bring it into my mouth to suck and bite it.

"I love you, Cat," Stryder whispers gruffly, as his free hand lands on the small of my back, guiding my movements.

His words fill me with a happiness I can't describe. I'm nearing nirvana with the man who loves me more than I could possibly love myself. There's something primal to this kind of lovemaking; don't get me wrong, we've been at it like bunnies since our first time in Mayrhofen, but there's something different this time around. It's like we're one soul divided into two bodies, two hearts bound by love, and two like-minded people loving the heck out of each other.

One more thrust is all it takes for me to come. I gasp his name against his shoulder, my teeth scraping his skin as the aftershocks of the best orgasm of my life tremble through me. Stryder quickly follows, grunting my name and pouring his essence inside me for the first time. There's no space for worry or fear, only happiness and bliss, and there's nothing more gratifying than to be claimed mind, body, and soul by the one you love with every cell in your body.

CHAPTER SIX

Jackson

I blow on my steaming mug of hot chocolate and reflect on the recent and most heartbreaking period of my life. I still hear in my head the shrilling cries of Rem and Chris when they were sucked under the avie that took their lives and almost robbed me of mine. I feel the ground tremble beneath me, and my skin prickles in response to my memories of that horrifying day. I wish I could go back in time and make the call to abort the run. I should've listened to my gut, but it's too late to change the past. I will have to live with this guilt for the rest of my life.

As I stand by the large picture window that shows off the most incredible view of the Casper Mountains I feel an indescribable sadness in my chest. Feelings of utter despair and hopelessness overcome me. There's a huge part of me that wants to ignore the doc's orders to rest and complete my rehabilitation, yet the other knows I need to wait before I can grab my board to do the one thing I know will make me happy again. Drinking is no longer an option.

I close my eyes and imagine shredding a line with my boots firmly planted on my favorite board. I try to crouch in front of the window like I normally do when I'm about to hit big air, but my legs rattle and hurt. I understand coping with this pain is part of the healing process, and knowing my body is betraying me truly pisses me off. I feel like a complete failure right now, broken beyond repair. Opening my eyes, I exhale loudly and a bunch of motherfucking bad words leave my mouth.

I have half a mind to throw my mug on the floor, but when I think about having to get on all fours to clean it up, the urge quickly fades. My thoughts return to that terrible day and the painful reminder that Chris and Rem are *dead* consumes me. My memories of them and the good times we had trekking the globe on our boards will stay with me until the day I die. It's tough trying to move forward and heal when I battle with myself over why I was given a second chance and they weren't.

Catalina is right. A part of me believes it wasn't my fault and Mother Nature played the bigger role here, but when I hear Rob's warning echo in my head over and over again like a broken record, it's hard to not blame myself. While a part of me wants to pack my bag and take the snowmobile to the small slope on my property to test Mother Nature, the other worries I won't be able to snowboard ever again.

I take another sip of my hot chocolate and sit on the reclining chair positioned by the window. My legs can't handle the weight of my body for more than five minutes at a time, and I hate that I've become so frail. I'm too young to feel like this, but when I think I could've shared the guys' fate a cold shiver of awareness rolls through me. I know recovery takes time, because I've sustained minor injuries over the years, mainly broken bones, and a sprained wrist here and there, though nothing to this degree.

I know broken bones mend and heal with time, but my head? I don't think it'll ever get better. I just hate having to sit on a fucking couch and talk to a person who will never understand me because they weren't there that day. As I sit on the recliner, I bring my hand to my head, trying to soothe the throbbing inside of it. These headaches are crippling, more so than the pain in my ankles and legs.

Abandoning the chair, I stand and limp towards my room, and with shaky hands I open the pill bottle on my nightstand. Popping a couple into my mouth I take a large sip of water from a bottle, and plop myself on the bed. I'm supposed to see Dr. B. tonight, but don't think I have it in me. I just want to sleep, to numb the memories and the screaming voices of Chris and Rem inside of my head. I *need* this madness to *stop*.

I know I was spared for a reason, but I don't know what the reason is, and the truth is I don't think I'll ever know. My life as I knew it is over. I feel this overwhelming sense of guilt for living, and for a guy who has lived so high on motherfucking life, I can't even stand straight on my two legs, let alone be the redeemed Olympic champion the world saw in me a little over eight weeks ago.

As the effects of the pain medication spreads through my body, I feel the madness in my head calm down. My body feels numb, kind of like when I used to get plastered, and for now that helps me relax. It doesn't take long before I don't have the power to think anymore, and I'm fast asleep like the dead. No memories, no nightmares just me, alone in the darkness, buried by the burden of the pain I'm living.

A warm set of hands touch my face, and I'm woken up by Catalina's kind voice.

"Jax?" she whispers.

My eyes flutter open, and I raise my arms over my head to stretch them. Despite having a slight fog in the head, I feel well-rested and in better spirits than when I went to sleep. I slowly sit up in bed and rub my eyes, all in between yawns. As my eyes adjust to the dim lighting, I smile.

I like these moments when I wake up. I have about three minutes of peace, as my body warms up and gets geared for whatever life has in store for me. Three minutes where my brain and my heart don't connect. Three minutes of momentary bliss. But as soon those three minutes are up and my mind connects with my heart and soul, I'm screwed. The images, memories, and everything that has tormented me since the avalanche bring me to my motherfucking knees.

I reflect back on yesterday, which was yet another bad day in the on-going list of shitastic ones I've had since the avalanche, where once again Catalina was on the receiving end of my frustrations.

"Jackson, you can't cancel any more of your appointments. How will you snowboard again if you don't follow through with your physical therapy?" she warns.

"Listen, Catalina. I appreciate you being around and stuff, but stop harassing me over the goddamn appointments! It's *my* body, *my* choice. You're not my fucking mother! Jesus Christ!"

As soon as those words left me I regretted them. I know Catalina is the last person in the world to deserve my anger. But I'm too proud, and I'm definitely a pussy for not apologizing when I fuck up. If she ever slaps me hard across the face I wouldn't put up a fight because I know better than anyone I deserve it. Instead, she always smiles, not once losing her cool despite my shit attitude.

I'll admit having Catalina around has made this recovery process easier, even though I've been a total asshole to her. I've pushed her away, yelled at her, treated her like I don't give three shits about her, yet she stays put, not losing her patience, loving and caring for me, and showing me the hard way I'm loved and worthy of everything. Deep down I know it's the depression talking, and mix that with the meds and the terrible pangs of pain in my legs, I'm one giant cluster-fuck of a mess.

"Jax?" her soft voice beckons again. I turn my head to face her, and raise one of my hands to cover hers.

"Hey," I reply, my voice raspy and dry. Just another side effect of the stupid meds. I reach out for the glass of water beside me, and chug it down.

Grabbing my empty glass, Catalina says, "Dr. Badcocke is here. I called his office to see if he could come over when I stopped by to check on you earlier. I noticed you were out like a light and figured you might cancel on him which I won't allow again. He's waiting for you in the gym."

I nod and sit on the edge of the mattress. As soon as I stand, I feel woozy and my ass lands back on the bed. "Whoa. Stop the world."

Catalina crouches in front of me, her worried eyes scanning the nightstand. She bites her inner cheek, and asks, "Jax, how many pills did you take?"

I give her the are-you-fucking-kidding-me look. I know I've been low, but things haven't gotten out of control. I inhale deeply, trying to think my words through.

"Just the two I'm supposed to take, Cat. I think I didn't eat well before taking them. Come to think of it, all I've had to eat today was the grilled chicken salad and the creepy-looking, good-tasting juice you made..."

Pardo tuts and shakes her head at me, and I reply by sticking out my tongue. She flips me two middle fingers with a 'blow me' look on her face.

"Okay, Jax. You can't do that, because these meds are like horse tranquilizers, and they will shred your stomach lining. You have to eat, babe."

I nod, feigning annoyance. She ignores me, and offers her hand. Once my hand is wrapped around hers, we walk towards the gym where Dr. B is waiting for me. As we walk through the doorway, Jupiter meets us and trades places with Cat.

"You okay there? You look a little green, buddy," he asks with a worried look on his face. I'm not going to lie. I feel like tossing my goddamn cookies.

Taking large gulps of air, I tell him, "Dipshit here forgot to eat before taking his pills. Bleh."

Jupiter chuckles softly, and walks slowly beside me guiding my steps. I look over my shoulder to make sure Cat is out of earshot. "Dude, she has been freaking out over you leaving. She's worried."

He sighs, and I know he's feeling like shit about it. "Make sure you keep an eye on her while I'm gone. I'm a mess myself because I keep reliving the bullshit I went through with Oli. I have half a mind to cancel the assignment altogether. Mom says it's a good idea to go back to work so..."

I stop dead in my tracks and turn to face him. "Lizzie put you up to this?" Lizzie has never been the kind of parent who meddles with anyone's lives, so hearing him say that is weird.

Jupiter eyes me and says, "No, asswipe. She didn't. I called her a while back and told her how I feel about Catalina, and how I think I've been smothering her since we met. I told her I was thinking about returning to work, but was worried she'd run off and lose interest in me. Mom said a little distance between us could make us stronger, and you know more than anyone Mom is almost never wrong. I'm leaving not because I want to hurt Catalina. The client is demanding only to work with me, and the pay is insane. I'd be a liar if I don't admit I miss working. At the end of the day, I need to prove my relationship with Catalina is ready for the next step. Having a little distance put between us will give us both a new perspective. Does that make sense?"

I nod, and smile at his honesty. He's leaving for their relationship, to make it healthy and grow. I totally get it, but my humor gets the better of me. Wiggling my eyebrows, I gab, "No worries, man. I'll make sure to keep her, erm, entertained, while you're away."

Jupiter stops and frees my hand, and I cringe, knowing what's coming. His usual, angry old man temper comes out.

Smack.

"Oww," I gripe, as my hand reaches to soothe the back of my head. "Why'd you do that for?" I ask between chuckles.

"You know why, you jerk. You will *not* be entertaining Catalina in *any* way, got it? I will saw your balls off and serve them on spaghetti."

I raise my hands in defeat as loud laughs escape me. "I was kidding! Jeez."

"Good, because I mean it."

He takes hold of my hand and when we reach the gym, he tells the good doctor his patient almost didn't make it in one piece. I shake my head, still laughing, and lay down on the mat where Dr. B will be working on my stupid legs. Catalina walks in and looks at us with a knowing smile. Jupiter kisses her, and whispers something into her ear, which makes her turn the color of ripe tomatoes. *Those two.*

Catalina crosses her arms and walks towards me with an unmistakably embarrassed look on her face. I raise my hands and cross them behind my head with a smug smile. She pokes me in the ribs, which are still super tender, and my arms come down to shield them as I grimace.

"Why do you work him up, huh, Jax?" she teases with a huge smile.

"Oh, you know, I like to mess with the old man. Damn, you two need to get anger management classes. You guys like to abuse me without reason," I scold in mock disgust. Catalina points her finger at me, her eyes zoning in on my ribs again. "*Don't you fucking dare, Pardo!*"

She holds onto her belly and laughs. I join in, but keep my eyes on her because, like Stryder, she can be unpredictable and playful. Cat kisses my cheek and leaves the gym, no doubt to make whatever time she has left with Jupiter count. I'm left to my own devices with the good doctor.

"Okay, Jackson. Today we'll be working on the range of motion of your Sartorius muscles in your thighs," Doctor Torture Cock says with a smile. "Are you ready?"

Sure. I'm pretty sure he's a sick, demented bastard who enjoys forcing my muscles into doing things they aren't ready to do.

"Mmm-hmm," I reply under my breath.

He lifts my leg and positions it at a ninety degree angle. I bite my tongue in preparation for the massive pain that will surely follow. "Try to bring your knee in as close as possible to your chest, okay?" the Doc encourages.

As I move my leg, I pray the next hour goes by quickly because the pain is unreal. "Have I mentioned I hate this?" I tell Dr. B through gritted teeth.

"I know, Jackson. But it's a necessary evil. If you want to snowboard again, you have to endure this," he replies while holding my leg.

"Fuck! Why not shoot me instead and take me out of my misery?"

"With all due respect, Mr. Reese, you don't pay me to pity you. I can empathize with your pain, but your biggest roadblock is your mind," Dr. B declares, meaning all business and zero pleasure.

I shrug my shoulders on the mat and mentally curse him and his entire lineage for the pain that follows. I can't believe I'm paying him thousands of dollars to make me cry like a goddamn baby. I can't wait for this rehab bullshit to end.

I look at the picture hanging on the wall to our right. It's me when I was about twelve going down Thunder Ridge Mountain. I keep my eyes focused on it during the entire session, thinking about that day. It seems like yesterday I was this goofy kid without a care in the world, just shredding lines and having fun.

Despite my insolence towards rehab, deep down I know the good doctor is right. It's all in my head. If I can get my heart to connect with my brain, I'll heal with time, and if I try my damndest, I can be a champ again. My family is counting on me, so is the country, but more importantly, so am I.

CHAPTER SEVEN

Stryder

The smell of freshly minced garlic and sweet basil wafts in the kitchen as I work on making us dinner. This is my second-to-last night here in Casper before my month-long assignment overseas, and I'm dreading leaving those who I love behind. I want to make my time here with Catalina memorable, so today I'm cooking for her for the first time. I've made sure to call my Dad and ask him for Nonna's sauce recipe, and even went through the painstaking process of making fresh Cavatelli on the granite countertop.

My mind is racing a mile a minute, thinking how amazing my life has been since I met Catalina. Sure, it hasn't been easy, but all in all, life is amazing at the moment. I try not to dwell on the duration of my assignment, because it will only make the wait seem longer than necessary. This upcoming assignment will give me more than ample time to set my plans in motion. If you thought I was going to sit idle while several oceans divide us, well, you're mistaken. I'm going to find myself and determine the next step I'll take to make the love of my life *mine*. People change with time, or with love, and it's mind-blowing to think I'm eager to ask Catalina the one question I swore I'd never ask again.

I can't help the ear-splitting grin that's on my face right now as I stir the pasta. The steam emanating from the pot is a great reminder of the warmth and love Catalina inspires in both my heart and body. And yeah, I'm going to miss her heart-shaped mouth and tan skin when I'm gone. What'll happen to her? Will she miss me? And just like that, the smile on my face disappears. As I'm about to lose my shit over my bullshit insecurities, I hear Catalina's footsteps approaching. She can't see me worrying; that would make matters worse. I take a deep breath, inhaling peace and exhaling anxiety, and try to appear normal when I'm anything but.

"What in the world are you cooking in here, Stryder?" Catalina exclaims, raising her head and taking a whiff.

Chuckling, I respond. "Oh, it's nothing really. Just Cavatelli and sauce, and in the oven I'm toasting a baguette for Bruschetta." Catalina moves to stand behind me and wraps her arms around my waist. I let go of the spoon and turn around to face her. Cradling her face and looking deep into her eyes, I say, "I hope you're hungry."

Catalina's eyes glisten with warmth. "I'm hungry, all right. Always."

Her response is so goddamn sexy, and the way she's looking up at me makes my blood rush south. I chuckle as she wiggles her eyebrows at me saucily. I turn around and grab the spoon, dipping it lightly into the crushed tomato sauce. I blow on the metal spoon to cool the sauce and bring it to her mouth. Her plump lips open and when the sauce hits her taste buds, Catalina closes her eyes and moans. I exhale trying to compose myself because she always manages to make the simplest of things so damn erotic.

"Mmm, that tastes so good, Stryder," Catalina whispers, as her tongue darts from her mouth to lick her lips. "A girl could get used to this."

I lower my head and kiss the tip of her nose. "Hmm. Something to consider... I'm not a chef, but I can hold my own. Mom and Dad taught me how to cook some family staples. I hope you like it."

"You're talented, in more ways than one," she says with a wink.

Smirking, I toss the spoon into the sink, then wrap my arms around her and place my lips over hers. I kiss her, nice and slow; the taste of my cooking mixed with her unique flavor has me thirsty for more. My hand grabs the back of her neck as I deepen the kiss, and her hands clutch my hips possessively. There's a thickness between us, and I'm not referring to the one in my pants. Our never-ending need for each other is prevalent with each lap of my tongue against hers.

The oven timer beeps, and, breathing hard, I break away to remove the tray of baguette slices before they burn. Catalina runs to the refrigerator and grabs the Bruschetta mix, and together we cover the toasted bread slices with it and set them aside. After checking the pasta I shut off the stove, and strain the Cavatelli. We set the table together, exchanging little touches and smiles. Once done, I ask Catalina to tell Jackson dinner is ready. Grabbing shallow ceramic bowls, I serve the pasta and sauce, making sure to sprinkle freshly grated Pecorino Romano cheese right on top.

Jax hobbles beside Catalina, and rubs his hands over his stomach. "Ah, nothing quite like good ol' Martynus Italian cuisine. Dude, it smells fucking amazing in here."

It's nice to see Jax smiling after all that he's been through, and I hope he progresses with his physical therapy while I'm gone. I haven't said anything to him, but I'm dying for all of us to hit the slopes again like the good old days. I pull out his chair at the head of the table, and he sits, grimacing slightly. I place his supper before him and wait for Catalina to take her seat and do the same.

Once dinner is served we all hold hands and say grace. It's something we've been doing since we arrived at Jax's after the accident. Regardless of the specifics, I believe there's a higher power watching over us, guiding our steps, and keeping us safe. If Nonna were alive, she'd be proud of me, not only for cooking but for behaving like the good Italian boy she always hoped I'd be. We dig in, and I'm satisfied with the result. Jax and Catalina have the biggest smiles on their faces as we talk about the memories we've made together since the day we all first met.

"... The look on your faces when you realized you were working together was priceless! I just stood there wondering what the fuck happened," Jackson recalls, laughing and pointing at both of us. Catalina throws her head back, giggling infectiously, and I follow suit because, looking back, I'm pretty sure I looked like an idiot at the time.

"I knew the minute you guys were face to face there was something there, you know?" Jackson recalls, forking pasta from his bowl and putting it into his mouth. "I'm just happy you guys got over your bullshit and gave things a chance."

Catalina looks across the table, and her honeyed eyes meet mine. One glance is all it takes; my heart is whacking furiously against my ribcage.

"Yeah," I agree, and clear my throat from the sudden emotion lodged there. "I never imagined the world being that small. Jax, did you know Catalina and I met once before we even got to Whistler?"

"You mean on the flight, right?"

Chuckling loudly, I shake my head. "No. We met in the city. It was a month before the assignment. I bumped into her outside a jazz club. I was checking my email and wasn't paying attention to where I was going. Catalina was walking up the ramp and didn't see me. When we bumped into each other she fell right at my feet," I declare smugly, and wink at Catalina across the table.

Catalina rolls her eyes. "I don't think your date was too thrilled you helped me up either."

"So hold up, let me see if I'm getting this straight. You guys met before Whistler? Why didn't you tell me anything about this, Cat?" Jax asks.

"That would be because she never saw my face, Jax. She was too embarrassed to look at me. I knew she looked familiar when I saw her on the flight, but it wasn't until we were at her apartment after the press tour that I recognized her dress lying on the floor. Jax, it had skulls," I affirm with a wink.

"Ah. I see... Destiny, man...That just proves you can't mess with fate and shit," Jax mutters. As if in slow motion, his entire demeanor changes, and silence fills the room.

Catalina looks at me wide-eyed and reaches out for Jax's hand. His face changes, and his smile is replaced with teary eyes. He tries to shield his crying with his free hand, and his heart-breaking sobs have me inching forward in my seat. Catalina abandons her chair and crouches beside him, whispering into his ear.

Jackson pushes his chair back, and allows Catalina to pull him up into an embrace. He uses his knuckles to wipe his tears away and looks straight at me trying to rein in his sobs.

"Thanks for dinner, Jupiter. It was delicious."

In the blink of an eye, I'm standing in front of Jax with both of my arms on top of his shoulders. "What's wrong, Jax?"

Jackson looks down to the floor, and says, "Nothing, man. I'm just tired and ate too much."

"Then why the tears, Jax? You're with family and we'll listen. Just talk."

"Nothing to be worried about, Jupiter, I'm just feeling a little overwhelmed with all the pills, the doctors, and how my body is crapping out on me."

I shake Jackson's shoulders gently, enough to get his attention. "Bullshit, man. Something triggered you. Just talk to us," I plead.

Jax looks at me with reddened eyes and returns to his chair. Catalina and I re-take our seats and wait for him to speak. With a shaky hand, Jackson raises his glass of water and chugs it down. "I can't control fate, and there's nothing I can do to bring them back."

Catalina gasps, and places her hand over her mouth trying to hide the smile I already saw. Hearing Jackson talk openly about his accident is a major sign of progress. Accepting what happened is an awesome step in the right direction. I was worried he'd be consumed by guilt, and listening to him accept that the avalanche was beyond his control proves he's coming to terms with what happened that day.

"Yes, Jackson, we can't control fate. What happened wasn't your fault and no matter what, you need to understand there was nothing you could do to prevent it. It's easier said than done, but trust me, please. I know what it's like," Catalina argues quietly, squeezing his hand.

"I agree with Catalina, Jax. It was no one's fault, kid, and the sooner you realize it the better you'll feel. No one needs to carry around unnecessary weight; you of all people should know that. It wasn't your fault, man," I assert, looking at him square in the eye.

"I know, Jup. I just need time to accept things, you know?" Jackson whispers, as two large tears roll down his cheeks.

All I can do is hug him as hard as his body will allow, and in my arms he cries. I feel the weight of his defeated hands thwack my back repeatedly and with each breath, his body shudders. I look at Catalina, who stands by us wiping tears of her own. With each wipe of her tears I know she's recalling her own struggles. Catalina nods at me, as if agreeing with my thoughts. She takes a step forward and wraps her arms around both of us.

"I love you, guys," she whispers, placing feathery kisses on both of us.

In unplanned sync, we reply, "We love you, too." It takes us a nanosecond to break into riotous laughter, which has Jax leaning against me for support, and Catalina patting my ass repeatedly with each giggle. To an outsider our little moment of hysteria might be considered odd and our laughter completely inappropriate, but to us it's healing and progressing, and if the world doesn't understand the nature of our friendship, well, that's their own damn problem.

We walk Jax back to his room and help him settle in for the night. He's in good spirits cracking jokes, and asking me to grab the remote control so he can watch the adult entertainment channel.

Catalina and I close the door behind us, shaking our heads in laughter. We return to the kitchen to tidy up while listening to soft music, Catalina washes the pots and I dry them, and then put them back into the cabinets.

It isn't until we're done cleaning that I realize how natural this domesticity has become. With each passing second, I'm more determined to do everything I can to ensure the future I'm planning becomes a reality. The more I think about it, the more the asshole grasshopper in my stomach does its number on me. *Me? Nervous? Hell yeah.*

The soft jazz tune ends, and Richard Marx's "Hold On To the Nights" starts playing in the background. As the opening verses echo softly in the large kitchen space, I hear Catalina's angelic voice singing along. I quirk my head and watch her sing as she rinses the last few plates in the sink. I'm pretty sure I look like an idiot gawking at her.

As soon as she hits the chorus, I turn off the water. She looks at me confused and abruptly stops. I shake my head and whisper, "Keep singing."

I take hold of her hand and pull her softly towards me, and she resumes singing, but this time she's smiling as she does. I take hold of her palm, and press our joined hands against my chest. I place my free hand on the small of her back, leading my lady to dance with me. I press her close, and we move our bodies softly to the beat of the song. Catalina stops singing and our eyes meet; she's moving alongside me, glancing now and then at her feet.

"Cat, look at me. Don't look at your feet, baby. Just look at me. It's my job to lead, okay?"

Catalina nods and lets out a nervous giggle, relaxing in my hold as if surrendering herself to my every move. She rests her head against my chest and lets out a happy sigh. "You smell good," she whispers.

I chuckle softly and rub her back, giving it a gentle squeeze. "And you sing beautifully, Catalina. It's so sweet and angelic."

Catalina scoffs and raises her head to meet my smitten gaze. "I rarely sing ballads, Stryder. I just really like that song... It takes me back to Junior High."

"Mmm. Did you go to school dances, Cat?" I ask.

Catalina shrugs, and replies, "I did... but I was the girl who sat on a bench while others danced."

"Why?"

"I have two left feet, so to speak," she replies quietly, with a shy smile marked on her heart-shaped lips.

"Well, you haven't smashed my toes yet, and your rhythm is perfect. You just need the right partner... that's all." I look deep into her eyes, hoping she understands what I mean.

Catalina's breath catches, and her eyes glaze over. Before I know it, she's on her tippy toes reaching for my lips. I bow my head to make it easier for her, and our brief kiss sends a hot message to my dick. As our lips untangle, we resume dancing. I twirl her, which makes her giggle happily. When I tip her backwards, I trace my fingertips over the silken skin of her neck, past her breasts, stopping at her navel, and she quivers. Keeping her torso dipped, I kiss her sweet-as-candy neck, making her sigh.

Raising her out of the dip, I swivel my hips against her soft curves and break my hold as I turn her around, pressing her back against my chest with my hand splayed over her abdomen. My free hand traces the outline of her body, starting at her neck, past her shoulder, down the side of her ribcage, around her waist and stopping to clutch her hipbone.

I can hear Catalina's sharp breaths with each movement of my fingers and body, and I have no doubt she feels my hard dick pressed up against her back. I've danced all my life, and it's never been a problem to keep my goods in check, but with Catalina, it's a different thing. I love how my body is so in sync with hers. Rumba is the dance of love, and while she doesn't know it, I'm giving her all the goods with this impromptu dance.

Twirling her around a final time, I bring her back to my chest for the end of the song. I stand before Catalina dying to rip her clothes off and take her against the kitchen counter. We are both breathing heavily as we look into each other's eyes with unmistakable want.

Yeah, I can tell she's turned on, and I would bet all my money her panties are drenched. Without further thought, I break our gaze and walk towards the counter to grab my phone from the stereo docking station and immediately put it in my pocket. I smile at Catalina and she raises her eyebrow in question. I pick her up and throw her over my shoulder. Taking a firm hold of her kicking legs, I race up the stairs and with each step I take, her hysterical laughter grows louder.

I gently smack her on the ass. "You're going to wake Jax up."

Catalina extends her hands and squeezes my ass cheeks really hard. I jump at the slight sting, but my dick knows it's mere foreplay and pulses against my fly.

"Don't think for one second you can slap my ass and not expect any consequences, Stryder Martynus," Catalina admonishes in that sweet yet sexy voice of hers.

"Yes, Ma'am," I reply, trying hard not to trip and fall on the stairs.

I kick the door shut behind us, and it rattles against the quiet of the night. I near the bed and lay Catalina against the white comforter, her long raven locks fanned over the bed. Her chest rises and falls, and her lips are slightly parted with excitement.

My mouth crashes against hers and she welcomes me with a reciprocating tongue. I groan into her lips, and my hands sneak underneath her blouse, eagerly seeking the swells of her breasts. I squeeze them possessively, completely lost in my need for her. The longer we kiss, the more she moans into my mouth, her body bucking against mine as I pull the cups of her bra down. As soon as my fingertips brush against her hardened nipples she whispers my name between ragged breaths:

"Stryder, please."

"Shh," I mutter, not wanting to pause for anyone or anything.

The world could crash down around me and I wouldn't give a damn. Right here, right now is where I want to be; lost in my lady's embrace. Catalina bucks beneath me, opening her legs wider so my body can align with hers. Her fingernails press against my shirt, and her moans increase with each movement of my hands. I wiggle against her soft curves, pressing my dick against her welcoming pussy. As soon as our bodies make that incredible contact, I groan. Catalina is my safe place, my little piece of Heaven on Earth. She's everything I could ever want from life and then some.

In my fit of desperation, it takes all of my willpower not to rip her clothes off. I tug her blouse from her body and cast it aside, and waste no time kissing, licking and nibbling her beautiful skin. It's hot against my lips and gives me the go-ahead to graze my teeth over it.

"Stryder, oh my God, *please!*" Catalina pants as she fiercely tugs my hair.

"I got you, Cat. I want you so much, baby. Just shut up and let me love you, yeah?" I breathe, as one of my hands covers her mouth.

Catalina looks at me with wild eyes, and locked in each other's gaze I roll my hips over, and over again. This makes her moan, and each thrust of my pelvis her eyes roll to the backs of her eyelids. If I keep this up she'll come before we even undress. I release her and stand to undress. She rests on her elbows, watching me with a salacious smile; her cheeks are red and her hair is mussed, and we've barely started.

I swear I've lost my damn mind and heart to her. She owns every square inch of my soul, my thoughts, and my body. My entire being belongs to Catalina, and every moment of my life I will devote it to her. I want us to be together until we are old and wrinkly. I vow to make her happy until my dying breath, no matter the cost. I don't care if this love I have for her makes me pussy-whipped. Crown me the poster boy of pussy-whipped men.

I stand before her and pull her legs closer to me, and tug the waistband of her leggings until they and her panties come off. She flails her legs, helping me rid her of her clothes, then undoes the clasp of her bra and throws it at my face with a giggle. Catching it, I nuzzle it and throw it across the room. I look down at her glistening pussy and a rogue breath leaves me.

I lick my lips and lower myself on top of her. As I kiss her mouth, I sink my dick balls deep into her pussy, wet and tight. This is Heaven, and if I'm wrong, well, condemn me to an eternity in Hell because I love it here. Catalina writhes beneath me, begging me to move. So I do, rolling my hips deliberately to give her that friction she goes crazy for. I want to make slow, sweet love to her, but my lady has other plans.

"Just fuck me, and don't be gentle. *Please*," she pleads, her words making me pulse inside her.

Who am I to deny Catalina what she wants? I plunge in and out of her and she meets every thrust, moaning fiercely into my ear each time. I get goose bumps with each sound she makes, and each movement of her dainty hands. She tightens around my aching dick and I know she is close to falling apart beneath me.

My balls tingle, but I will not stop until Catalina screams for me. I hope I can last beyond her orgasm because I want to give her a few before I call it a night. I once said Paradise is being in Catalina's arms, and today that statement still rings true. She is my Paradise, my Heaven, and my Home, and in the next month when I'm far from her, I'll hold onto the memories we've built together, and like a true North Star, she will guide me home back into her loving arms.

CHAPTER EIGHT

Catalina

You know the feeling you get when you're itchy and you scratch, and it feels so damn good, but you just can't stop? Even if it means you'll be sore or bleed afterwards, it doesn't matter because the pleasure outweighs the pain. I get the exact same feeling every time we are intimate. It's a delicious itch that gets scratched over and over again, and it feels amazing. Who knew I'd get a kick out of rough sex? But the sound of Stryder pounding his cock deep into me again and again has me all kinds of delirious.

"Fuck me good, Stryder. Please... don't... *stop!*" I cry into his ear, a never-ending chant that makes him plunge deeper and further into me. His groans and ragged breaths undo me; I'm dancing across the midnight-blue sky, twirling around the fucking moon, and floating back down to Earth with the grace of a hummingbird. Stryder withdraws and kisses the space between my breasts and I instinctively wrap my arms around his neck, showering him with kisses.

"I love you, Stryder," I whisper in between ragged breaths.

"I love you too, Raven Girl," Stryder replies with a smile, trying to catch his breath. "Are you okay?"

"Yeah... but why'd you stop?" I pout lips.

"I needed a moment. I'm not quite done with you yet," he replies with a chuckle. "Thirsty?"

I nod as he rises from the bed and walks towards the bathroom, then returns with a glass of water. I drink it so eagerly some of the droplets dribble down my chin and pitter-patter against my breasts. Not one to be wasteful, Stryder eagerly laps them up; trailing his tongue down my chin, past my neck, and stopping in between my breasts. Halting abruptly, he snaps his head up and, with his hands, demands the glass of water.

I tilt my head, and hand over the tumbler. Before I can put two and two together, I feel the cold sting of the thick glass pressing against my nipple. I moan in shock and pleasure, and Stryder lets out a sexy growl of approval. With an ear-splitting grin, he straddles me and tips the glass, allowing small droplets of ice-cold water to land on the tip of my hardened nipple. Stryder lowers his head and I squirm with delight when I feel the warmth of his tongue lapping, then suctioning, the cold wetness away. He unlatches with a loud pop, and lifts his shimmering eyes and satisfied smirk to meet my scandalized gaze.

He lifts the glass and repeats the same delectable torment on my other nipple. I watch him in wonder, asking myself if our intimacy will ever go bland in the years to come. My mind goes haywire thinking beyond the present. I have no doubt Stryder is happy with me; his actions, both in and out of bed point to it. I don't know what tomorrow holds let alone months from now, but I can't help but dream of a future beyond what we currently have. My heart skips a beat as hope blossoms deep within my belly.

"Hey, where'd you go?" Stryder asks with a heart-melting smile. "Don't tell me it was me, because you make o's with your mouth when I'm sucking your nipples. The smile on your face is priceless, so spill the beans, Pardo. Tell me what's going on inside that pretty head of yours."

I exhale a shaky breath and hesitate before speaking. I can't tell him what's on my mind; what if I'm rushing things too fast? I don't want him to believe I want to take our relationship beyond what he's prepared for. I refuse to admit that I see myself married to him, the mother of his children.

"Nothing, really, I'm just happy with you, Stryder. I love being with you, sharing my ups and downs, kissing you and spending time with you. I'm going to miss you when you leave."

Stryder's hazel eyes look deeply into mine. "Ditto, Cat. I love you too."

Sighing deeply I hold him tight. I feel terrible hiding my true feelings and desires, but at the same time, I know I'm doing the right thing.

"You know you can tell me anything, right?" Stryder whispers against my cheek. "*Anything.*"

I nod in agreement, yet a cold shiver runs up my spine. Stryder knows I'm not being forthright, but he's too much of a gentleman to press the subject further. Instead, he raises his head and pours a small stream of water on my belly, resuming his affections.

As dawn approaches the sun begins to glow through the curtains of our room. I'm wide awake, but my heart feels like it weighs a ton. This will be the last day I'll spend with Stryder before he takes off to Australia for four weeks. As he lays beside me, fast asleep with his arm around my waist, I know how much I will miss mornings like these. I cuddle closer to his warmth and he lets out a sigh, as I try to hold on to this precious connection. I stay curled up beside him as long as I can, until the call of nature disconnects us.

I tiptoe into the bathroom, closing the door softly behind me, and after my morning routines are covered, I step into the steamed-up shower. As the water rinses my body, the overwhelming sadness that's been threatening me for days comes out full force. In a matter of seconds I'm a weepy, sobbing mess. I cover my mouth with my hands, afraid my hiccupping cries will wake Stryder. The last thing I need is him cancelling his trip because I can't handle us being apart. I try shampooing my hair, but overtaken with sadness, I can't even manage that. I take deep, steadying breaths to regain my composure, and chastise myself for being such a hot mess.

Old habits die hard. The defeatist in me is trying to undo the progress I've made in recent months, and I can't let that happen at least not until he's gone. I'm the happiest I've ever been, and consider myself pretty damn lucky after all the shit I've been through in my life. Now is *not* the time to take a step back. I talk myself into weighing the positive influence Stryder and Jackson have brought into my once-dull life, and the more I think about it the easier it is to breathe. I can't let this departure eat away at me; Stryder loves me, and there's nothing to be afraid of.

Turning off the water, I step out and wrap myself in a large, fluffy towel. I peek through the door to see if Stryder is up, but thankfully he's not. Walking into the closet I grab an outfit and quickly dress for the day, then tiptoe out of our room, jogging down the staircase en route to the kitchen. I come to a halt when I find Jackson, naked and head-first in the refrigerator. As I'm backing up, I stop dead in my tracks when I hear a female voice. *What the hell? Jackson has company?*

"Good morning!" she greets; her voice cheery and bright.

"Umm, good morning to you too," I reply awkwardly. As soon as I hear Jackson's hearty chuckles, I shield my eyes trying to avoid the direction in which his voice is coming from.

"Hey! Sorry for the birthday suit, Cat. Sam popped in late last night to hang out," Jackson explains matter-of-factly in between munches. "I'm standing behind the counter. You can look now."

My hand falls from my eyes, and I blink a couple of times to allow my vision to adjust. Jackson's smile meets my own, and then I wave hello to Sam.

"I didn't mean to barge in on you guys. I'm going to grab a cup of coffee and get out of your hair. My name is Catalina, but everyone calls me Cat. I'm pleased to meet you, Sam."

Unlike Jackson, Sam is fully dressed thank God, and she opens her arms to greet me with a hug. "Samantha, but everyone calls me Sam. Nice to meet you too, Cat."

For the briefest of seconds our eyes connect, and then she quickly walks away towards Jackson. She has sun-kissed blonde hair that barely kisses her shoulders, large expressive honey-brown eyes, and raised cheekbones. Sam is *really* pretty, and from what I can see her personality matches her stunning looks; an athletic build and a graceful walk, and while she's wearing one of Jackson's t-shirts, I can tell she has an enviable body underneath.

"I'm surprised you're up so early... let alone walking," Jackson jokes with a small laugh.

Heat rises to my cheeks, and after grabbing a mug from the cabinet, I turn around and stick my tongue out at him. He smiles, then winks devilishly, that is, until Sam elbows him on the shoulder and gives him a threatening glare. Jax looks at her with wide eyes, and raises his hands, mouthing, 'What?' Judging by the way they are interacting, it's easy to see they've known each other for a very long time. Turning around to give them a semblance of space, I face the counter waiting for my cup of brew. As I'm standing there the sound of them kissing makes me blush, but at the same time it makes me smile.

"Do you want breakfast?" Jackson asks her, and I grin even wider, thankful they can't see the excitement plastered on my face.

But curiosity gets the best of me. I turn around and see Jackson taking a lock of her blonde hair between his gruff fingers and tucking it sweetly behind her earlobe. I've *never* seen this side of him before and, holy hell, I feel like a voyeur watching them. His eyes twinkle as he looks tenderly into hers. Gone is the mischief and joking, and in its place is deep affection. Even though I'm standing, metaphorically-speaking I'm on the edge of my seat waiting for Sam's response. *Say yes, woman, yes!*

"No, Jaxy-boy. I have to get going," she replies quietly. Through my eyelashes I catch the disappointed look on Jackson's face. The frown he's been sporting since the accident is back. His eyes meet mine, and I smile, but he rolls his eyes and twirls his index finger in the air silently asking me to turn around. I hear him leaving the kitchen, followed by the sound of a door slamming shut.

Crossing my arms over my chest, I turn around and without sugar-coating shit, say, "Why'd you say no?"

Sam replies, "Because you and I both know what that means. I'm not the girl that stays. What's it to you, Cat?"

"Jax is my friend, and he's been through a lot of shit in case you didn't know. Yes, I don't know you and yeah, I'm shocked to see you here, but seeing him smile was really something. The least you could do is accept his offer of a meal. It's just food," I emphasize as calmly as I'm able to.

Sam smiles. "You really care about him, huh? I do too. We have an understanding... It's fun and nothing more. I refuse to commit to anyone and neither can he. It is what it is."

I tilt my head to the side, and before I can ask a follow-up question, Stryder's throaty voice fills the room. "Call me crazy, but I swear I heard Sam's voice in here." And when they see each other, they hug fiercely in front of me.

"Jupiter!" Sam exclaims happily. "What a pleasant surprise!"

Great. They know each other too. An unsettling feeling builds inside me and I'm pretty sure there's a little troll inside of me dressed in green named Jealousy. I've never been the jealous-type, but seeing them hugging and smiling at each other prompts my mind to imagine all kinds of fucked-up scenarios that have me close to leaving the room.

Stryder's arm curls around my waist, and he pulls me close to his chest with a kiss. "Sam, meet my girlfriend, Catalina Pardo."

"Yes, we made our introductions earlier. Wow. I thought I'd never see the day you'd be linked to someone who wasn't Olivia. Thank God! Good for you, Jupiter," Samantha exclaims with a grin.

Okay. I like Samantha. A lot.

"Sometimes you come across people who make you want to be a better, happier man." Stryder declares, with another kiss on my temple. "Maybe you should stop fighting and start trying, Sam."

Samantha looks down and exhales. "No, Jupiter, certain things need to be left as is." She pauses to clear her throat. "Listen, it was nice catching up with you. As you can see," she says gesturing at Jax's t-shirt, "some habits die hard. I've got to go. Pleased to meet you Cat. I'll see you around."

And with that she walks away towards Jackson's bedroom with confident steps. I look up at Stryder and a knowing smile quirks his lips. "Oh, such a curious little one you are!"

I poke him in the rib, "Hey! What's that supposed to mean?"

"You know damn well what I'm saying." He chuckles.

"I kind of have an idea. Jax seems to like her a lot, and I'd be a liar if I said I'm not intrigued..."

Stryder releases me to grab a mug from the cabinet. I watch him make coffee, patiently waiting for him to spill the beans. Of course, he takes his sweet-ass time. Once he's done with the first few sips of his coffee, he finally speaks.

"They used to date a long time ago, but their careers and schedules made it impossible to have a stable relationship. Sam was born and raised here just like Jax. She's a cross country skier for the US Olympic Team, and last I heard she lives in Denver, but that was a while back. It's been a long time since we've talked."

"I see. She's the one that got away, am I right?"

Stryder quirks his head, but keeps his eyes fixed on the coffee maker. "Yeah. I guess you can say that. They are both willful people with similar backgrounds. They butted heads a lot, but when they are together it's something special to watch."

I stand there thinking about Jackson's happiness and how having a woman in his life, especially now, could help him. I'll make sure to have words with him when Stryder leaves. I want him to be himself whether he's with Sam or not. Jackson needs someone to ride his ass when I can't, and someone to care for him when we can't. The thought of him finding love thrills me. Perhaps Cupid needs a Cupid of his own.

After finishing his coffee, Stryder places the empty mug in the sink and walks over to hug me. I wrap my arms around his neck inhaling his scent and committing it to memory. I'll miss him more than I'll ever care to admit.

"I woke up this morning thinking about something, Catalina," Stryder muses, as he rubs circles against the small of my back.

I smile. "And that would be?"

"Valentine's Day," he whispers gruffly. "We were so busy with the press tour, the day came and went without us even realizing it."

"Wow. You're right. Valentine's Day... In my defense, I'm used to not celebrating it."

Stryder takes a step back and his steady gaze meets mine. "I know. I used to feel the same way that is, until I fell in love with you, Catalina."

My heart beats furiously at his words. "You are not alone there, Stryder. I think I fell in love with you the moment you put your arm around me in that SUV to calm me down. I was a hot mess then. I still am, but I'm better with each passing day. Thank you for loving me."

Stryder cups my face with his large hands and kisses my lips lovingly. "And *I* fell in love with *you* the moment you sat beside me on that plane. I'll never forget the warmth of your cheek against my shoulder, your scent, and more importantly how *you* made me feel on the inside. I was a jaded man before I met you, Catalina, and now I'm such a happy, lucky bastard."

We stand in the middle of the kitchen gazing into each other eyes, confessing our feelings for each other out in the open, and damn it feels wonderful. "I love you, Stryder."

"I love you too, Catalina."

The sound of a throat being cleared makes us aware we are not alone in the kitchen, and we turn around to see Jackson and Sam holding hands, looking at us with warm, tender smiles.

"They've got it bad, Sam." Jackson nuzzles his nose into the crook of her neck.

"I know. This is nice to see, Jupiter." Sam winks, combing Jax's wayward hair with her fingers.

They love each other in their own unexplainable way, and I wonder if either of them realizes it. Smiling, I wrap my arm around Stryder's waist. "The view of you two isn't so bad from here either, you know..."

Sam separates herself from Jackson and walks over to say goodbye, hugging us both. The three of us walk towards the foyer to see her out.

"It was nice to meet you, Catalina," Sam pipes, wrapping her gloved hand around the doorknob.

"Likewise, Sam. Don't be a stranger." I wave, and she waves back as she opens the door.

With his hands in his pockets and a pained expression on his face, Jackson mutters, "I'll walk you out to your truck."

Stryder and I make our way up the staircase towards our room, and on the way there I take a glance out of the window. Jackson and Samantha are kissing beside her snow-covered truck. Feeling intrusive, I quickly look away. I can't help but think she's the owner of Jax's heart, and nothing would make me happier than to see them experience the same kind of relationship Stryder and I share.

"He loves her," Stryder mutters as we walk into our room. "He always has."

I figured that out the moment I saw them kissing in the kitchen. Jackson's eyes were soft and tender in ways I've never seen before. I wonder if that is what Jackson saw in us back in Whistler. Perhaps he needs a reminder—a sip of his own medicine.

Sitting on the small chair next to the bed, I prop my legs over the arm and watch Stryder walk into the closet. "What do you want to do today?"

He walks out with some clothes in his hands and lays them out on the bed. "We are going out on a date, Raven Girl. It's almost March, but I'll be damned if we don't celebrate Valentine's Day before I leave." He grins, walks over to me, and bends down to kiss my forehead.

"Sounds perfect," I reply, my heart skipping a beat. Thoughtful, handsome, and loving... He says *he's* lucky. I respectfully disagree.

Stryder goes all out for our belated Valentine's Day date. We drive to a rustic movie theater downtown, where we steal kisses from each other during the movie. His constant displays of affection have me like a pot on the stove set to simmer.

The weather isn't terribly cold as we walk down the quaint sidewalks of downtown Casper. Stryder pulls me by the hand practically dragging me into a flower shop. As a native New Yorker, I'm used to seeing colorful bouquets sold on each street corner... flowers for people on the go, but to see them beautifully displayed inside the shop like this really takes my breath away.

I peruse the aisles and find a colorful bucket full of gerberas, and smile, remembering the first time Stryder gave me flowers back in Whistler. Stryder hugs me from behind, and whispers, "Are you thinking what I'm thinking?" With a grin on my face, I nod.

Stryder motions the shopkeeper over."I'd like to buy these, please," he says pointing at the bucket. The woman walks over and trims the gerberas' stems; the colorful splashes of orange, red, yellow, pink and purple contrast beautifully with each other in the cellophane wrapping. After paying, Stryder pulls a red gerbera from the bouquet, and, snapping the stem, he pushes it softly into my hair. "Red is definitely your color, Catalina," he whispers sultrily.

I wasn't expecting to celebrate Valentine's Day today, and I'm at a loss as to what to do for him. As we walk past a corset maker's shop I take a peek through the frosted windows, and that's when the light bulb in my head clicks on. It's my turn to drag him inside, where he looks at me with a raised eyebrow and a salacious grin.

"Since this is our Valentine's Day, I'd like for you to pick something out for me," I say, gesturing at the racks and feeling brazen all of a sudden. Our eyes meet, and the way he looks at me makes feel like butter melting in the middle of the lingerie shop.

Bending down, he whispers into my ear, "Naked is how I want you, Catalina. Naked is how I'll take you, and naked is how I'll make you writhe beneath me begging for more. That is how I'll make you come... over and over again."

His words hit me like a tidal wave, traveling through my cells at the speed of light. My body trembles as the seduction simmering in my belly slowly unfurls. My thighs instinctively clench against each other, seeking reprieve from the overwhelming ache pooling there. Through my layers of clothing, my skin tingles, and my hardened nipples push against the padding of my bra and sweater. My lungs feel like they are void of air, and I can hear blood rushing through my ears. I glance to my sides nervously and when I see the coast is clear, I grope his cock, slanted and hard in his jeans. He lets out a hiss of approval when I squeeze him gently. Thankful his pea coat is hiding my movements, I rise on my tippy-toes, and whisper into his ear.

"You have your talents, Stryder Martynus, but don't forget I also have mine. So pick something out, and let us get the hell out of here before I shove you into the dressing room, and ride my wet pussy over your thick cock."

I smile in victory when he swallows hard, his Adam's apple bobbing up and down. Adjusting himself he moves towards one of the racks.

"Turn around, Cat," he says. "I'd rather surprise you."

Nodding and smiling like a sweet little girl, I turn around as asked. It isn't long before he snakes his arm around my waist and walks us towards the door with his purchase in hand. As soon as our feet land on the sidewalk, Stryder's hand squeezes my bottom.

"I hope I didn't scare the saleslady, Catalina." He chuckles, looking down at himself. "You don't play fair."

With an innocent smile, I bat my eyelashes coquettishly and reply, "And I never will."

CHAPTER NINE

Stryder

Back at Jackson's ranch, I'm shocked to see a note from him saying he will be spending the night at his parents. Either he's feeling down after Sam's visit, or he knows tonight is my last night here and wants us to have the place to ourselves. I want to think it's the latter.

I get busy plating the Chinese takeout we picked up on our way back while Catalina showers. Grabbing my phone, I shoot Jackson a quick text.

    <SM: Hey, man, how's it going?>

A few seconds later my phone chirps.

    <JR: It's good. I'm having dinner with Mom. I won't be home tonight so you have the place to yourselves. Make it count, Jup.>

I knew it. Smiling, I send him a quick reply.

    <SM: I will. Thanks, man.>

‹JR: Good. Have fun. *devil emoticon*›

I chuckle softly and dock my phone into the sound system, setting soulful music to play in the kitchen. I bring our plates into the dining room and set them on the table, lighting some candles. The sun is setting and hues of orange and yellow filter into the room. Standing by the large picture window, I try not to think too much about tomorrow. Leaving is my decision, and I have to stay true to it. This past week I've been tiptoeing around the idea of leaving, but I need to prove my relationship with Catalina is different from what I had with Olivia.

Things will definitely change when I get back because I'm determined more than ever to commit to a life with Catalina. We've been in a bubble of sorts since we met, and leaving could change everything, but deep down I know this time things are different. I'm no longer the jaded son-of-a-bitch I once was. I have so much to look forward to, so many dreams to fulfill, dreams which have Catalina front and center.

My spine straightens when I hear Catalina's footsteps coming down the stairs. When she walks across the threshold, I find myself short of breath. Her long raven hair is curled down the sides of her face, and with each step she takes it bounces happily. She's wearing a black satin robe with a red sash around her waist, and bright red stilettos which stand out against the black silk stockings I bought for her today.

My mind wanders, imagining the red garter belt holding her stockings in place. *Fuck.* My dick stirs in my pants when she stops in front of me. All I want to do is bury myself deep inside of her, but there will be ample time for that later. I want to give her a proper date first. I reach out to caress the soft skin of her cheek, my thumb tracing over her beauty mark.

The Catalina that stands before me is slightly different from the Catalina I met almost two months ago. She's significantly thinner, yet the curves I fell in love with are still there. Her eyes used to be sad, but now those dark chocolate beauties burn bright. At the end of the day her external features don't outweigh the beauty of her soul because it's the most beautiful and perfect part of her, the part that loves me in return.

Catalina cradles her face into my hand and smiles, a red hue coloring her cheeks. Her cherry-red lips are slightly parted as she tries to even her breathing. There's an energy surrounding us, and if I could describe it I'd say it's like a seismograph needle drawing waves of tectonic plate activity. The same could be said about my racing heart; Catalina Pardo is the only woman in the universe who can make it beat this hard.

Licking my lips and gathering my thoughts, I speak. "You look, wow." I tilt my head to the side and place my free hand at the base of my neck. Clearing my throat, I continue. "Damn, Catalina. I can't even... you sure know how to make a grown man stumble."

She giggles.

"Hardly, Stryder... I wonder how a man like you, with such enviable vocabulary skills suddenly finds himself unable to use his words," Catalina quips playfully, forcing a chuckle out of me.

I bring my free hand to cup her other cheek and gently coax her forward. She looks at me through her long onyx eyelashes, blinking rapidly, and when my lips hover over hers she closes her eyes. Our lips are so close they're almost touching, our breaths one and the same, and her candied scent plays a grueling game of chess with my willpower. The air seems too thin, and my hands begin to shake.

My body knows and recognizes Catalina's, and I swear if I don't take a step back right this minute, we'll end up skipping dinner, dancing, and the proper date she deserves. While every single cell of my body wants to kiss her, my resolve remains firm. Instead, I wrap my arms around her frame and hug her fiercely, and when she hugs me back I bury my face in her hair. Our hearts are so close, and each beat feels like a love letter to each other in Morse code.

I break our hug and pull out a chair for her. She sits down, her curious eyes scanning the dinner table appraisingly. I never knew I had it in me to be a romantic kind of guy, but ever since I met Catalina I've been doing things for her I've never done for anyone before, including Olivia. It wasn't my style, but when I'm given the gift of Catalina's love the romantic side of me surfaces, and to be frank I like this newfound side of me. I feel like the man I always aspired to be, but was never given a chance, and it feels fucking good. The more I think about it, the more I believe a man isn't fully a man until he meets his soul mate. Sex might make you *feel* like a man, but it's ultimately love that *makes* you one.

We sit and enjoy a quiet dinner, taking turns to feed each other. I like how natural these moments come, how effortless it is to be myself with her. While I'm dying to unwrap my Valentine's Day present, I'm making sure to pace myself. Every so often, Catalina snakes her hand inside her robe to touch her shoulder, and each time I see her tanned skin, I find myself gripping onto my fork a little too tightly.

With dinner behind us, we retreat to the kitchen to wash our plates. I reach into my pocket and grab the rectangular box from my pocket. Catalina is too occupied wringing out the water from the sponge to notice it on the counter right next to her. As she reaches for the paper towels, she gasps.

"What's this?" Catalina asks, pointing towards the red velvet box beside her.

I clear my throat. "It's a gift, Catalina. Open it."

She dries her hands and opens the box. She covers her mouth with her hand, and gasps when she sees the white gold pendant in the shape of a star.

"Oh, Stryder! It's beautiful. Thank you!"

"Did you read the inscription?" I ask, pointing at the pendant.

"My North Star..." Catalina reads aloud, her words measured and slow. She turns to face me with a curious expression on her face.

Grabbing the velvet box from her hands, I remove the pendant and walk behind her. Catalina moves her hair aside to grant me access to her neck. I put the pendant on her, and once the clasp is secure, I kiss the curve of her neck. My hands land on her shoulders, and I spin her around.

"Catalina, I'll be away for a month and while that sounds like a reasonable amount of time, to me it isn't. Do you want to know why?" I ask, and when she nods, I continue. "My home is wherever you are, and I know it's too soon to make promises to you, but I want you to know while I'm away I'll be thinking of you always. Stars... They shine bright in the night sky, and they are constant, always twinkling, even when we can't see them. Catalina, you are my bright North Star, and I know I will never get lost because you will always guide me home."

Her eyes glisten with unshed tears, and she smiles revealing the lone dimple on her left cheek. "Stryder, I already loved the necklace, but now that I know its significance, I'll cherish it with all of my heart," she promises, and lifts the star to her lips and kisses it once before letting it fall against her neck.

She gets on her tippy toes and kisses me. I pull her close and press her tightly against me. I rub my thumbs up and down on the small of her back enjoying the soft material of her robe. As our tongues tango, I feel a fire building inside me, a fire that demands to be quenched. I break away from our kiss and, with measured steps, approach the counter where my phone is docked. After a couple of taps Halestorm's "Break In" starts to play. With confident strides, I return to Catalina and lift her hand to my mouth, brushing my lips against her knuckles.

"Will you dance with me?" I ask. Catalina nods, then smiles. She lifts her right hand and places it on my left shoulder.

"Your left hand goes on my right shoulder, and your right hand goes on my left shoulder," I whisper. Catalina nods and positions her hands like I explained.

I place my free hand on the small of her back, and lead her away from the counter. We slow dance, looking into each other's eyes with a considerable amount of space between us. A few bars of the song pass before I decided I can't take her being so close yet so far away. I press her flush against me, and breaking my dance hold I guide both of her arms around my neck, our foreheads resting against one another's.

As our mouths breathe each other's air, Catalina whispers against my parted lips, "Is this proper dance technique? I definitely prefer this method."

The way she says those words captivates me. With a soft chuckle, I reply. "No. It's not proper technique, baby, but I've never been one to follow the rules."

Catalina grins, and replies, "Good to know."

We slow-dance until the song ends, and by then I'm more than ready to unwrap my Valentine's Day present. Bringing Catalina to the living room, I light the fireplace. Its pops, cracks, and fizzes inundate the room, and Catalina stands in the middle of the room playing with her hair as if she's nervous.

I excuse myself to run upstairs and grab our pillows and blankets. With them in tow, I fly down the stairs to find Catalina waiting for me, now wearing nothing but the black lace corset, apple-red garter belt, and black silk stockings I bought her, as well as her red stilettos. I halt in my steps, taking a moment to process the vision before me and commit it to memory.

Her raven curls hang over the swell of her breasts, the vintage corset making them look rounder, and at the base of her neck is the star pendant I gave her earlier. Her body curves like a violin, and I'm eager to pluck her alluring strings. Silk stockings cover her shapely thighs, and when she moves, the garters stretch tantalizingly slow. All I can think is, *fuck me*. From across the room, Catalina seems confident, but upon closer inspection I notice she's quivering under my gaze. That tinge of innocence mixed with confidence has me close to ending this party before it even starts.

When I picked out the lingerie, I knew it was going to be perfect for her, but not once did I imagine she would look as gorgeous and as sexy as she does right now. I know a lot of guys say they prefer their ladies naked and sure, I do too but damn! Catalina looks smoking hot dressed up like this. I swallow hard, my mouth parched all of a sudden, and resume my strides like a man on a mission. Before her I extend my index finger and trace it over her heaving bosom. As I make contact with her skin, she lets out a raspy sigh, and I follow. Either my vocal chords have stopped working, or touching her fried my brain.

I'm incapable of coherent speech as I watch Catalina's eyes following the movement of my finger. I draw an imaginary line down the center of her corset, hooking my finger over the soft material of the red garter belt, and tug on it gently. Her whispered breaths have me groaning softly as anticipation builds in the narrow space between us.

"Catalina... Baby..." I breathe her name like a litany.

"Stryder..." she whispers my name in supplication.

I hold the back of her neck with one hand, and tilt her chin up with the other, my lips claiming hers. Our kiss is urgent, filled with passion and laced with unmasked devotion. Her mouth is my temple and her body is my home, and I pray that never changes for as long as I live. I kiss her deeply, branding her mouth with my memories so she's unable to forget me when I leave tomorrow morning. I don't know what will happen tomorrow, but seizing this moment is my top priority.

Her hands clutch my waist as I swallow the soft moans she exhales, relishing her taste and affection. I release her neck and chin, and grip her shapely thighs, lifting her body onto mine and wrapping her legs around my waist. As I deepen our kiss, she wraps her hands around my neck in response. Apart from the crackling and hissing of the fireplace, it's the sound of our ragged breaths that fill the air.

I prop her against the nearest wall, pushing her hair to the side with one hand while the other pins us securely against the hard surface. Catalina breaks our kiss to catch her breath, and offers me her neck to kiss and lick it. Between the scent of her skin and her unmistakable need the air is filled with a heady combination that has me bursting quite literally at the seam of my pants. I'm eager to be naked, and I hope she is too.

As I lower my head to the swells of her breasts, I have a moment of reckoning. I pepper them with kisses, then raise my head to see Catalina's head thrown back with her eyes closed. It takes her a split second to realize I've stopped kissing her, and when her eyes snap open its impossible for me not to grin. Her eyes reflect bewilderment which makes her blush under my gaze.

"What?" she asks, biting the inside of her cheek in an obvious effort to compose herself.

"As much as I want to undress you, I have an idea," I reply, slowly unwinding her legs from around my waist. Catalina slides down my chest, and her stilettos clink against the hardwood floor. She wraps her arms around her chest, shielding her body from me. "In Port De Soleil I took pictures of us and you gave me a hard time because I went through the trouble of a photo shoot when I could've just committed things to memory. Remember that?"

She smiles, and a small giggle escapes her. "Yes... I also remember what I did after the last picture was taken," she answers with a wink.

"While I'm away, there won't be a moment where I don't think of you, but I'd like to have something to hold me over when I'm missing you a little too much..." I admit.

"What? You want to take pictures of me? Dressed like this?!" she asks, gesturing at her body with an incredulous look on her face.

I nod, pouting my lips like child, and Catalina laughs again, her dulcet tones filling my chest with indescribable satisfaction.

"All right, get the damn camera, Martynus," she mutters, resting her hands on her hips. "Go get it before I change my damn mind."

She doesn't have to tell me twice. I bolt from the room, not caring if I look like a horny teenage boy. I race up the stairs two steps at a time, and after grabbing my camera I run back down. She's standing in front of the fireplace, looking at the flames as if lost in thought, and her skin seems to glow. I power on the camera... *Perfect.*

I adjust the lens to focus on her body, her right hand resting on her waist while the other plays with one of her curls. Her face is mesmerizing, and while this type of photography isn't my forte I know without a doubt these pictures will turn out nice. I press the button, and the sound of the shutter startles her.

Maybe I see Catalina differently, or perhaps I'm inspired by her love... What I do know is I want this night to perpetuate itself. I swear the time continuum is skewed when she turns to face me, her hair swishing softly, as if in slow motion. Her contemplative expression slowly transforms into a beaming smile, and as she approaches me, I readjust the lens to capture the garters, which expand and recoil with each of her measured footsteps. The non-stop sounds of the camera blend with the staccato clicks of Catalina's stilettos against the floor.

"Did you get your shots?" Catalina asks.

Lowering the camera, I rest it against my chest in awe. I extend my hand and lead her towards the sofa near the fireplace.

"Lay down on your side facing me, baby," I whisper, while holding the camera.

Shaking her head, she plops against the leather couch and props her head on her shoulder with a sassy glint in her eyes. Her free hand rests against her heavenly hips as her index finger pulls on one of the garters, allowing the elastic material to snap against her tanned skin. She does this repeatedly, and I twitch my neck to ease up the tension there, all while forcing myself to focus on getting the job done.

"Look at me, Catalina," I command.

When she does, I snap away. I know my view of her is completely subjective, but when I see Catalina through the lens, I see so much beauty and potential, and I revel at the fact that this woman loves me. I feel like the luckiest bastard in the entire solar system. Picture after picture, frame after frame I'm left thunderstruck.

Satisfied with my pictures, I rest the camera against the cocktail table, and sit on the edge of the wooden surface. I look at her long and hard trying to memorize everything about her, from the sound of her breathing to the way her pulse jumps at the base of her neck. Am I torturing myself here? Probably, but I don't want to miss a single detail.

"Thank you," I croak, as I clear my throat. Looking into her sensuous eyes, I continue. "You look stunning, Catalina. I'm having a tough time here seeing you like this... propped on the sofa looking so sexy. You're perfect. I want to rip those stockings off, unlace your corset, and trail my fingers over those beautiful breasts of yours. I crave nothing more than to rip that thong with my goddamn teeth and lap up your need for me."

Catalina exhales, her eyes darkening with heat at the sound of my blatant words. Through her long, black eyelashes she challenges me.

"Then take me as you see fit."

I stand and adjust myself, but as I'm about to approach her, Catalina raises her hand, signaling me to stop. "But first, bring the camera."

I halt, taking a New York minute to process her words. With a shrug and a wicked smirk, I hand the camera over. She rises, and deliberately pushing me against the sofa, my back hitting the leather surface. I raise my hands to support her waist as she straddles me, gripping her hips as I caress her soft, naked skin.

"What are you up to, Catalina?" I swallow hard.

"I think you should have the memories of *us*," she whispers with misty eyes. "I want you to remember *us*, and how beautiful and perfect this love between us truly is."

Her words cut into the deepest part of my soul, halting my need for her body and replacing it with tenderness. The simplicity behind her words overcomes me, and I'll never get over how incredible and inspiring it is to find love when you least expected it. A simple favor for a friend truly changed my life, and this love has defied all odds and we're all the better for it.

Having Catalina before me, all of her protective barriers and self-defense mechanisms completely obliterated, her heart raw and out in the open, trusting and believing in me is the best thing that could've happened to either of us. She has no clue my heart is also open; I'm learning to give myself in other ways. I have to learn to ignore the nagging voice in my head screaming our relationship will fail during my absence.

"Our love is..." I pause, feeling overcome with emotion. "Our love is nothing like I ever expected real love to be. Forgive me, Catalina. I'm at a loss here for words... just bear with me. I just... damn it... Our love has the ability to-"

"Make us or break us," Catalina finishes, her statement echoing my thoughts. Our eyes meet, and when she nods my grip on her hips becomes tighter. "I know, Stryder. It scares me, but when you think about it life is too short to be scared, or to hold back. I look back at my life now, and realize there were moments I was too worried and afraid to fail. As Tennyson once wrote, *'Tis better to have loved and lost than to never have loved at all'.*

"It's scary to think you can trust someone with your heart at the risk of it being broken, but at the same time, imagine: if you don't take the chance, you'd never discover the joy of finding real love. I learned that lesson with Blake and I'm revisiting it with you. Fight or flight. Isn't that how it always goes? I'm choosing to fight for you... for *us*," Catalina affirms, her beautiful eyes filled with tears.

Exhaling loudly, I speak. "I've come to the conclusion that moments like these define us, Catalina. Like film, these moments are cut into frames, capturing the beauty and the essence of the things that play before us. They have the power to control our thoughts and define the things we do, and they're inescapable and unforgettable. You're the best thing that's ever happened to me."

Catalina smiles and wipes her tears from her cheeks with the back of her hand. With the other she positions the camera near both of our heads. Sighing, she leans in and kisses me sweetly, all while the camera clicks away. She breaks the kiss and smiles devilishly.

"This camera... I have *tons* of ideas," she taunts.

"Yes? Indulge me," I ask, squeezing her round hips and inching forward to nibble on her lips.

Catalina giggles, and angles the camera to capture us smiling and kissing again. Hey, I don't mind the pictures, but right now all I can think of is sinking my dick deep inside her again and again. Without a moment's hesitation, I take the camera away, bringing it to rest on the cocktail table, and then busy myself unlacing the strings of her corset.

My fingers work at a frantic pace, and when I lower the corset past her ribcage I kiss her breasts, nibbling, licking, and sucking. Her hands clutch my head, her fingernails scratching my scalp, and between the rolling of her hips against my thick dick mixed with her sexy moans, my hands and heart work faster. Once undressed, with the scorching flames of the fireplace as our only witness, we make love all throughout the night, taking turns to worship each other's bodies. Losing, and rediscovering ourselves again and again.

Completely exhausted yet incredibly satisfied, I pick her up from the sofa and carry her upstairs to bed. With each step I take, the more I know Catalina is the woman I want to spend the rest of my life with, and be the mother of my babies. For many years I felt I was waiting for a bus that would never arrive, and just as I was about to call it quits–behold Catalina. As fortuitous as us meeting was, it was fate and Jackson who brought us together.

With Catalina fast asleep in my arms, I decide to hold onto her for a minute longer. Her heart-shaped lips are curled into a small smile. Now more than ever I want to snap a picture, but like she's told me before: *Commit that to memory,* so I do. Pulling the comforter back, I tuck her in and lean over to place a kiss on her forehead. She cradles into me, and a strangled groan leaves my throat. I fly down the staircase to put out the fire, and then gather our clothes making sure to bring the camera too.

Curling beside Catalina, I snap a few pictures as I kiss her shoulder and back, praying the constant flashes of the camera don't wake her up, and then I rest the camera on the nightstand and fall asleep with my cheek rested against the warmth of her shoulder. *God, I'm going to miss her.*

CHAPTER TEN

Catalina

The alarm clock goes off sooner rather than later, and when I reach out for Stryder's side of the bed I come up empty handed. I sit up in and perk my ears for the shower, but I don't hear a thing. As I scan the room, I notice his bags are lined up by the door, and my heart sinks to my stomach as I think every morning will be just like this during the next month. I try to choke back a sob, but it's too late–a rivulet of tears trickles past my cheeks and onto my naked thighs.

Inhale. Exhale, Catalina, I repeat in my head in a pitiful attempt to stop crying. I don't want to upset Stryder with my gloominess; he cannot be aware of how much his impending absence will affect me. I vow to be strong and not to allow sadness to overshadow the happiness we have built over the past few months. It's natural to cry don't get me wrong especially when you've fallen head over heels with someone as kind, tender, and unbelievably romantic as Stryder. Yet the heart wants what it wants, and mine wants to wake up beside him every day.

I swing my legs over the side of the mattress, and let them dangle there for a second. As I try to stand my ass lands right back on the bed. *Holy shit.* My body aches everywhere. It's a delicious kind of pain, the kind that reminds you what you were up to the night before. I get up again and walk stiffly towards the bathroom, mumbling to myself when I hear his soft chuckles. I turn on my heel and see him leaning against the doorjamb; one hand resting against the door while the other is tucked in his front pocket.

"Rough night, babe?" he asks smugly, with a knowing smile on his lips.

My hands instinctively rise to cover myself, and my cheeks feel like they are on fire.

"I guess you could say that," I reply with a scoff.

Stryder saunters to where I'm standing, and envelops me in a tight hug which I happily return. There is no place I'd rather be than wrapped in his loving embrace.

"Does it make me an asshole to feel proud you're walking odd this morning, and it's all because of me? Hmm?" he mumbles against my lips.

I nod into his neck, and take in his scent. He smells fresh, like right out of the shower, and the scent of his cologne mixed with the smell of his skin is a heady combination; it's manly, but not overpowering; sweet, yet incredibly seductive. His hand lands on my backside and squeezes my ass cheeks like quite the caveman.

"Are you feeling sore?" he asks, as he kisses my hairline.

"Yes," I mumble and squirm in place, which in turn makes him chuckle. I swat him playfully on the arm and continue, "Last night was absolutely beautiful. I loved every second of it." I break our hold and walk towards the bathroom. "What's your departure time?" At the last syllable my voice breaks, and I clear my throat as I wait for his response.

"One o'clock, but I have to be there by ten thirty. Jackson just got here. The three of us will go," he answers quietly, his hands fidgeting in his front pockets.

I nod and quickly enter the bathroom. A part of me is undeniably sad, yet another is optimistic this separation could benefit us in the long run. I've been thinking a lot about our future, and there's no doubt in my mind I want *us* to work. Let's face it, we both have demanding careers, and our jobs require lots of travel on both short- and long-term assignments. If we cannot survive this separation, then at least I know we gave us a shot. I want this to work. No... I *need* this to work.

After my shower, I wrap myself in a big fluffy bathrobe feeling more optimistic than I did. I've been thinking about picking up a hobby that will keep me busy while Stryder is away, plus I have Jackson to consider, too. He needs me now more than ever, and I'll make sure he gets back in tip-top shape, and back on the slopes where he belongs. Having Jackson by my side will definitely make this upcoming month easier.

After styling my hair into a suicide roll I get busy with make-up. My spine straightens as I watch Stryder, in the mirror, collecting his toiletries from the shower. The cherry-red lipstick I was about to put on falls from my hand, landing into the sink as Stryder embraces me from behind. His eyes are dimmer than usual, and his forehead is scrunched as if concerned.

"Are you okay with this? With me leaving? Be honest."

I look into his eyes in the mirror and brush my fingers over his tight hold.

"I'll be fine, Stud. I have so much to do, I doubt I'll miss you," I reply with a wink.

Liar. You big fat liar. The cold hard truth is I'm not fine, but I can't tell him that because he will cancel his assignment in a heartbeat. While I'd love to spend my days, nights, every waking moment beside him, I need him to let him go so our relationship has a chance to grow. Sometimes we make sacrifices for the greater good, and it's in those sacrifices we show what we're made of and what we're capable of achieving.

I can't tell if he's aware of my lies, and if he is, he says nothing. Our eyes stay put in the mirror, a mess-load of unsaid words floating between us. Will I miss Stryder Martynus? *Of-fucking-course.* It will take some getting used to falling asleep at night without his arms holding me, or his whispered words of affection that make my heart and soul fly when my eyes flutter open in the mornings. It will be tough sitting at the dining table without his hand brushing against my leg, or our mutual feeding routines reminiscent of our times in Whistler. What I'll miss the most is the requited love and undeniable connection we share.

Stryder rests his chin against my shoulder and pouts. "You won't miss me? Ouch." I cradle my head against his and nestle into his warmth. He kisses the tender spot beneath my ear and breathes, "You can say you won't miss me all you want, but this body of yours knows mine, and it will crave my touch every single day."

I scoff at his words, but my heart thrills at the confidence behind them. He's right in more ways than one. I will miss him, and my body will miss him more. Turning to face him, I let my thumb brush the soft skin of his lips. Stryder mumbles something unintelligible, and judging by the pained groan he lets out, I know it has to do with my affections.

"Oh, Stud. Your mornings will be the hardest. Pun intended," I tease with a wink.

Stryder chuckles and shakes his head at my words. "Oh, Catalina... you and that mouth. I'll miss all of you, from your sass to your body, and everything in between."

He opens the bathrobe to expose my neck, his gaze falling on the star pendant hovering above the slope of my breasts. One of his fingers lifts the pendant to his lips and kisses it. "You are my North Star, Catalina. God, I'm going to miss you."

I clear my throat and force a smile. He needs to hear reassurances which will hold him over while he's away; while Stryder is sweet and kind, he's also filled with insecurities just like me. I have to tell him something that will ease his mind allowing chance, destiny, fate, or whatever the hell you call it to take the lead.

"When you get back I want us to go away, just you and me, to somewhere beautiful and far away. Is that something you'd like to do with me?" I ask with an awkward smile. Stryder lets out a huff and brushes his knuckles against my cheekbone.

"I thought you'd never ask, Catalina. I'd love to," he replies, eyes bright. "Tell you what. There's this place in the Caribbean I think you'd like a lot. I'll take care of all the details. "I can tell he's excited, and right now I'm thankful I let my heart do all the talking. He stands tall; the confident man I've grown to love is back with that sensual, passionate look on his face. "I can't wait to have you all to myself. Just us on a private beach with the warm sand beneath our toes, and the pale of the moonlight reflected on your skin..." he finishes with a hum.

I push him away softly, and giggle when he closes his eyes and licks his lips. This man, I swear. He has the innate ability to create the most delicious of scenarios in my head. Sometimes distractions prove to be useful most especially when there are goodbyes involved.

"Come on, handsome. I need to get dressed so we can be on our way." My voice cracks at the last word, and Stryder lets out a ragged sigh. Just when I think he's letting me go, his strong arms hug me again.

It's hard to explain how this feels, but bittersweet comes close. Our hearts beat frantically against each other's chests; not driven by desire, but by the innate awareness where we belong. This is how we should always be, standing together and braving the uncertainties that life throws our way. Love, true love, truly changes you. It's not just an intense feeling or a sense of attachment; it goes far beyond that. Real love is not only sharing a connection with someone or having remarkable sex don't get me wrong, though, we enjoy those things too. Finding love is a game-changer.

We understand each other, and we're considerate of our needs, not only by our actions, but by the way they nurture our relationship. I've been in love once before, and I know it grows and evolves with time, but like a plant it can also wither away. I don't want that to happen to us. I love Stryder with all of my being, and I'll be damned if I let this die. In the past it was easy to resort to self-sabotage, but this love has changed my way of thinking, and this love will have a happy ending. I'll be damn sure of it.

"Hey, where'd you go?" Stryder mumbles into my ear, interrupting my thoughts. I dry my tears against his sweater and melt against the hardness of his chest and strength of his arms. He squeezes me tightly. "I love you."

Three words: subject, verb, and object. Only eight letters, yet they yield the power to make my heart sink to the pit of my stomach, and ricochet back to its rightful place.

"I'm right here. I was thinking... that's all. I love you too."

Stryder breaks our hug and holds my face with his hands. Tilting it, he massages my cheeks with his thumbs. "I know you're not okay with this, and you're trying damn hard to hide it. I know because I'm right there with you, hiding how I truly feel. Watching you pretend to be indifferent when you're anything but kills me. I can see it in your eyes. Our careers bind us, and my client is hell-bent on working only with me. Plus, there are things I *have* to do and I know going away is for the best. Cat, you'll be on my damn mind every day, from the moment I wake up until I pass out at night.

"I can't stop thinking of you because you're the blood that runs through my veins, and life isn't life without you in it. You better wait for me because at the end of the day, baby, you own me." Using one hand, he gestures at himself, from his head all the way down to his shoes. Stryder then rests both of his hands over his heart, and confidently says, "This is all yours, Catalina."

My heart somersaults at his words, and the sob I've been holding back unravels, tears streaming past my cheeks. "I'm yours too, Stryder. I just- I didn't want to worry you with my emotional bullshit, that's all." I don't know why, but hearing myself say that makes me laugh. "See? I'm a basket-case," I declare amidst giggles.

There we stand in the middle of the bathroom laughing and crying and wiping our eyes, enjoying these last moments with no concern for the time. I reach for his chest and take hold of his hands, and intertwine them with mine. We bow slightly toward each other as our lips meet for a sweet kiss that tastes like 'see you later.'

As if on cue, Jackson knocks on the door, calling our names, and we reply in unison, "Come in!" We look at each other and laugh while Jackson parades into the bathroom with an ear-splitting grin on his face.

"Well, aren't you two just fucking adorable standing there holding hands? Are you ready to go? We have to get going if we want to make it to the airport on time," Jackson says, looking at his wristwatch—his old-self back, and in rare form.

"Yeah, we are, sort of..." Stryder replies and then turns to face me. "I'll leave you to get dressed." He kisses the tip of my nose and then leaves the bathroom to collect his luggage. Jackson walks towards me with a half-smile, his eyes focused on mine. I take a deep breath and exhale shakily.

"You're going to be just fine, Pardo. Before you know it, he'll be back," he says matter-of-factly.

I return his smile and nod. "I know... It's just hard."

In his best Michael Scott impression, he replies grinning, "That's what she said."

I laugh until my abdomen hurts, and Jackson gives me a peck on the cheek before he walks out of the bathroom so I can dress. Once ready, I retrieve my purse and climb into the back seat of Jackson's truck.

"Dude, why am I not allowed to drive my own truck?" Jackson complains, on our way to the airport. "Catalina, earmuffs back there."

I raise my hands to my ears pretending they are indeed earmuffs, but I can hear everything.

"Listen, my ankles are pretty much healed and so are my legs. My dick works just fine, so I don't understand why there's a problem with having my hands on the wheel. I'm just saying."

I bite my lip, trying to contain my laughter while Jackson glares at me in the sun visor mirror. I stick out my tongue, and he rolls his eyes in response.

"Your ankles, legs, *and dick* have nothing to do with it. You're still taking pain meds which clearly state you are not allowed to drive. Until you are done with them, you will not drive. Lei capisce?" Stryder answers nonchalantly, with his eyes focused on the road.

"Io capisco, old man. Gah!" Jackson grumbles and crosses his arms across his chest. "I'm not an invalid, asshole."

As the truck traverses the winding roads of Casper, I sit back and contemplate my new life. They say time can change a person and make old things new. I agree wholeheartedly, but I hope my life doesn't change again, and I pray with all of my heart this works out in the end.

"Text me as soon as you make the connection to L.A., okay?" I ask Stryder as we unload his bags from the truck. He stands on the sidewalk of the drop-off area and looks at me with sad eyes. He opens his arms, and I walk into them crying. "Be safe, Stud. That's all I ask," I whisper in between breaths.

His arms hold me in place, ignoring the airport transit officer urging us to wrap it up. He scowls at the officer, and says through gritted teeth, "Give us a moment, all right? This isn't easy for either of us."

The officer replies, "Farewells are never easy, my man. You're holding up traffic. Don't force me to write you a ticket."

The incessant honking horns of annoyed drivers make us rush, something neither of us is prepared to do. I choke at the officer's words, and wipe away my tears trying to keep my cool. I cup Stryder's cheeks with my gloved hands and kiss his lips softly, trying to let his taste linger there for as long as possible. Breaking our kiss, he speaks.

"Catalina, I love you. Be strong and know that you are loved by me, okay? I have to go."

I let go and jog towards the truck door trying to appease the transit officer and the upset drivers blasting their horns at us. Lifting the door handle with a shaky hand, I raise the other to wave goodbye. He blows me a kiss, then turns on his heel to walk through the sliding doors that will separate us for an entire month. I watch for as long as I can until he disappears from my view. Sliding onto the driver's seat, I drive away knowing I'm leaving behind a piece of my heart.

Crying while driving is something I'm not accustomed to, and like clockwork, Jackson reaches out for my knee and squeezes it tightly. I sigh, but keep my eyes on the road. From the corner of my eye I see his goofy smile that gets me every time. Despite my wet cheeks and stuffy nose, I smile. He cocks his head against his shoulder, and exhales as if relieved.

"What would you like to do today?" he asks. "I don't want to go home. I'm starting to think the ranch is my prison, and I fucking hate that. Let's do something fun."

Keeping my eyes on the road, I consider his words, but when I see a coffeehouse up ahead I wiggle my butt against the leather seat. As I'm pulling in Jackson shakes his head, and chuckles.

"Caffeine for the addict... Is this your idea of fun, Catalina? Let me inform you it is not." When I nod, he lets out a huff and looks at me with wide eyes and a flared nose. It's more than obvious he's teasing me. "Girl, you need to get out more. Mmm-hmm."

"Shut up, Jax. You underestimate the power behind a nice, hot cup of coffee. It rights many wrongs in the world... just a few sips of the stuff and I'll be as good as new. Trust me on this one," I declare with a wink.

Once parked, Jackson opens his door and jumps out cursing loudly when his foot hits the snow-covered pavement. I run to the passenger side, and place my hand on his shoulder. My heart clenches when I see the pained expression on his face.

"Are you okay, Jackson? Anything I can do? Why'd you do that? What were you thinking?!"

Jackson opens his eyes and laughs at me. Is he mocking me? What the hell?

"You spewed out so many questions my brain kind of exploded. I'm fine," he replies with a smile.

When he sees the irritated look on my face, he laughs harder, so I push him playfully, and we walk into the coffee shop with linked arms. The young lady behind the counter blushes, and her hand rises to cover her mouth in surprise. It takes me a second to understand her reaction. When you know Jackson Reese on a personal level like I do, it's easy to forget he's a celebrity and well-known in these parts. I look over at him; he's sporting the biggest smile, and watching his features light up makes me very happy. *This* is the Jackson Reese I met and grew to love with all of my heart. I take a step back and let him work his charm.

"What can I get you, Mr. Reese?" asks the blue-eyed brunette behind the counter. I watch in amusement and notice her body is shaking so much that her bangs quiver over her eyebrows.

"I don't know, babe. What do you recommend? I'm not much of a coffee drinker, but can we get my girl here a coffee? Light and sweet with regular sugar, right, Cat?" Jackson informs the barista in a deep voice, and then winks at me in confirmation.

The girl looks somewhat deflated by Jackson's term of endearment for me; she tilts her head, avoiding eye contact with me.

"Yes, please," I reply, and walk towards the other counter to wait for my cup of liquid happiness. The barista asks my name, but Jackson answers for me.

"This is going to be a mouthful, okay?" When the girl nods, he continues. "Her name is: She saved my life. She's my best friend and I love her very much."

She looks at Jackson with wide eyes, and worries her lip as she busies herself writing the ridiculously long name he gave her with a black marker. When she's done she exhales upwards, her bangs flying up and down then back to their spot.

"And for you Mr. Reese?" she asks softly, as if he were a regular patron. Their eyes connect and she blushes again. *Good Lord*. Resting both of his gruff palms against the granite countertop, he leans in to get a better look at her name tag.

"Surprise me, Ashley," he purrs, as I bite back the urge to laugh my ass off. The man is shameless, but nevertheless it's interesting to watch him in conquest-mode.

Another barista puts my cup on the counter, not bothering to call out the name, but smiles when I sip and mumble my approval. I debate whether or not to sit on one of the couches by the large picture windows, yet there I stand sipping my coffee watching Jackson flirt with the barista.

"Do you like chocolate, Mr. Reese?" Ashley asks shyly while worrying her lip.

"On my *stuff*? Yeah, I sure do," he replies without skipping a beat.

The sip I'd just taken sprays from my mouth, and dribbles down my chin like a toddler's milk. Leaning against the wall I laugh long and hard, making the other patrons look at me like I'm a loon. I cover my mouth with my free hand, trying to keep my wits in check, but I can't stop laughing, and Jackson is laughing with me. He hands over the stack of napkins Ashley gave him to clean up the mess from my coat, chin, and hands.

The other barista comes out with a mop, and starts cleaning the spray of coffee by my feet. Through my tears of hysterical laughter, I notice Ashley is the color of beets. I want to walk away to find a waste bin to throw away my dirty napkins, but I can't move an inch. Jackson stands there, his ass leaning against the counter and his arms crossed with the smuggest look on his face.

"Was it something I said?" he asks with a straight face, which in turn makes me laugh harder. Other patrons look at me, shaking their heads.

"Oh, Jackson Reese, you're going to hell for that one," I mutter before walking away.

There is an isolated couch in the corner of the shop; I perch myself on it. As I wait for Jackson to join me, I look out the window and think about Stryder. His flight should be about to take off. My heart tightens in my chest as I'm reminded we'll be away from each other and I'll be left to my own devices with Jackson. My musings are interrupted when my phone chirps with an incoming text.

> **<SM: I'm buckled and ready for takeoff. There's an empty window seat beside me, and I keep hoping you'll come barreling down the aisle and sit next to me. I miss you. *kiss emoticon*>**

I exhale a shaky breath, and through teary eyes I reply.

> **<CP: I miss you too. More than words can express. Be safe, and let me know when you make the connecting flight. I love you.>**

> **<SM: I love you too. I'm listening to this: *No Air* by Jordin Sparks. Don't judge. *winking emoticon*>**

I scramble for the ear-buds in my purse, and look up the song. I've heard it before, but never paid attention to the lyrics and when I realize what he means I smile. I can't breathe either.

> **<CP: Stud, you're killing me. Come back soon, okay?>**

I press 'send' and hold my cell against my chest. I wait for a few minutes and when he doesn't reply, I gather he's up in the air far away from my reach. It is funny how your life and perceptions can change right before your eyes, how love makes you whole and empty at the same time. It's during times like these that you become thankful and embrace the happy moments you lived because they're what you cling to during sad times. There's this emptiness in my soul brought on by his departure, and I keep having these moments of realization, reminders that love is powerful and it can change everything about you. Loving Stryder is the best thing that has ever happened to me, and I'll never tire of admitting that. I'm still lost in my thoughts when

Jackson sits beside me, raising his legs on the sofa, like at home, with a paper cup in his hands.

"You okay there, Cat?" he asks, concerned.

I nod, and reply, "Yeah... Stryder's flight just took off." My voice cracks, and I change the subject quickly. "Jackson Reese, you are shameless, you know? That poor girl..."

Jackson grins shifting his paper cup for me to see Ashley's name and phone number written in black marker, and laughs wickedly. I shake my head in disbelief.

"Girl, I think I just regained my mojo," he says with a wink. "She's cute. I think I might call her."

I quirk my head, and look at him inquisitively. "You're serious," I declare rather than ask, and when I see his eyes free of mischief, I blurt my thoughts. "What about Sam?"

Jackson scoffs and blows raspberries. "What about Sam, Catalina? I know the score there. She's not the type to commit, and to be honest I don't think she ever will be. She's not wired that way."

"Have you thought maybe she's playing hard to get? Maybe she wants you to pursue her to death?"

Jackson shakes his head, and with saddened eyes, he replies, "It's been ten years. I know you don't know a thing about us that's a story for another day but the truth is it's been ten fucking years, and I can't sit here and grow roots waiting for her to come around. I told her that the other day. I don't mind having sex with her, but I need more than that, you know?"

I nod.

"Jupiter is right. The heart needs something more than just a warm body, it needs love. Your man is wise, Catalina. Treasure that."

"Was Stryder always insightful as a kid?" I ask.

Jackson rolls his eyes. "Yes... irritatingly so. He's an old soul, and as much as I hate admitting it, the man is wise beyond his years. His biggest flaw, if you can call it that, is insecurity. The way he masks it is by pretending not to care, but deep down he does. My sister is the one to blame for that, but I've seen a change in him since you two got together. You're giving him back what Olivia took from him. It's nice to see, girl," Jackson replies, and takes a sip of his drink.

I take a moment to ponder his words, and while I don't answer, I hold all this information to be true. One of the qualities I admire most about Stryder is his blunt honesty. He made it a point to show me the skeletons in his closet when we were first getting to know each other in Whistler.

"What did she make you?" I whisper, quirking my head in Ashley's direction.

Jackson follows my gaze with a smug smile on his face. "White hot chocolate, and let me tell you, it's promising," he says, making me believe he's referring to Ashley and not his drink.

"Have you figured out what you want to do for fun while the old man is away?"

"Dancing," I say under my breath. I turn my head to face him, and grinning I repeat myself more assertively. "Dancing... I want to learn how to dance, and you're going to teach me, Jackson Reese."

He leans forward to rest his cup on the table. Placing his palms on his knees, he sits forward with a look of deep contemplation. "Dancing... It's been a while for me. Not to mention, my bum ankles..."

"Then all the more reason to get off your ass, and put your heart into physical therapy. Think about it. I'm not a doctor but we can ask the medical team, but maybe dancing could help with strengthening your muscles, and ultimately help you get back to where you belong, which is back on the slopes. I'm not taking no for an answer, Jax. You *will* teach me. That's not up for negotiation," I challenge. "Are you in?"

Jackson sits back and crosses his arms over his chest. Scoffing, he replies, "Like I have a motherfucking choice?"

"Good. Now that we have an understanding, let's call the doctors and schedule a consult. Let's grab this bull by the horns." Standing, I throw my empty cup into the nearest trash bin.

Jackson rises, and looks at me with a smile. "Yes ma'am."

CHAPTER ELEVEN

Jackson

"**I** was waiting for you to come to your senses, Jax," Rob booms proudly, looking at my treatment plan. He rests his hands on my shoulders like my dad would, and looks at me square in the eyes."You aren't to blame for anything. Do you understand me? I need my boy back, and this is my last season, kid... Let's make it count."

I nod at the silver-haired man before me. I've let him down many times before, mostly because of my shit attitude and behavior when I was a certified drunken asshole. Now that I'm sober I can see the pride in his eyes and the joy in his voice when he sees I'm not letting depression and fear get the best of me.

From across the room I see Mom, Kaelan, and Cat watching me jog on the treadmill. Doctor B. walks in and smiles when he sees me breaking a sweat on the machine.

"Well, well, Jackson. How are your ankles?" He asks, looking at my feet.

"They're super tender, but nothing I can't manage, Doc," I answer, panting.

"Good. Remember to pace yourself. It's not a race. A fast horse may win, but it's a consistent gallop that makes him a winner. Does that make sense?"

I smile at his analogy. I feel more like a mule trotting on the treadmill, but I totally get it. "Yep. Perfectly."

Completely exhausted, I hit the shower and get ready for my appointment with the shrink. Catalina waits for me in the vestibule of the medical center and, together, we walk towards the office down the long corridor holding hands. For the first time in weeks since the accident I'm feeling optimistic, and I make a mental note to share that during today's session.

"How was your week, Jackson?" Dr. Head asks, as she scribbles something in her notebook.

As I lay on the chaise, I look up at the fluorescent lights in the ceiling and smile. "Good, Doc. Pretty good."

"Care to elaborate?"

"There's not much to say... My mobility has improved dramatically over the past week. The pain is no longer crippling, and I'm starting to feel like my head is finally catching up with my body."

Dr. Head walks over and smiles. "Tell me exactly what's going on in your mind right now."

I sit up on the chaise and look into her eyes. "I'm starting to feel like myself again. One part of me feels it's okay to move on from the avie, but the other argues it's too soon. I will admit I feel happy to be alive which I haven't felt since the guys passed on."

I think I'm getting a better grasp of reality now that I'm putting my heart into my sessions with the shrink, and to be honest having Cat mothering me around is a huge incentive. Mom has been on tour with Dad, but whenever she's in town and hooks up with Catalina and Kaelan... God help me. It's like these women gang up on me and enjoy riding my ass like there's no tomorrow.

As I'm leaving the medical center, I see Rob waiting for us in the vestibule. "How'd it go, son?" he asks, smiling.

"Good! I don't know if I'll be ready for next season, but I sure as hell am going to try. I miss the pow, Rob, and can't wait to get back on it."

Rob keeps me at arm's length, his eyes firm and steady on mine. "You will, son. Hell, you're a goddamn miracle. Walking away from an avie, and living to tell the tale just shows you owe it to yourself and the boys to rise up, and push yourself to give your best. I'm not saying it won't hurt, and I will push you like never before. I expect the best from you because I know in my heart you haven't shown me or the world what you're truly capable of. They are waiting for you to give up, son. Show them they are wrong."

Rob's words fill my chest with indescribable feelings. For one, I don't want to disappoint him, especially when our days as a team are numbered, but I also want to let him retire with a bang. I owe it to him, and to myself to give this recovery my all. I'm cringing at the thought of pushing my body to its limits... I'm not one hundred percent recovered, but I can't prove the world wrong if I don't try.

After I fill Rob in on the details, Catalina and I leave the medical center. Tomorrow will be my first day of phase two of rehabilitation, and I need all the rest I can get. On the drive home I can't stop smiling, but Catalina says nothing, which is a complete shocker since her job is to ask questions. With her hands firm on the steering wheel, she looks at the road ahead with a grin.

The music playing on the truck's stereo system stops as an incoming call is routed through the speakers. I look at the dashboard and see it is Jupiter calling. *That's odd*. Why would he call me, and not Catalina? I ignore the call and text him instead making sure to un-pair my phone from the truck's system.

<JR: What's up?>

<SM: Why'd you ignore my call?>

<JR: I'm in the truck with Cat.>

<SM: Oh... How is she?>

<JR: She's good, riding my ass. You know, the usual.>

<SM: *laughing emoticon* I sent something your way. Take a look and let me what you think.>

<JR: Define "something". If it's porn, I'm game.>

<SM: No, jackass! Just text me when you see it. Got to go. I have a cyber date with Cat.>

<JR: What you really mean is FTF... kinky. Who knew? *devil emoticon*>

<SM: *eye-roll emoticon* I'm not sure what that is, and I'm not even going to ask... TTYL>

<JR: You're right, you don't! *angel emoticon*>

I remind myself to check my email tonight. As we pull into the drive-around in front of the house, I notice the large maple tree in the front yard has buds on its branches a sure sign spring will be here soon. I grimace at the change of seasons; I must be the only idiot in the universe who needs snow as much as breathing.

"Is Stryder okay?" Catalina asks, halting my thoughts. I nod, and close the passenger door. "He wanted to ask how things are and all. He said you two have a hot date in a bit... Oh, to be a fly on the wall. Do you guys... you know?" I ask, but instantly regret asking such a dumb-fuck question.

"Do we what, Jackson?" Catalina asks with a raised eyebrow.

I raise my hands and shake my head. "Never mind, Cat. It was a stupid question." I unlock the front door and rub my boots against the foyer rug. "Take-out for dinner?"

"Sure," she chirps as she removes her coat, and hangs it on the coat rack, then races up the staircase. "I'm going to shower. You can pick dinner. I trust your judgment."

"Okay."

When I hear her door close, I walk towards my office and shut the door behind me. I look for the folder with the takeout menus and remember to check my email. As the laptop powers on, I look at the two framed pictures on my desk. One is me standing beside Rob on a slope in Sweden at twelve or so, and the other is a picture of me from the dancing days. I think I'm five or six.

I contemplate Cat's proposal asking myself if I truly want to dance again. It's not like I've forgotten, but Jupiter is a better teacher than I am. Maybe my sister Kathryn can help? A part of me really misses dancing, but there's a reason why I quit. I'm not sure if I'm ready to share that part of me with anyone yet, including Catalina. That fucked-up shit that happened to me as a kid is a part of my past I'll take with me to the grave. However, Catalina is right. Teaching her to dance will benefit not only her, but me as well.

I log into my email account and scroll down past snowboarding stuff to see Jupiter's email. It has an odd title. *Raven Girl*. Hmm.

> Jax,
> Here are some pictures I want you to look at. Let me know what you think.
> -SM

There are five attachments. When I click on the first one I blink twice. Rings, and just not ordinary ones *engagement* rings. Picture after picture, each one more eye-catching than the one before. I'm no expert on the subject, but it's nice to see Jupiter following through with his feelings. Five months ago it would've been easier to spot a farting unicorn flying in the sky than to imagine him in love and considering marriage again... especially after what happened between him and my idiot sister. Shit. If Jupiter finds his happy ending, then there's hope for the rest of us.

I don't wear jewelry apart from the bracelet Cat gave me, and I vow never to take that off since it's the reason why I'm still alive. I look at all the options and decide I like number three. It's a simple square diamond ring, and knowing Catalina I'm positive she isn't the type of woman who'd measure love by the weight of carats on her finger. She loves with her heart, and the man she agrees to marry will be the luckiest fucker in the world. I guess you can say the little green monster in me envies their connection, but not in the way you'd think.

My near-death experience has me reevaluating my life. My days of living selfishly and pushing the envelope with stunts aren't over, but I definitely want to make a life for myself outside of snowboarding. I'm alive but haven't lived, if that makes any sense. I'm not saying I'm cured from the nightmares or over the feelings of guilt that haunt me, but I have a new lease on life and I'm going to take full advantage of it.

> Jup,
> You've gone soft on me! Why must you burden me with this girly shit? Last I checked I have dude parts... Kaelan, Mom, or Lizzie would be better at this stuff than me. Pussy-whipped, much? Okay, but seriously though. I like option three, and I think she will too. I'm deleting this email before our cunning reporter comes across it and spoils your surprise. Safe travels, bro.
> Still a man last I checked,
> -Jax

Earlier today I asked Kaelan to hire a personal chef to get my diet in order in preparation for rehab, but tonight I'm going for comfort. After pressing 'send' and deleting Jupiter's e-mail, I power off the laptop and order pizza. The prospect of having pepperoni and gooey cheese in my mouth makes my inner fat kid do the Harlem Shake.

I turn off the office light and walk towards the den, to pop in a movie. I hear Catalina's voice coming from her room, so I raise the volume to give her privacy. I'm not really feeling the movie though. Grabbing my cell, for reasons I can't explain to myself, I dial Sam's number. She answers on the third ring.

"Hey, you!" she practically sings.

Hearing her happiness over the line makes my heart thump hard, but that's something I'll never willingly admit to anyone, let alone her.

"Hi! How's my sexy girl doing today?" I aim for playful; she despises me when I'm sappy.

"Good, about to call it a day. Training's a bitch. How are you Jaxy-boy?"

"I'm good, starting phase two of rehab tomorrow. The docs think I can make a decent turn-around. I'm psyched. I miss being on the pow."

On the other end of the line, someone–a dude–says, *'Come on, babe'*. It makes me want to end the call and throw my phone against the bricks of the fireplace. I know the score when it comes to Samantha. I've always known there's no future there, but damn! Her carefree, no-strings attached mentality is something else. She's the only woman I've ever had feelings for, and while I've dabbled with others, no one comes close to making me feel the way she does.

"Jaxy-boy, I have to go. Talk to you soon?"

"Yep," I reply curtly, and hang up.

Resting my cell against my chin I wonder if this is the future I want. The more I think about it, the more I'm convinced I need to move on. I could have any girl I want, but right now the one girl I truly miss and want is the snow. Exhaling loudly, I press the play button, and wait patiently for the pizza to arrive. Half-way through the movie, the doorbell rings. I clap my hands in excitement, and walk towards the door.

I swing it open, and greet the delivery girl, who is wearing glasses and a baseball cap with the logo of the pizzeria. When she looks up her eyes meet mine and widen with recognition.

"Oh my goodness, Mr. Reese," she mutters. *Well I'll be damned.* It's the girl from the coffee shop. Ashley.

"Hi, Ashley. Stalking me much?" I quip, my arms crossed against my chest. Her cheeks turn bright red. Despite the dim lighting, I can tell she's embarrassed. *Geez. I was only joking.*

"I just... I have two jobs, Mr. Reese," she stammers. "This is my night job."

I'm trying to understand why someone so young would need to have two jobs. She looks well-put together... I'm not going to lie. I'm curious.

"Wow, two jobs. Are you sure you're not a spy, with the glasses and all?"

Maybe it's just me, but beyond the geeky facade there's likeability about her, and the more I look, the more I enjoy what I see. I grab the pie from her hands, and place it on the console near the door. Leaning against the doorjamb, I retrieve the cash from my pocket and give it to her. She starts counting the money and tries to hand me back the tip.

"I can't accept this, Mr. Reese."

"Sure you can, and you will. Are you going to tell me about the glasses?" I encourage, winking.

Ashley crosses her arms against her chest as if cold, appearing uncomfortable. I raise my hands in defeat and walk inside. As I'm about to close the door, she speaks.

"I popped a contact lens at work today, and don't have a replacement, which sucks when you have astigmatism. I have two jobs because it's just me and my kid. She depends on me. Good evening, Mr. Reese," she replies, before jogging towards a questionably safe heap of metal shaped like a hatchback. I own snowmobiles that look safer than her car.

I touch my jaw to make sure it's still there. Of all the possible answers she could've given me, that was the furthest from my mind. To say I'm shocked is a goddamn understatement.

"Stop with the 'Mr. Reese' crap. Just call me Jax," I call, jogging towards her. As I stand before her, I notice her lower lip is trembling, and through the brim of her ball cap and glasses I see her watery eyes. I can't help what I do next. My large hands dwarf her dainty face as they hold her jaw and tilt it upwards so I look into her eyes. "I'm sorry for being a prick. I didn't mean to pry."

She looks at me, no doubt panicked at my blatant disregard for her personal space. She'll probably call the cops and sue my balls for sexual harassment, but I don't care. I'm not one to look the other way when someone is down or sad, and right now she looks both. One of my thumbs brushes against her cheek, and it's the softest skin I've ever touched. I remove one hand from her jaw, and take off her black-rimmed glasses. I want to look directly into her eyes with no obstacles. I honestly don't fucking understand why, but I do.

"It's okay, Mr. Reese," she breathes, her blue eyes searching mine.

"Jackson, or Jax. You remind me of Cat..." I chuckle to myself.

"Your pretty girlfriend? The one with you at the coffeehouse?" she asks uncomfortably, with her eyes looking over my shoulder.

"She's my best friend, but not my girlfriend, Ashley," I clarify, emphasizing the last four words. "How old are you? And what happened to your kid's dad?"

"I'm twenty four. Kyle left when he found out I was pregnant. That was five years ago," she replies quietly, and swallows hard.

"What a fucking douche bag," I grit, feeling incredibly pissed off at that low-life motherfucker. "If you work two jobs... who watches your kid?"

"My Mom and brother help out whenever they can. I'm saving so I can move far away from this place," she answers firmly, her sudden strength a shock. Ashley reaches for my hand, and puts some distance between us. "I see that look in your eyes, Jackson, and recognize it for what it is... pity. I know that look all too well because that's how everyone looks at me in this godforsaken town."

Her honesty and bluntness is a huge breath of fresh air. I return her glasses, and step back to give her the space she obviously needs. I want to correct her poor assumption of me, because if anyone knows what that's like it's fucking me. I could be mad at her for being overly judgmental, but I pick my battles. Shoving my hands into my pockets, I walk away.

"Goodnight, Ashley."

"Enjoy your dinner, Jackson."

I stop in my tracks unable to bite my tongue. "I will, Ashley, but this isn't goodbye. Consider it a see you soon."

I wave goodbye, and then close the door. I rest my forehead against the door for a minute, then pick up the pie and walk past the staircase.

"Cat!" I call, and jump when I hear her voice nearby.

"I'm here. Who was that?" she asks.

I turn around and smile. "That was Ashley."

"The barista? Why was she here?" she asks with a raised eyebrow.

"She has a part-time job delivering pizzas. She's a single mom of a five year old. She works two jobs to make ends meet," I reply nonchalantly.

"You got all that 411 from her with just a pizza. Damn, Jackson. You're smooth," she mocks, but I see the amusement in her eyes.

"Yep," I answer, and open the pizza box. Grabbing a slice, I put it in my mouth and chomp on it before Catalina has the chance to say anything further. With the pizza box in hand, I walk in the den with her trailing behind. As we sit on the leather recliners in front of the big screen TV, I consider opening up to her about my feelings for Sam, and this growing curiosity for Caffeine Queen by day and Pizza Geek by night.

"Do you want to talk about it, Reese? I can hear the rusty gears turning in your head all the way over here," Catalina mumbles in between bites. Have I mentioned how irritatingly right she can be at times? Yeah. Nothing flies over her head. I guess that's why she's a journalist. She's got that asking-truth-seeking-questions thing down to a science.

Grabbing another slice, I consider her words for a moment. Maybe I should tell her and stop acting like a pussy. Guys like me don't often talk about our feelings, though I make an exception with Jupiter because he's like a brother to me. And I've trusted Catalina with my struggles with the freaking bottle... *Oh, fuck it.*

"Sam..." I mumble uncomfortably, not sure how to go about this conversation.

"Do you love her?" Catalina asks point-blank.

"Jeez, Cat, can you ease into the topic before you start asking me stuff like that?"

Catalina puts the pizza back in the box. With pursed lips she says, "Why beat around the bush?"

When I don't respond she sits up straight in the reclining chair, and looks at me with a raised eyebrow. *Damn.* Her seriousness cracks me up, and the louder my belly-laughs grow, the more she looks at me like I'm an idiot. When my laughter gets under control, I grab a napkin to wipe the tears from my eyes.

"You said 'beat around the bush' so I had this mental image of-" I pause and notice she isn't amused. "Never mind. Okay. I adore Sam, but I also know it's a fool's mentality to think after so many years she'll change her mind out of the blue. I think it's time for me to take a hike, you know? I'm not saying I won't love her anymore, but it's clear to me how I fit into her equation. I'm just a side piece, and that's all I'll ever be to her," I exhale loudly, leaning back on the headrest.

Catalina looks at me with understanding eyes, and I'm relieved she doesn't question my decision further. I think, if anything, she's stunned I'm turning the page so decisively. I need to get my life in order, starting from the inside, and all the way out to my recovering body. I stand, and walk to one of the picture windows facing the mountains. The powdery peaks at dusk look so serene and peaceful. Resting both palms against the cold glass, I bow my head in respect. My throat constricts as I think about Chris and Rem. I look at the ceiling and say a quick prayer for my dearly departed friends. Wherever they are, I hope they're happy. I vow to never forget them, or the memories we created on the slopes.

Looking at my reflection against the window I breathe, "Jackson Reese. I forgive you."

I feel Catalina's warmth beside me, and while I know she heard me, she says nothing. Putting my arm around her waist, I pull her in close and kiss her hair. "I'm glad you're here, Cat."

Catalina hugs me tight in silent agreement. I don't know how I'd have done it without her friendship for the past few months. She truly is the embodiment of what it is to be a friend. A true friend. A *real* friend.

CHAPTER TWELVE

Catalina

"Catalina."
"Catalina!"

I roll in bed and throw the pillow over my head trying to drown out Jackson's voice. All I want to do is sleep the day away between the comfy mattress and the Sherpa comforter. I haven't been sleeping well at night since Stryder left; I always find myself searching for his warmth in the middle of the night. Sometimes I have nightmares where he never comes back, and wake up in a pool of sweat. Let's just say, his absence is really weighing on me with each passing day.

"Catalina Pardo, get your ass out of bed. We're going to the doctor's and then to run errands. Don't tempt me to walk up there with a water jug, because I will!" Jackson threatens with a loud chuckle that bounces through the open space of the ranch.

I throw the pillow on the floor and sit up in bed. Ugh. No sleeping in, I guess. Grabbing the night robe, I slip it on and open the bedroom door, then lean over the staircase to see Jackson fully dressed and ready for the day.

"Well hello there, *Sunshine*." He grins.

I yawn loudly, and stretch my arms before I reply. "Morning, Jax. It's too early for this shit," I mumble, half-asleep.

Jackson chuckles and with a wiggle of his eyebrows he says, "You're saying that as if I give three shits... Come on, and get your ass in gear. I'm in the mood for white hot chocolate. We'll stop at the coffee shop on the way to the medical center. I promise I'll buy you coffee."

"All right, let me get ready," I reply, walking into my room, and closing the door behind me.

I'm showered and dressed in fifteen minutes flat. As I jog down the steps, I hear Jackson's voice coming from the kitchen. I stop in my tracks to listen.

"Sorry, Sam. I just can't... I can't do this anymore... No, I'm not seeing anyone... Are you out of your fucking mind?! She's Jupiter's girl! ...We're not kids anymore... Yep... No... Okay... What'd you expect? I'd wait around forever? Oh, please... I heard him... Not jealous... We're not exclusive, Sam... You do you, and I'll do me... Don't pull that shit... I don't have time for this!

"Fuck!" Jackson yells, and I hear a crashing sound from the kitchen. I run in there and find Jackson leaning against the granite countertop with both of his hands clutching his hair. He hears me walk in and looks up with a weary look on his face. I don't know how to interpret his mood right now so I walk to the cupboard, and retrieve a glass. Opening the refrigerator I pour myself a glass of water and drink it in silence.

Through the glass, I see him watching me, and a smile appears on his lips. "Step one, complete."

I tilt my head to the side like a dog does when they hear a high-pitched sound. "Come again?" I sputter, and place the empty glass in the kitchen sink. When I look down, I see what used to be Jackson's phone strewn all over the floor. "If you wanted a new model we could've gone to the store and got you one."

"Nah, Cat. That's just a metaphor," he says with a wink. Okay, I don't know what Jackson is up to, but at least he's talking. "Come on, we have places to go today. Plus, I promised you a coffee."

"Are you sure you promised me a coffee, or is this some ploy to see Ms. Hot Java again?"

Jackson smiles widely, and rests his hands against his hips. "Maybe... Does that bother you?"

"Now why on Earth would that bother me? You are the owner of your life, and the decisions you make are yours to live by. I'm just here as a spectator, Jax," I reply with a genuine smile.

Returning my grin, Jackson claps his hands. "Then let's quit the dilly-dallying and get to it. Admit it, Pardo. You're curious about her too."

I consider his words for a moment, and nod. "When it comes down to your happiness, I'll back you up one hundred percent." Walking towards Jackson I take both of his large hands in my own, and squeeze them firmly. "I'm protective of you because I love you, and I don't want to see you get hurt. I've seen glimpses of Tropical Storm Sam, and the aftermath she leaves behind. I think you need to give Ashley some thought before you make a move, though. I'll be supportive, but you need to heal first both physically and mentally. Understood?"

Jackson nods, his eyes searching mine. I can see a flicker of irritation, but I also know it's not my place to tell him what to do. Like a child, he sometimes needs reminders about the little stuff, and I know he's always depended on Kaelan for advice. I know I'm not Kaelan, but I'm positive my words get through to him

"Yeah, I know, Cat. I just can't get this geeky girl out of my head. I'm not going to pursue her. I just want to know if what I felt last night was real. I know I have my dumb motherfucker moments, and I know the timing is off. I just want to make sure I wasn't seeing something that wasn't there, you know what I mean?"

"Yes, of course," I respond with a smile. "Let me tell you a thing or two about timing, Jax. Even control freaks like me can't control it. Things happen when they happen, and we can't force these things. They need to happen on their own, okay? Now let's go. I need my coffee."

Jackson smiles, and after putting our jackets on we're out the door. As I sit in the coffeehouse parking lot waiting for him to return with our drinks, my phone chirps with an incoming email from my editor at *Xsports Magazine*, Marcia Reed. I'm on mandatory vacation, so I find it odd that she's emailing me.

C-,

I hope you're enjoying your well-deserved vacation. I wanted to touch-base with you on the article coming out in a few weeks. I saw the final proof, and between the images of the tour and the compelling story in between the pages, I think this edition will be our highest selling to date. Subscriptions are up a whopping 47%, and after what happened to Reese in BC, everyone wants to know what happens next.

I wanted to give you a heads-up... Dominick and I will be in contact with Reese's team to see if they would be interested in a follow-up story post-avalanche. If negotiations go well, I want you to write the story. I don't know where you are, and I hate to interrupt your vacation again. Just let me know if this interests you. I also need the address of where you're staying so I can ship the proof.

Until then,

-m

I slump in my seat, and lean my head against the headrest. *Work*. That's something I haven't considered since Jackson's accident. A part of me is annoyed because the media has no respect for timing. They fail to understand that while it's our job to report facts, we forget our subjects are also human beings. Jackson needs to focus on his recovery, and while I understand the world is dying to know about him, he shouldn't be forced to appear in the public eye until he is one hundred percent ready. Having said that, I also understand where Marcia is coming from

As I'm about to put my phone in the cup holder, it rings, and my heart skips a beat because it's Stryder calling.

"Stud!"

His chuckles echo through the line, making me smile. "Hey, baby. How's my Raven Girl doing today?"

"I'm good. Missing you... What's new?!" I laugh. "How's The Sunburnt Country? Where are you today?"

"I'm on a white sand beach waiting for the first heat to start. I wish you were here," he breathes. "What are you up to?"

"I'm waiting for Jax. He's getting us coffee and then we're headed to the medical center for a physical therapy session."

"How is Jax coming along? Is he getting better?"

"Yeah, he's good. Listen... I think he cut Sam loose."

Stryder hums, and then says, more to himself than to me, "Hmmm. That's interesting."

"Why do you say that?"

"Well, he's been hung up on her for years. The optimistic side of me wants them to get together, but I know Sam is a free bird... Did he tell you why he cut her loose?"

"He says he knows where he stands, and she doesn't believe in exclusivity."

Stryder chuckles and says, rather than asks, "Did he meet someone new?"

I sigh, and look out the window to make sure Jackson hasn't left the coffee shop. "He did. She seems like a nice girl, but I don't know. It's too soon to say. Maybe the accident put things into perspective for him, you know? *Carpe Diem*?"

"Well I'll be damned. This is good news, Cat. Why do I get the impression you aren't thrilled?"

"No, no. It's not that," I huff over the line. "I just don't want him to rebound. It's not fair to the other person, if that makes sense. He needs to recover first."

"Here's the thing, Catalina. We guys aren't wired the same way women are. When we turn the page, that's it there's no turning back. He's a big boy and he knows what he's getting into. My advice is to stay out of it."

I huff in irritation. "Stryder, do not confuse my need to protect Jackson with narrow-mindedness. Hell, there's nothing I want more than for him to find love, happiness, and stability. Unlike you, Jackson is sensitive. I think there's more to him than you're aware," I mutter.

"Whoa, Cat! That's *not* what I meant. When I said stay out of it, I meant to let Jackson arrive at his own conclusions, not that you're narrow-minded or meddling in his business. Don't get upset, baby."

I tug at the long strand of my braid, feeling the knots. I don't know what to say.

"Babe, are you there?"

"Yeah, I'm here," I reply flatly.

"Jeez, you're mad at me. I'm sorry, Cat," he says awkwardly. In the background I hear a voice on a loudspeaker, followed by deafening cheers. "Babe, I have to go. The heat is starting now. I'll call you tonight," he yells over the phone.

"Bye, ba–" I try to say, but the line goes dead. Frustrated, I toss my phone into the cup holder, and rest my head against the steering wheel. As my hands wrap around my chest, the passenger door opens and Jackson hands over a tray with our drinks. I force a smile, but he isn't buying it.

"What's wrong, Pardo? What's with the sad puppy face?" he asks, frowning.

I shake my head. "It's work, but first... tell me. How'd it go with Ashley?"

Jackson beams, his crisp blue eyes glimmering. "Awesome actually... It was less awkward and *very* entertaining," he replies, wiggling his eyebrows. "Look," he says, pointing at my paper cup.

I lift it from the tray and inspect the "name" written in black marker in what I presume is Ashley's handwriting. *My name is Catalina Pardo, and I'm a Caffeine Addict.* Cute. Very cute. I smile and lean over to kiss his cheek. "What does yours say?" I ask, dying to know what's written on his. Jackson hands it over, and I laugh loudly.

Gimpy McGee.

"Did you ask her to write this, Jax?"

"No... She came up with that one all on her own," he replies with a giggle. "I asked her to write the first thing that came to mind. The little shit wrote that." *Oh, I like her tons already.*

"Not for nothing, but I think we need to visit this coffee shop every day, Jax," I say encouragingly. "If her marker talents make you happy then I'm all for it." I take a sip from my cup and smile. "Plus, she makes a mean cup of coffee."

I turn the ignition, and the engine roars to life. As I'm pulling away from the coffeehouse, Jackson looks out the window. He raises his hand and waves, and when I look at the rearview mirror I see Ashley leaning against the glass doors, waving goodbye. I smile to myself and stop at the stop sign longer than legally required to give them a moment.

I turn on the radio and The Stroke's "You Only Live Once" plays. Jackson straightens in his seat, and we drive away into the early morning sun, singing at the tops of our lungs. I guess I can't be all that irritated with Stryder. He's right. I need to let Jackson work at his own pace, not mine. When you love someone, the urge to protect them from harm can easily turn into smothering. I wouldn't say I'm smothering Jackson... Well, maybe a little, but it's because I adore him and want to see him happy.

We arrive at the medical center, and after Jackson is called to enter the therapy room, I step outside and head towards the large fountain in front of the building. I need to speak with Kaelan.

"Catalina! So nice to hear from you!" she answers the phone. "I presume by now you've heard..."

"Yes, though I was unsure you were in the know. What are your thoughts?"

"I think it's a great idea, Catalina. Why do I sense you don't approve of a follow-up story?"

I smile as I look at the fountain. Kaelan's shrewd intuition reminds me of my own. "Jackson needs to focus on healing at his own pace, not because the press demands to know whether or not he'll snowboard again. *Xsports* can down play this all they want, but I *know* it's a ploy to secure an exclusive. I feel I'm being used for my friendship with Jackson."

Kaelan laughs softly over the line. "That is true. However, you have to see this as an opportunity for Jackson to get off his ass and get back in the game. I agree with you on everything you're saying, but you and I both know he needs this. Everyone loves a great comeback story, and who better than you to write it? I saw an online proof of your article. Clever title by the way. I'll admit you captured Jackson better than anyone ever has. Hell, I think you see him better than he sees himself..."

"That's very kind of you, Kaelan. Thank you."

"Nonsense, Catalina, no need to thank me. Your work speaks for itself. While I haven't discussed it with Jackson, I'm moving ahead with your magazine's proposal, and like last time I am making it a condition that you, and only you, write the article. There is no one I trust more."

"Okay, I'm in. I'm with Jackson at the medical center... Would you like for me to tell him about the proposal, or do you prefer to tell him?"

Kaelan hums, and with a happy sigh, she says, "I think he'll be more receptive if the proposal comes from you. Tell him that you have my blessing, and this is something he must do, okay?"

I nod. "Indeed."

We chat for a bit, talking about my stay in Casper and Jackson's recovery, and then we end the call. Placing my cell in my pocket, I walk through the revolving door of the medical center, and wait for the elevator to arrive. When it chimes and the steel doors open, I'm greeted by a smiling Jackson. I look at my watch and realize an hour has zoomed by.

"Where'd you go?" he asks.

"I was on a call. I'm sorry. I lost track of time. How'd it go? What's the word?"

Jackson gives me an ear-splitting grin.

"Is everything okay?"

"Yep. I'm regaining mobility in my ankles and if I keep on track, I won't need surgery. I talked with the good doctor and asked him about dancing. He says it won't be a problem, though I'm not allowed to do lifts. I'm thrilled!"

I jump up and down, and clap my gloved hands excitedly. I wrap my arms around Jackson's neck, and kiss his cheek. He returns my hug, and just when he's about to lift me, I smack the back of his neck. We both laugh, and unlock from each other to walk towards the truck. As we drive away from the medical center, I ask Jackson where we're headed.

"Downtown... I'll show you the way, okay?"

We make the journey down the serene streets of downtown Casper. There is a vintage feel to this town, and unlike New York City you can pull up to any one of the many shops and find a place to park. Everyone knows each other, and outsiders are seen as curious yet welcome. I love the old-time charm of this place and while it isn't really home, I feel like it could be.

"Pull up here," Jackson says, pointing at a vacant spot in front of a shop.

Reese-Moore Dance Company.

Instinctively, I grip the steering wheel harder than usual tense at the possibility of facing Olivia without Stryder. It's not that I don't count on Jackson to keep her in line. It's just that she's not a nice person.

"It's not the Reese you're thinking of, Cat. This place belongs to my oldest sister, Kathryn, and her husband, Gregg Moore," Jackson chuckles. Stepping out of the truck he walks around to open my door. "This is going to be great!"

"Do they know we're coming? I don't think I'm dressed properly..."

"Girl, you're fine. Stop being a pussy, and come meet my sister. She's dying to meet you!" he exclaims, dragging me along the sidewalk and through the doors of the studio.

As soon as we walk in, I see a class in progress. Six adult couples are dancing to Lee Ann Womack's "I Hope You Dance." I watch in fascination as their bodies sway to the beat of the country song. There's a mystic feeling in the air as, couple by couple, they move across the amber-colored dance floor. I keep my eyes focused on the teacher and her partner, who dance perfectly in each other's arms.

Jackson leans closer, and pointing towards the couple I can't take my eyes off from, he whispers, "Kathryn." I nod and keep watching, fascinated by the effortless movement of their feet, and of Kathryn's lean body and long arms as she points her fingers in the air while her partner holds onto her body. When the song ends they bow to the other couples present, and I find myself clapping. All eyes turn to focus on me, and I'm positive my cheeks are red.

Kathryn's gaze meets Jackson's and she races towards him, her steps so graceful she looks like a wild gazelle. Her shoulder length sandy blonde hair bounces with each step. Jackson opens his arms and she crashes into them with a gleeful squeal. I've only heard of her before, and like her Dad, she often travels with her husband around the world for dance-related events. We aren't acquainted, but it's easy to see she is nothing like her younger sister. The only common trait they share is their stunning looks, and while Kathryn is shorter than Olivia, she has an incredible smile and crisp blue eyes like Jackson.

"Jaxy!" she cries amid tears, and they hug like they haven't seen each other in years. When they finally let go, Jackson drapes his arm over my shoulder and makes introductions.

"Kathryn, this is Jupiter's better half, Catalina Pardo. Cat, meet my wiser and awesome big sister, Kathryn Moore," he says with a smile.

I extend my hand, and shake hers. "Pleased to meet you, Mrs. Moore,"

"The pleasure is mine, Catalina. Please, don't call me Mrs. Moore. It will only make my husband's, erm, ego grow. Kathryn, just call me Kathryn." She giggles, letting go of my hand and wrapping me in a tight hug. "Thank you for saving my baby brother's life. Now, tell me, Catalina... what's it like to tame a wild bull like Jupiter?"

I'm at a loss for words, so I simply laugh. "Well–well... it's nice, or so I'm told."

Kathryn and Jackson laugh loudly, and another song starts playing. "All right, ladies and gents, let's show our guests how a Rumba is danced, okay?" Kathryn calls to the people in the room. Redirecting her attention to me, she speaks. "Jaxy told me you want to learn how to dance. With those beautiful hips of yours it shouldn't be a problem," she says appraisingly.

"Oh, no... You don't understand. These hips are for show. My feet are the problem..." I explain seriously, but again Jackson and Kathryn break into laughter.

"Come on, Cat. *Anyone* can dance. Our parents have ingrained that belief in us, and I have yet to see someone prove them wrong. Have some faith and confidence in yourself, will you?" Jackson encourages, and Kathryn agrees with a nod.

"You see that handsome grump over there?" Kathryn says, pointing at the man standing in front of the mirrors. "That's Gregg, my husband. He had two left feet, and now we co-teach. We'll whip you into shape in no time. Trust me."

I nod, but I'm still skeptical. Kathryn goes on. "I'm not sure if you're aware, but Jupiter is the best dancer of all of us right behind our parents. The man is fierce on the dance floor."

Jackson looks at me and gives me an I-told-you-so look. "That's why I want to learn. I don't want him to be embarrassed with my dance-on-one-tile routine," I mumble, blushing.

"Then you're in the right place, Catalina," she says. "Jackson told me we have several weeks before Jupiter returns. By then we'll have the basics covered, and you'll blow his socks off the next time you go out. Sounds like a plan?"

"Yes," I exclaim, thrilled and terrified at the same time.

"Wonderful! I'll pair you up with Gregg, and you can work on basics as soon as the class is over."

"No, Kathryn," Jackson says. "I'll be her partner."

"But your ankles, Jaxy, not to mention you haven't danced for a while. I figured Gregg might be a better fit for her," Kathryn says, resting her hands on her hips.

Jackson cups his sister's face and kisses her forehead. "I'm okay to dance. The doctor has given me the go-ahead, plus you and I both know dancing is the best medicine.

Kathryn nods. "Okay, brother, but no lifts and I'd hold off on the jive too. Got it?"

Jackson nods and hugs Kathryn again. "I'm happy to do this with you, sis. I'm going to take Cat back there and find her some shoes. Send me the bill, okay?"

"Oh shut up, Jax. Just get her the damn shoes. New clay to mold, Gregg! I'm excited!"

There I stand, feeling a mixture of self-doubt and exhilaration, just like when I went snowboarding for the first time. Ever since Stryder Martynus and Jackson Reese walked into my life, I've experimented with new things... things I would never have done on my own.

Jackson takes hold of my hand and leads me to a backroom filled with dancewear and equipment; from ankle bands to footwear. He picks up a pair of heeled shoes... and suddenly, I'm no longer feeling so confident. I don't mind wearing stilettos to go out, but dancing in them is a whole different thing. I pick up a cream-colored pair and sigh.

CHAPTER THIRTEEN

Catalina

"It's going to hurt, Cat. Not going to lie. You will have blisters, and you'll learn to love and hate the very shoes you're holding. What's your size?" he asks, smiling.

I lift one shoe and look inside the heel. It's a size nine. "I think these will do."

Jackson takes them from me, and shakes his head. "Nope. You'll need a half-size larger. Reason being, you don't want the back to rub against your heel. Not to mention, you want to have enough leeway for tape. Trust me on this." I smile, and giggle as he flips lids off shoeboxes looking for the perfect pair. As he goes deeper into the room, my phone chirps with an incoming text message.

<SM: I miss you. I have a hellish sunburn.>

<CP: Oh, no! Get some aloe cooling gel, put it in the fridge, and rub it where it hurts. I miss you, too.>

<SM: "Rub it where it hurts." Mmm. There are parts of me that hurt far more than sunburn. I'd like to rub THAT instead. *angel emoticon*>

I giggle and look around, making sure no one including Jackson notices our sexting.

<CP: Save it for later... Video chat. *wink emoticon*>

"Found them!" Jackson calls from the back of the room, and I jump.

"Okay," I call shakily, and then my phone chirps again. I'm eager to read Stryder's response, and when I do my cheeks grow warm.

<SM: I have half a mind to return just to feel your luscious lips hugging my dick. Video chat you say? I'm looking forward to it VERY MUCH.>

My hand rises to cover my mouth, and I close my eyes imagining just that. A small moan escapes my throat, and when I open my eyes Jackson is standing in front of me with a shoebox in his hands and a knowing smile on his lips.

"Do you need me to call the Fire Department?" he asks with a click of his tongue. My eyes widen in horror; if a few moments ago my cheeks felt warm, now they are on fire. I'm mortified, and shove my phone into my pocketbook avoiding eye contact. "What? It's perfectly normal to *sext* with your boyfriend, Cat," he chuckles.

I look at him and laugh, bringing both of my hands to my hot cheeks. "Damn... Was it that obvious?"

"Yeah, a bit." He nods. "Come on, you dirty girl. Let's dance."

Jackson grabs my hand and leads me toward the office, where he opens a locker and shoves my purse inside. After placing the dance tape Jackson gave me over the tops of my toes and heels, I take a few steps, trying to get a feel for the shoes. These feel different from normal heels and with the tape in the mix, walking feels downright awkward. Jackson's laughter stops me dead in my tracks, and resting my hands on my hips, I scowl.

"What."

Jackson tries and fails to stifle his laughs. I give him the blankest of stares, and tap my fingers impatiently against my pelvis.

"Nothing... You're walking like a newborn horse, that's all," Jackson mumbles, then laughs harder, prompting tears to spill from his eyes. He's right. I *am* walking like a foal taking its first steps. This shit feels weird. Huffing loudly, I walk as best as I can towards the door. Jackson grabs my hand and leads me out with a whispered, "Come on, pony, attagirl," which earns him a nice smack on the ribs.

He's laughing now at my walking... wait till he sees me dancing. I'm preparing myself mentally for the mockery that will ensue when they realize I'm no good at it. My footsteps click loudly against the hardwood floor. The class that was in progress has ended, and the studio is vacant. Kathryn smiles when she sees me and, with a quizzical look on her face, she observes my walking. Unlike Jackson, she doesn't laugh, and when I stand in front of the mirrors and cross my arms against my chest, she walks toward me in strides.

Sweet Lord! Her grace is infallible, and nothing short of a model's runaway walk. Kathryn stops in front of me, and rests her hands on my shoulders.

"Listen closely to what I'm about to say, Catalina."

I nod.

"Anyone can dance. It's all in your head. Jackson told me you didn't know a lick of snowboarding and you got the hang of it pretty quick. This is no different, yeah?" Again I nod, but stay quiet because she's in her zone.

"Good. Dancing is meant to be fun, and it's an honest way to express oneself. Think of it as art; your body and feet are the paintbrush, the dance floor is your canvas, and on it we will make a masterpiece. I will push you, break you and put you back together again, but we will put all that we have on this floor. I will give you my very best and I expect the same in return. Half-assed dancing is unacceptable. Do I make myself clear?"

There's something extraordinary about Kathryn; her sharp yet fantastic approach has ingrained itself in my mind. I feel empowered, brave, and eager to show her I don't do half-assed. I look at her square in the eye, and reply, "Crystal."

She squeezes my shoulders and lets me go, and from the corner of my eye I notice Jackson watching our exchange. I redirect my attention to Kathryn as she walks around me like a shark swimming around prey.

"Your posture isn't bad, but it can be improved. Raise your hands as if you were dancing with Jupiter, please." I comply, and jump when I feel her palm pressing against my spine. "Good... now breathe through your diaphragm." I breathe in and out and my arms quickly grow tired. When they fall down, though, I quickly raise them and shuffle my feet to regain my balance. When I do this, Kathryn mumbles, "Very good."

"She's going to be great," Jackson shouts from across the room.

With measured steps, he approaches us and when he's standing before me, I admire our reflections in the mirrors. Despite his injuries, Jackson stands tall with a posture I've only seen once before on the day I agreed to go snowboarding for the first time. Smiling, Jackson extends his arms and takes my hand, directing my other hand on his shoulder. Once locked in each other's hold, he inches us closer to the mirror.

"Frame and posture, meet Catalina," Kathryn says. "Catalina, meet posture and frame." I giggle at her methodology. "Frame and posture is everything; it can make or break a dance. You will learn how to keep your frame and posture while in hold; whether it's a Viennese Waltz or an Argentine Tango. Believe it or not, this will be the hardest part of dancing. Your feet will follow along, Catalina," she says, as if reading my thoughts.

We stand in front of the mirror working on my frame, and every time my body slumps, Kathryn is quick to swat it back into position. Two hours later and completely drenched in sweat, Kathryn finally gives me a break to catch my breath. My toes and feet are killing me. Jackson hands me a bottle of water, and walks towards Kathryn with a smile.

"Be gentle, Kathryn," he says, as he opens his hold for her. Gregg presses a button on the sound system and Mazzy Star's "Fade Into You" starts to play. They dance a slow waltz, my jaw drops as I watch Jackson dance for the first time. His steps are slow and measured, and judging by his taut facial expressions, I can tell he is pushing past pain to get through the dance. It's so mesmerizing to watch them cover the expanse of the wooden dance floor, and more than once I find myself sighing. I've seen Stryder dance with Olivia, and Kathryn with Gregg, but there's something incredibly inspiring about watching Kathryn and Jackson dance, capturing the somberness of the song. It's as if I'm watching a story unfold before my eyes.

Gregg walks over and sits beside mine.

"It's something to behold, isn't it?" he asks with a smile, and I nod.

"Definitely... If I didn't know any better, I'd say he does this every day instead of snowboarding! When they told me they were dancers I had a good laugh, but having seen Stryder and now Jax I feel like an ass. These boys are really talented."

Gregg chuckles and replies smugly, "You'll be showing them up in no time. You have what it takes to be a great dancer, Catalina. My wife is right. It's all in your head. Believe in your capabilities." He shifts in his seat, and winks wickedly. "Dancing has other benefits too, and Jupiter is the best of the best, or so I've heard."

My face feels like it's on fire. "Indeed," I mumble, my finger suddenly interested in rearranging my bangs. "I just want him to be able to do what he loves with me. For too long I've sat down to watch others dance. It's time for me to start doing... I want to surprise him when he gets back."

"And you will, Catalina. I can't wait to see the look on his face when you do."

As the Reese siblings dance, we sit in silence, my eyes following their footsteps and trying to memorize their placement. When the song ends, I give them a standing ovation. They take a graceful bow, and then I race towards Jackson with my arms open wide.

Engulfing him in a tight hug, I cry, "Oh my goodness, Jax. That was stunning!"

Jackson wipes his sweaty brow with a hand towel and mutters under his breath, "Glad you thought so. Dad would lose his shit if he saw how crappy that truly was. I need to sit down... everything hurts." I pout, but follow him towards the chairs and sit beside him.

"Are you blind, Jackson? I know nothing of dancing, but I know what I saw and you were wonderful. You should be proud of yourself!"

Kathryn kneels in front of him resting both of her palms against his knees. "Catalina is right, Jaxy. I know what you're saying about form and execution, but you're not back one hundred percent. Not to mention you haven't danced properly in a long time. With practice and rest, you'll be back in shape in no time."

"I know, I know. I just feel like an old man," Jackson mutters.

"Just pace yourself. You still have the goods," Kathryn asserts, and then rises to hug her brother fiercely. "I'm so proud of you. I love you."

I clench my hand into a fist and rub it against my chest, moved by this affectionate exchange between them. I don't know what it's like to have a sibling. The closest to that is my friendship with Faith and Jackson.

If I ever have kids, I'll make sure to have more than one so they don't miss out on the experience. Wait. What? I feel a light fluttering in my stomach, and in my head I hear my voice repeating my thoughts. Kids... I quickly revisit the conversation I had with Stryder several weeks ago, and how shocked he was when I told him getting pregnant again would be near to impossible. And now I find myself considering it. Another voice plays inside my head. *Don't be afraid*. My whole body shudders as I recognize the voice.

"Are you okay?" Jackson asks.

I turn in my seat to face him. "Yeah... Why do you ask?"

"Nothing, you just shuddered and sighed really loud." Jackson points at my arms, "Look, you have goose bumps."

I look at them and cover myself instinctively, closing my eyes with a sigh. "Just a cold chill, that's all." I rise to face Kathryn. "When will we dance again?"

Kathryn giggles and wraps her arm around my shoulder guiding me towards her office. I'm not going to lie. It feels awkward that someone I just met is being so affectionate, and more than once I have to remind myself this is Jackson's sister we're talking about. They are like two drops of water, both physically and emotionally.

"What are you thinking about? Am I coming onto you too fast?" Kathryn says coquettishly.

"Um, no," I laugh. "I was thinking how identical you and Jackson are."

Kathryn giggles, and I join along. "Yep, and he calls you family, so I guess that makes you my family too, huh? Speaking of sisters, I know my sister hasn't been nice to you. I'm sorry about that." I nod. "It's okay, Catalina. We love her, but we also know she's a see you next Tuesday."

I laugh. "Oh my God. You went there!"

Tightening her grip on my shoulder, she grins. "I sure as hell did."

With a practice schedule in hand Jackson and I say goodbye to Gregg and Kathryn and head back home. We're exhausted, and as soon as I walk through the front door, I march my weary ass up the steps to my room for a well-earned bubble bath. Freshly bathed and completely exhausted, I fall asleep as soon as my head hits the pillow.

My phone rings loudly. Mumbling my disapproval, I answer. "Faith?"

"Goodness gracious, Cat. You answered!" her high-pitched squeal rings over the line. I adjust the pillows against the headboard and sit up.

"Yeah, why wouldn't I, Faith? How are you?" I reply between yawns.

"I'm great. I haven't heard from you in weeks! I miss my best friend like a plant needs water... How's your vacation? Are things still hot and heavy with your scrumptious cannoli? I bet the filling is quite delicious..."

I snort at her description of Stryder and laugh. "Things are well. He's overseas right now on assignment."

"What? Why?" she asks, her voice laced with confusion. "Where are you?"

"I'm in Casper with Jackson."

"Wyoming? What the—why are you there?"

"I'm helping with Jackson's recovery, plus I love it here. It's nice to be away from the hustle and bustle of the city."

"Are you two...?"

"No, Faith! No. I love him like a brother. I'm just taking time out here to rest, and figure out what I want to do with my life."

"You're considering moving away? You haven't been home for months, and I miss you..." Faith says rather sadly.

"I'm on vacation, silly. No need to be sad or worried, lady. You can't get rid of me so easily."

Faith laughs, and says, "Good, because I sort of need you around for the wedding and all. I've been meaning to ask, shall I make your invitation a plus one? Now that you have a sexy man in your life, surely you'll want him to come along. Mom and Dad will be thrilled." I cross my ankles in bed and play with my hair. "You're family, Cat. Just because you met someone new doesn't change the fact that you are part of the Mackenzie Clan."

"I know, but I think it would be disrespectful to Blake's memory, you know?"

"No, it isn't. Plus one it is. Listen, if you don't make time to come back soon, I'll fly my merry ass out there to visit." I hear the sounds of a PA system in the background. "Listen, I'm due for surgery in ten minutes. I have this hot patient that requires open-heart surgery. Talk to you soon?"

I giggle at her inappropriate remark. "Yeah... sure thing, and stop checking out your patients, you pervert." Faith laughs and hangs up.

I look at the alarm clock; it's close to dinnertime. Tip-toeing down the stairs I approach Jackson's room- his door is wide open and the lights are off. I wonder where he wandered off to. In the kitchen, I busy myself making dinner and half an hour later, I'm sitting on one of the barstools eating.

With each bite I feel exactly like Jackson's house- large, cold, and empty. The more I think about my loneliness, the more I lose my appetite. I push the plate away. My phone on the counter is silent. It hasn't been too hard to get by because Jackson and I are always up to something, but now as I sit here in the quiet I hear the clicking of the wall clock and each second passes agonizingly slow. I call Stryder and my heart races with each ring. Sadly, I get his voicemail.

"Stryder Martynus, here. At the beep, leave a message. Thanks."

"It's me. I just wanted to say I miss your voice. I hope everything is well. I love you," I breathe into the line. I'm not in the mood for dinner anymore, so I busy myself by clearing the kitchen counter, putting the food away, and washing the dishes. By the time I make it back to my room, it's close to nine o'clock and Jackson still isn't home. I crawl into bed and opt to watch a movie, but my eyelids feel heavy, and before I know it I'm fast asleep.

As dawn breaks through the soft curtains, I open my eyes and search for my cell phone. There's a missed call and voicemail from Stryder. I press the button and with my heart beating like a drum I wait for the message to play.

"Hey, baby. Sorry I missed your call. I was grabbing lunch when you called, and didn't hear my phone ring. I'm so sorry. Is everything okay? You sounded sad. God, I miss you so much, and I hope Jackson is behaving. We'll video chat tonight. Love you, and I can't wait to come home."

I sigh and rest the phone against my chest. The days go by slower the more I think about the oceans dividing us, but my heart skips a beat when I consider our upcoming getaway. The two of us alone where no one knows us, far away from the distractions of the world, and building our love on the fragments of our pasts.

I have lessons with Kathryn today, and despite the ache in my body and feet from yesterday's impromptu lesson I'm eager and motivated to learn more. Jackson's sitting in the kitchen when I walk in, reading something on his tablet. When he hears me, he sits up straight and smiles.

"Good morning, Sunshine! How's the newborn horse? Ready to start galloping?" he asks, and when I cast an evil glare in his direction, he laughs.

"Good morning to you, Jackson."What I really want to ask is where he was last night, but it's not any of my business. "What are you reading?" I ask.

With a sincere smile he replies, "Just looking over a proposal your bosses at *Xsports* just sent. They want a follow-up story, and they said you'd write it." He rests his tablet against the table and stands. "Did you know about any of this?"

"I did. I didn't say anything because I wanted it to come from your camp first, even though Kaelan asked me to tell you. The truth is I totally forgot about it. I'm onboard as long as you are."

"It's fine by me. I guess the pressure is on to get back on the board."

I throw my duffle on the counter and rest my hand on his shoulder. "There is no pressure or timeline to get better. You come first, Jackson. *Xsports* and the rest of the world can wait. What is important is for you to recover on your terms, not anybody else's. We dance to the beat of your drum, not the other way around, got it?"

Jackson nods and from his lips an amazing smile emerges.

"A million stories could be written about me, and at the end of the day no one will see me like I see myself. I'm just an athlete, Catalina. I don't have to prove anything to anyone. I've lost two of my best friends, and a part of my soul along the way. People mistake my failures as a sign of weakness, or take it as me giving up. Nah, Catalina, there's only one person I'm up against, and that's *me*, and regardless of what's happened, in my eyes I'm still an Olympic and world snowboarder."

Looking into his eyes, I say, "I'm so fucking proud of you, Jackson. You're starting to realize that your ironclad determination is what will get you back into the sport. I can see the fire in your eyes. There is hunger, and I know you'll rise on top again. Just be the best you can be."

"Sometimes I just need a little convincing, that's all. I work well under pressure. You of all people should know that, Catalina." Jackson pulls me closer to his chest and gives me a fierce hug, and I sag in relief. "Hmm. Looks like you needed that hug more than I did. Come on, toots. I'm eager to see my sister whip our sad little asses back into shape."

We leave Jackson's home with determined steps. His walking has dramatically improved and the cockiness I adore is not so far behind. I'm taking my cues from him on the dance floor. *It's all about having self-confidence* I repeat to myself like a broken record, remembering Kathryn and Gregg's words to me yesterday. My heart races as a wave of determination hits me in the best of ways. It blows my mind when I consider how much my life has changed. A year ago I was stuck in a crippling depression, yet now I'm eager and willing to try new things. My smiles are no longer forced, and I don't feel the need to hide my feelings under a mask of make-up and clothes.

I wasn't living my life back then. I was only going through the motions of living and breathing. The truth is I was nothing short of a zombie, alive yet dead, but not anymore. I thank my lucky stars and God for bringing a new breath of fresh air into my life in the loving arms of Stryder and the gift of Jackson's friendship. I'm confident there is no luckier girl out there.

We arrive at the studio, and I make a beeline for the lockers. My body is buzzing with excitement, and I'm not letting my lack of self-confidence take away from this joy I feel inside my chest.

As I'm about to step into my dance heels, Kathryn walks in.

"No heels today, Catalina. We're going to work on basic choreography and see how quickly you learn. It's all about footwork and lines. Your upper body is graceful, but at the end of the day footwork is just as important."

I smile at her words and counter-challenge, "You think I'm graceful? That's crazy. You must be blind."

Kathryn shushes me. "Cut the shit, Catalina. Are you the instructor? *No.* I've been doing this long enough to recognize talent where there is any. If you want this experience to work then I suggest you come to terms with the fact I know what the hell I'm doing."

CHAPTER FOURTEEN

Catalina

I feel taken aback by the stern tone behind Kathryn's words. All of a sudden I feel like a child who's been scolded. My arms fall limply to my sides, and for being such a loud mouth I find myself at a loss for words. I guess I must've made a face because Kathryn bites her upper lip, and I see a smile creeping from her mouth.

"Oh my goodness, that was mean! Jackson told me you need metaphorical slaps every now and then, but damn that was harsh!" She laughs at herself, and I follow.

I grin and breathe. "Metaphorical slaps? That was like you punched me square in the tits, Kathryn." We both laugh, and in true Reese fashion Kathryn hugs me.

"I'm so happy I get to groom you for Jupiter even though he's such a broody son of a bitch sometimes. I'm dying to see you blow him away with your hips, which certainly *do not* lie."

We emerge from the locker room laughing, and I stop in my tracks when I see Jackson doing what I can only describe as kicks and flicks in front of the mirror to Eddie Cochran's "C'mon Everybody". His brow is furrowed in concentration as he focuses on his footwork in the mirror. He's definitely dancing through his pain with every jump and shimmy.

Turning to Kathryn, I whisper, "Should he be doing something as physical as that?"

Kathryn shakes her head. "No, I specifically told him not to do a jive. But, this is Jaxy's favorite dance ever since he was a kid. Jupiter is the best dancer all-around, but when it comes to the jive no one comes close to Jax. He'll know when to stop. I hope!"

We redirect our attention to Jackson, watching the fun, fast jive in amazement. It's a physically exhausting dance which has me breathless at the mere sight of it. Kathryn starts chanting steps under her breath and hands me her bottle of water before walking onto the dance floor. She circles Jackson, as if memorizing his routine, and they begin to dance side by side, their footwork in perfect sync.

I start to clap and jump in place as they dance. Jackson looks at me, his cheeks flushed with the physicality of the dance, and winks. I grin. As the song progresses, Jackson takes hold of Kathryn in a proper hold, and as they dance I find my left foot tapping to the beat of the music. The next thing I know, Gregg is coaxing me onto the floor.

Laughing hysterically, I attempt to mimic the kicks and flicks I saw them doing earlier, with Gregg coaching me on. I'm not going to lie. It's only been seconds and I'm sweating profusely, and find myself nauseated and completely out of breath. The realization that dancing is as physically grueling as snowboarding helps me understand exactly why Stryder and Jackson are in top shape.

When the song ends, I clap twice before bending over, my hot breath warming my leggings. Jax walks over and lays his back against the maple floor, his eyes finding mine. With a satisfied smile, his breaths long and hard, he says, "Fuck, that was fun."

I try to laugh but I don't have the energy. I fall to my knees and then lie on my back, mimicking the pose of a dead body at a crime scene. Kathryn and Gregg watch us sprawl on the dance floor, and their belly laughs echo in the open space.

"Pussies," Kathryn declares. She crouches beside us and says, "Again."

I wonder if she's gone blind, given how out of breath I am, but the glint in her eye is unmistakable. I rise, and help Jackson up. And then, true to her word, Kathryn beats us to a dancing pulp for a good three hours before Jackson can't take it anymore.

As I'm getting my purse from the locker room, I see a couple of text messages from Stryder. With all the excitement of learning how to dance, time has flown by. I feel guilty for not checking my phone sooner; the last thing I want Stryder thinking is that I'm purposely ignoring his messages.

> <SM: Hey! I was on the beach today and saw a couple learning how to surf. I'm thinking for our vacation, I'd like us to try that. What do you think? Love you.>
>
> <SM: I'm growing roots here waiting for a response, baby.>
>
> <SM: *sad face emoticon* You must be busy...>
>
> <SM: There's this gorgeous girl I like but she's ignoring me...>
>
> <SM: I miss you?>

I smile at his last message and quickly reply.

> <CP: Baby, I'm so sorry. I was with Jackson visiting Kathryn's dance studio. The music was loud. I'm here now.>

My phone chimes.

> <SM: You met Kathryn? That's awesome. She's like Jackson 2.0>

I nod and smile as I type.

> <CP: OMG! You don't say! I love her already.>
>
> <SM: Why was Jax visiting?>

I grimace at his question because as much as I don't like keeping secrets from Stryder, I want to surprise him when he gets back. If I tell him what I'm up to, then I'll certainly ruin that plan.

> <CP: Yeah! Jackson wanted to visit Kathryn and Gregg, which by the way, they are awesome! I saw them dance and was drooling. Damn. I'm seriously missing out on the twinkle-toe genetics here.>

<SM: Hahaha. I can teach you. All you need to do is ask. You have what it takes, and dancing is not so different from having sex... I have an ache for you. God, I miss you.>

<CP: I miss you too. Let's video chat when it's your morning. *angel emoticon*>

<SM: You don't have to tell me twice. I REALLY miss you. Love you!>

<CP: I love you too. xo>

I put the phone in my purse with a sigh, and lean against the wall, facing the large picture window. The reminder that someone out there across the ocean is missing and loving me fills my heart with joy. There's only a few more weeks until Stryder returns, and then we're off somewhere for our first vacation as a couple. I tuck a lock of hair behind my ear, and walk towards Jackson, Kathryn, and Gregg.

"You ready?" I ask Jackson, dying to grab something to eat, and to shower. After today's exertions, I'm feeling less than fresh.

"Yeah," he smiles, and wraps his arm around my shoulder as we leave the studio. "You okay there, Cat? You look off..."

I shake my head and return his smile. "Yeah, I'm just tired. I'm worried about walking tomorrow. Going up and down the stairs? I'm shuddering at the thought."

"Yeah, you'll be hurting like a bitch tomorrow. Kathryn knows how to manage these things, though, so tomorrow it will be lines, making sure your arm and hand placements are fluid and stuff. You looked great today, Cat. Jupiter's jaw will fall to the fucking floor when he sees you. The jive is ballsy, toots. I'm proud."

"Thank you, Jax. It's a lot of fun, but holy shit! What a workout. Come on, let's get takeout. I need to eat, shower, and get in bed."

Jackson smiles and then nods. "Agreed!"

After grabbing food from a local joint and enjoying dinner in front of the TV, I excuse myself for the evening. After a long hot shower I dress in my favorite t-shirt and panties, and crawl into bed. I don't even bother to turn on the television. As my eyelids grow heavy, my phone begins ringing to the sound of Amos Lee's "Violin." I sit up in bed, and in a groggy voice I answer. "Hello?"

The rich timbre of Stryder's voice floods the line, making my insides heat with a yearning I never thought possible. "Hi, baby."

A few yawns escape my mouth. "It's so nice to hear your voice, Stud."

"You sound demolished. I'll let you go, baby. You need your rest."

"NO!" I half-whine, half-yell. He laughs, and I try to compose myself. There's a lulling ache in my insides that is getting deliciously worse with each passing second. I swear, even the sound of his breathing is enough to make me want to climb into the phone and kiss the hell out of him. "Don't hang up. I want to hear your voice..."

"Catalina, are you hot and bothered right now?" Stryder asks wickedly, and my nipples harden at the bluntness of his words.

"Yes," I breathe, and run my fingers through my hair.

"I want to kiss every square inch of your body... starting from your forehead, all the way down to the tips of your toes." His words make me melt against the blankets.

I exhale loudly, "Oh, God."

"After I'm done kissing your body, I'll let my fingers explore the softness of your skin; grabbing here, scratching there... marking you with my need."

"What else...?" I challenge, my fingers stroking the length of my neck.

"After I'm done tasting your amazing mouth, I'll kiss your incredible breasts, nipping and teasing your nipples with my tongue, and when I'm done I'll squeeze them softly because I know you like when I do that."

With my right index finger, I trace circles around the hardened nipple poking through my t-shirt. My body shudders in response, and a satisfied sigh escapes my lips. Through the phone I hear a rustling sound followed by a sensual groan.

"Are you touching yourself, Catalina?" Stryder purrs. My legs involuntarily buckle against the bed, and I tuck my fingers underneath the hem of my shirt. As soon as they make contact with the sweltering skin of my abdomen, I moan.

"Yes," I whisper, both mortified and excited.

"Good, baby. By now your pussy is aching for some attention, am I right?"

"Mmm-hmm."

"I'm kissing and licking your hipbone. Your skin is so soft to the touch, Cat," Stryder mumbles, and I close my eyes imagining my hands tangled in his obsidian hair, and his hazel eyes occasionally rising to meet my own lust-filled ones. "Take your panties off," he commands, and the pang of my need for him makes me comply in double-time. "As soon as I hang up, get off the bed, and wait for my call in the bathroom," he commands gruffly.

And just like that, the line goes dead. Feeling adventurous, I do exactly as I'm asked. As I walk into the bathroom, I feel a breeze tickling my bare bottom. Stryder only asked me to take off my panties, and while pacing on the bamboo flooring of the en-suite bathroom, I debate whether or not to take off my black t-shirt as well. My cell rings, and I gasp at the request blinking on the screen.

Stryder Martynus would like to Video Chat. Swipe to answer.

With trembling fingers, I accept, and Stryder's gorgeous face appears on the screen.

His skin is more tan than I have ever seen it, and it suits him incredibly well. His eyes twinkle and when I look closely, they are full of heat and mischief.

"Hi!" I squeak.

"Hey, you," Stryder greets me, his voice deep and seductive. "Now, where were we?"

I swallow hard, confident my cheeks are the color of my favorite lipstick: fire engine red. "Panties off," I reply quickly, and cover my face with my free hand.

His chuckles are music to my ears; I uncover my face but keep my eyes closed.

"Open your eyes, Catalina." When I do, I see his panty-combusting smile filling the screen. "Let's save the pleasantries for later. Climb into the bathtub." With a furrowed brow and an embarrassed smile, I do as I'm told. Once settled in the bathtub, I grab a fluffy towel to use as a headrest.

"Put your phone near the faucet to where I can see all of you laying down in the bathtub." I reach forward and position my phone at the perfect angle. "Now stand up and take your t-shirt off."

My body is humming with anticipation. I rest my phone on the ledge of the waterworks station, and when I have it where I want it, I stand. As I'm taking off my t-shirt, Stryder groans loudly. Throwing my shirt on the floor, I sit down in the bathtub and frown at the screen. "What's wrong?"

Stryder smiles. His eyes are small, his upper teeth continuously grazing his bottom lip. "You stood up and your amazing pussy was smack-dab in front of the camera. If I was there right now, I'd lick you without restraint or care. I want to taste your wetness, have it dribble down my chin, and feel your-not-so-delicate clenches as you come in my mouth."

I inhale sharply, and close my eyes at his words. My core tightens, and my legs involuntarily sag with each consonant and vowel dripping from his naughty mouth. I reopen my eyes, and they widen when I see him laying on his back on what I presume is a couch. One of his hands is wrapped around his hard cock, stroking it gently, and the other is cupping his teardrop shaped balls. It's the sexiest thing I've seen in weeks. My body aches with his absence; this is the most I've missed him since he went away.

"What are you thinking about, Catalina. You're awfully quiet."

"I miss you now more than ever, Stryder. I want you here doing all those things you say you want to do, and there's nothing I'd like more than to reciprocate," I half-moan, half-whisper.

"If I was there, what would you do to me?"

A part of me feels shy to say this, but fuck it.

"I want to wrap my lips around your cock and suck on it hard. I want to feel your twitches against my tongue, and swallow your taste when you come. I know that won't be enough for us, so I'll plant my pussy over your mouth and have you suck my clit until I can't stand it anymore. And when you're ready, I want you to sink inside me in one hard, sharp thrust."

"Fuck..." he hisses, his hand stroking his cock faster. "What else, Catalina?"

I let my fingers roam towards my aching, swollen breasts, my fingertips tugging and squeezing my hardened nipples. "I'd ask you to pump into me hard, like my pussy is the last one in the world, and just when you're about to come I'd like you to pull out. I'll wrap my tits around your cock and have you come on my chin."

Stryder stops stroking and sits up on the sofa. Resting both arms on the back of his head, he speaks. "Fuck, Catalina. Of all the things I thought you'd say, that was not what I had in mind." I sit up in the bathtub and worry my lip. I may have crossed the line. My hands fall to my sides, and the urge to cover myself is overwhelming.

Stryder continues. "I know I love you, Catalina, but now I love you even more. You're my perfect match. Don't shy away from me, baby, and stop thinking too much. I wish I was there to fulfill your desires and make them my own."

My eyes glisten, and I close them because I'm certainly feeling his absence. There's nothing I'd like more than to have him hold me right now. Sure, the sexy stuff is nice, but the fulfilling warmth of his loving embrace exceeds sexual urges any day of the week.

"Me too," I whisper as I open my eyes.

"Don't get sad on me, Cat. Put your hands back on those round breasts and pretend your hands are mine."

I quickly comply and touch myself. Feeling an ounce of bravery, I give some instructions of my own. "I want you to stroke that cock for me, Stryder... nice and steady."

He responds quickly, his effortless tugs clearly visible on the screen. The sound of his slapping skin heightens my senses; watching my guy pleasuring himself is one of the sexiest things I've ever seen. My fingers trail past my breasts, tenderly caressing the barely-there curls beneath my abdomen. I scrape the tender flesh with my fingernails and when my fingertips meet my clit, I can't help but rub it in endless circles. My breath catches with each movement, and the moment doesn't go unnoticed.

"Oh, Cat. If you could see yourself the way I do. You... look... so... hot... right... now..." Stryder grumbles in between tugs, his tempo increasing with each syllable.

His words have quite the effect on me. My fingers quickly grow wetter with each movement, and I tilt my hips up to add pressure where my body craves it most. That borderline feeling that what I'm doing is wrong dissipates. I'm lost in the moment, consumed by pleasure and urged by need, and if this is wrong then by God arrest me and lock me up. I'd do the time happily. Despite the great distances separating us, I feel he's here, loving me with the force of his entire being, and that thought alone is comforting. As our bodies continue to climb towards nirvana, I mumble my warning.

"I'm there..."

Stryder sits up a little, his free hand on the back of his neck while the other strokes his length. "Don't hold back, baby. I'm there too."

Just two more brushes of my fingers and I fall apart with him bearing witness. With my eyes closed and my pelvis tilted against the cold porcelain bathtub I cry my pleasure, my voice hoarse and my mouth feeling parched. As I come down from my high, I open my eyes to see Stryder fall apart by the grace of his own hand. With rapid breaths, I sit up in the tub to get a better view of this moment.

Unlike me, he usually doesn't make much noise, and when we're together he groans his release into the curve my neck. But tonight he comes loud and hard, his whole body quaking. I can see the rippling effect of his shudders across his sun-kissed skin, his muscles and well-defined lines up front and center for my viewing pleasure. The first thick spurt of his essence lands on his abdominal muscles, and more follow. I watch in awe, my eyes moving upwards to his face. He looks relaxed, yet his eyes are somber–a mirror image of how I feel on the inside.

Yes, instant gratification feels good, but the emptiness that follows can be overwhelming. It's a fleeting moment of pleasure that morphs into severe loneliness and frustration, and I can tell with a glance that he agrees. I give him a moment to come down from his high before I step out of the bathtub to wash my hands. We exchange no words, just the sounds of our movements echoing in our respective rooms. Dressed and washed up, I pick up my phone and take it with me to bed. I turn on the bedside lamp, and curl underneath the blanket. It's been several minutes of silence between us, and quite frankly it's deafening.

"I miss you, Stud," I mumble, as my free hand tucks a wayward curl behind my ear.

"I miss you too, Catalina. So damn much it hurts," Stryder replies quietly. I wish I could hug him.

"Did you- did you enjoy yourself?"

Stryder looks into the camera and shrugs. "Nothing compares to you, baby. Not even my hand. I just... fuck. I miss you."

Tears pool in my eyes and when I nod, they slip past my cheeks. I wipe them away, and with a quivering lip, I whisper, "I know exactly how you feel. It's a second of happiness followed by days of longing and desperation. I get it because I feel it too."

He clears his throat, and despite the somber moment, he moves the conversation forward. "It looks like you keep losing weight, Catalina. What have you been up to?"

I straighten on the bed and worry my lip. What do I tell him? I don't want to lie, but I don't want to spoil a surprise either. "Nothing really... I joined a studio," I answer as vaguely as I possibly can.

"Working out? I guess my little adrenaline junkie needed an alternative until Jax gets better, huh?" he teases with a smile.

I nod, and exhale in relief because for now, at least, my little secret is safe. "Yeah, I guess you could say that."

We chat about his assignment and Jackson's progress until I start to yawn. Having Stryder in a different time zone, seventeen hours ahead, can be tricky for both of us, but after today's dance lessons and our naughty cyber tryst I'm beyond exhausted.

"I'm so exhausted. I'm going to hang up. Can we video chat tomorrow?" I ask, yawning.

"Yes, but you're not hanging up on me. I haven't seen you fall asleep in weeks. Please." He urges and lies on his side not once breaking eye contact through the screen.

"Okay, Stud."

Placing my cell on the nightstand I see through the screen he does the same. Looking at his handsome features, and hugging my pillow a little too tightly, my eyes begin to close.

"Sweet dreams, Catalina. I love you," He whispers sweetly.

"I love you too, Stud," I mumble. In matter of seconds, I'm asleep with a smile on my face.

CHAPTER FIFTEEN

Stryder

Three weeks.

It's been three weeks of pure hell. After my break up with Olivia, I learned to embrace assignments like these- the kind that keep me away from home for weeks at a time. That was before I met the woman of my dreams, way before I gave my heart away for the second time in my life. Now I want to kick myself in the ass for accepting this assignment. The clock hands move agonizingly slowly and the time difference takes some getting used to. It's been three weeks since I left Catalina in Casper with Jax, and the news I received today is seriously depressing. I have to spend yet another week here in Australia. I don't know how I'm going to break the news to her.

I worry she'll be upset because her forced vacation for Xsports is coming to an end. Staying another week here means less time we'll have together before she returns to New York City. My experience in Australia has been nice, all things considered. The weather is warm, and spending the majority of my days on the sandy beaches watching surfers from around the world compete hasn't been bad. My tan is ridiculous to say the least. Last time I video chatted with Catalina she kept giving me that sexy stare, and her gawking didn't go unnoticed. I love it when she looks at me like that.

When the days are short and the nights are long, I lie back in bed and replay in my head our cyber rendezvous from a few nights ago. It was the craziest thing I've ever done with a woman before. Catalina has her shy moments, but when she stops over-thinking? Holy shit. My lady is sexy as hell. The way she commanded me to stroke my dick, and how she came during that call has kept my imagination, hand, and dick extremely busy. I really wanted to get on the first flight out just to taste her.

Physically missing Catalina is something I haven't gotten used to. There are mornings when I wake up and my wood is so uncomfortable it reminds me of the movie "The 40 Year-Old Virgin." If anything, my sexual appetite has increased since I've been away, and I'm thankful for the days I'm too exhausted to think about it.

This assignment has put many things in perspective for me, and I'm surer than ever Catalina is the woman I want to be with. I just hate that our reunion will now happen in two weeks instead of one. At least having an extra week here means I get to finalize our vacation plans. I hate to disappoint her with the news of the assignment extension, but I also know she won't throw a fit like Olivia did when I had to break similar news to her. I'm so thankful for that. I pick up my phone and glance at the time. She's probably sleeping. I hate to do this via text message, but I really don't have a choice. The sooner she knows the better.

<SM: Hey, baby. Assignment has been extended by a week. *sad face emoticon* I'm sorry. Love you.>

As I place my cell in my pocket I see the evening sun from the balcony of my suite. I haven't had much of an opportunity to visit to that jewelry store with the cute blue boxes. It might be considered cliché, but I really want to buy Catalina a gift from there- hopefully something she'll wear forever. Grabbing my access keycard I leave the suite and walk the couple of blocks to the jewelry store.

I stop by the gallery windows to admire the incredible jewelry on display. My heart is whacking furiously in my chest. It's a healthy mix of *holy shit*, and *what the hell are you doing*. I suddenly feel queasy and there's a beading of cold sweat covering my brow probably due to the humidity I tell myself unconvincingly. I'm confident I look like a lunatic pacing back and forth in front of the store. It's balls to the walls or nothing. Taking a deep breath, I open the glass door and slip in. I'm greeted by a woman who reminds me of Kaelan. Her smile instantly calms me.

"G'evening," the cheery shopkeeper greets me. "Are you here for y'self or shoppin' for your lady?"

I chuckle, and extend my hand, making sure to look at her nametag. "Stryder Martynus. Pleased to meet you, Louise. I'm here to look at engagement rings."

"Ah, an American... Are you here on holiday?"

"No, I'm on assignment, but when I get back, I'd like to take Catalina–that's my girlfriend–away on holiday. Hopefully if I have the guts, I'll ask her to marry me, and hopefully she'll say yes."

"Ah, I see. It's always nerve-wracking, Stryder. Come, dear, let's look at some options. If you find the one you're looking for you can order it here, and pick it up at your local shop as we can ship it there too."

I don't tell her that I've done this before. She doesn't know why I'm so fucking nervous this time around. I mean, why would she? The first time I did this sort of thing I was blindly in love with Olivia, the woman who betrayed me, and this time around I'm unquestionably and undoubtedly in love with Catalina Pardo. Just thinking about her makes me smile and my heart thud.

"Ah, thinking about your lady, I see," Ella says, stating the obvious.

I nod. "Indeed. Here's what I'm looking for."

I'm walking like a jolly idiot back to the hotel. If it didn't make me look like a lunatic, I'd probably do a couple of cartwheels and back-flips because the happy buzzing in my heart has me on a natural high. My phone rings in my pocket and I smile when I see who it is.

"Jax! How are you, little brother?"

"I'm good, Captain Chipper. Damn, you sound really happy!" Jackson chuckles.

I laugh at his spot-on assessment. "I'm great, man. I got it. Number three."

"Umm, not sure I'm following, Jupiter."

I stop walking. "I got the ring, Jax."

"Holy shit, man. For real?"

"Yeah, I've never been surer of anything in my life. Catalina is the one, Jax."

"Dude, I'm so fucking proud of you! When are you going to pop the question?"

"I don't know. I'm going to wait until I get back and pray for the best. How is she?" I ask, and continue my walk towards the hotel.

"She's good. Cat's been on top of my appointments and stuff. She's been super supportive, and she's doing another piece for *Xsports*. The girl was moping, but her new hobby is making her really happy."

"She's been working out, right?"

Jax laughs, and replies, "Yeah, what else did you think?"

"I don't know, Jax. You can be cryptic at times."

"Whatever, man. Less than one week to go. Your dick must be thrilled."

I sigh, and Jax says, "You're not coming back on the thirteenth?"

"No... Work got extended by a week. I sent Cat a text letting her know when I got the news, but haven't heard from her yet. Is she up?"

"Nah... She is zonked out. I couldn't sleep so I hit the gym and then called you. She'll be fine."

"The gym? You got cleared to do that?"

Jackson chuckles. "Yeah, I did. The doc says I can hit the slopes in a few weeks. I have one more week of physical therapy, and then a follow-up with the medical team. So far, so good!"

I smile, listening to his old bubbly self. "That's great. I'd love to be there when you take your first ride, and I'm sure Cat would love it too."

We banter back and forth for a bit and then end the call. As I walk through the door of my suite, I throw my access keycard and cell on my bed. The sun is beginning to set, so I open the glass doors of the lanai. The sky is painted with red, orange, yellow, and blue. In the photography world, this is considered magic hour- the perfect moment to take stunning pictures. Resting my palms against the balcony railing, I close my eyes and point my chin to the sun.

Just be patient, Stryder, it's only two more weeks. You can do this.

"Simon said you were second-guessing this assignment when it was first proposed to you, Mr. Martynus. I appreciate you coming over here for the competitions. By now you must be homesick," Mr. Smith says, while puffing on a cigar.

I take a sip from my rye, smiling. "I wasn't expecting spending an extra week, but the experience has been great. The reason why I made the sacrifice to be here was to work with you, Mr. Smith. It has been a real honor."

"Well, how can I make up that extra week for you? If you have a special lady, maybe you can whisk her away to one of my properties. You have eleven to choose from," he chuckles.

I straighten in my seat and say, "Funny you mention that. I've been making arrangements but one of the rental properties I was looking at in the Caribbean fell through. There's this one place I want to take her."

"Tell me where, and I'll make it happen." Mr. Smith asserts, while flicking the ashes of his cigar.

I can't conceal my satisfaction as I mark a dramatic 'X' over today's date on my calendar. The sound the marker makes as I snap it shut makes me smile. I am determined more than ever to make the most of my time left in Australia. I don't know when I'll be back, and Aussies have been welcoming and have made my stay far more enjoyable than I ever imagined possible.

Part of the assignment has kept me on its Gold Coast beaches which are probably the best for surfing in the Eastern Hemisphere. I've made it a point to take small excursions inland on my days off, and even took a flight to Perth to explore that part of the continent. It doesn't matter where I've been, watching kangaroos hop across the arid desert lands, or taking a walk through a vineyard, my mind has kept me far away from where I am. I haven't heard from Catalina in a few days, and while the time zones keep us far apart, my insecurities take me to that dark place in my mind all thanks to my past with Olivia.

I pick up my phone with nervous hands, and text Catalina.

<SM: Hey, Raven Girl. What are you up to? Miss you.>

My phone chirps and my heart drops in my chest when I see it's her. Olivia.

<OR: I was in Casper for the weekend. I've debated whether or not to tell you something. But I think you need to know about it. Better the devil you know. -Oli>

I look at my phone in confusion, and type up a reply.

<SM: WTF, Olivia. What are you talking about?>

<OR: This.>

There are two pictures underneath Olivia's latest text. I look at the blurry pictures, and shake my head in confusion. Jax and Catalina are in a tight embrace, and Jax's face is buried in Catalina's as if kissing her on the mouth. My hands begin to tremble, and bile threatens to rise.

I want to think that everything isn't as it seems, but some irrational part of me quickly dismisses the idea. *Jackson-motherfucking-Reese.* How could he do this to me? The devil's seed of doubt planted by Olivia many years ago returns full force, and I look at the picture again trying to piece it out. It's obvious it was taken at a club and Catalina doesn't dance unless it's with me...so what the fuck were they doing? There's only one person who can give me answers. Olivia.

<SM: When and where was this taken?>

<OR: Hellbenders. Last night. I'm so sorry, baby. I really am.>

I throw my phone on the bed, and stalk towards the mini-bar. I find a slew of miniature liquor bottles and go to town. The burn in my stomach and throat pale in comparison to the pain I feel in my chest. I never imagined they would be capable of doing something like this. Jackson better run and hide because the next time I see him I will snap his fucking dick in half.

Catalina... My anger is quickly replaced with heartbreak. *Fuck, baby. How could you do this to me?*

One by one I throw the empty liquor bottles against the pristine white wall, and the splitting sounds of broken glass ring in the silence of the room. After the last bottle is thrown, I collapse to my knees, and raise my hands to cradle my head against the barrage of thoughts consuming me. These past weeks I've spent missing my Raven Girl, counting the minutes until I can be with her again, only to be cheated on. Again.

I cry bitter tears of frustration on the floor of my suite; my drunken state forcing me to curl into myself. A part of me wants to call the airline and get my fucking ass on the first flight out, but I have responsibilities that keep me grounded. As I consider my predicament, a part of me begins to reconsider the pictures, and the more I think about them, the more I think I need to calm the fuck down.

As my tears subside I put what few facts I have on a scale, and arrive at the same conclusion every time. *Olivia*. I contemplate a theory of destruction devised by her. Surely there's an explanation for the picture, and there's only one person I need to confront about this: Jax. I glance at my watch; he'll be asleep. But the more I think about it, the more I know I can't take care of this bullshit over the phone. I need to see the look in their eyes when I confront them, even if the wait kills me.

Right now I need to calm down, center myself and brace myself for the worst. Until then, I will not contact either of them, or Olivia either. I'm done with her, whatever the truth about Catalina and Jackson. You can only fool me once.

CHAPTER SIXTEEN

Catalina

It's been a week and a half since I last heard from Stryder, and I'm starting to believe something is wrong. Since he's been on assignment, we've kept up constant communication and we've never gone such a long stretch without talking. All of my text messages and voicemails have gone unanswered. Perhaps he's too wrapped up moving from location to location. Whatever the case, it disappoints me to have to wait another week to see him again. The last time we spoke was the morning Kathryn and Gregg invited me to Hellbenders. Kathryn says it will help build my self-confidence, or lack thereof, if I dance in a room full of people.

Jackson and I danced a rumba, and it took everything in me not to laugh hysterically at his blatant invasion of my personal space, but that's the nature of the dance or so I've been taught. After we danced, we bumped into Olivia Reese who was home for the weekend, and I have this unsettling feeling in the pit of my stomach Stryder's radio silence has something to do with her. She didn't say much, but had a smug smile on her face, like the cat that ate the canary. I don't know... Perhaps I'm putting too much thought into it? I'd like to think she's changed her ways after her brother's near-death experience, but then again, people don't change overnight.

I've focused all of my frustration into dancing, and it shows. I feel like a different person when I'm on the dance floor, a feeling I've experienced before when I snowboarded for the first time. Dancing isn't as difficult as I thought it would be, and I can't wait to show off my new skills to Stryder when he returns. I don't know when he'll be back, and not knowing has me on edge. He is due to return any day now, and I'd like to think his lack of communication is because he wants to surprise me. I pray with all of my being that's the case.

"Earth to Catalina!" Kathryn scolds as I miss a step. I raise my head to meet her gaze, and worry my lip in acknowledgment.

"Sorry. I'm just a little out of it today. Can we start again?"

"Come on, girl. Jupiter is due back any day now. We need to get this choreography perfect so you can blow him away with your sexy hips." Kathryn stands beside me and looks into the mirror. "From the top! One, two, three..."

I'm shocked I'm able to finish the class without major incident. I know I could've done better, but thinking about Stryder has me off my game. As I'm packing my bags to leave the studio, Kathryn stops me.

"What's bugging you, Cat? You were out of it today."

I put my bag over my shoulder and huff. "I haven't heard from Stryder in over a week. I can't help but think your sister has something to do with it. I'm sorry if I'm bad-mouthing her here, but I wouldn't put it past her to fuck with our relationship."

"Sit down," Kathryn says, and I do. "Olivia may be many things... Manipulative and a total brat, but I think she's over Jupiter. I mean, she has to be, right? You're here and part of our family, not to mention Jackson was found thanks to you. I don't think she'd be dumb enough to stir shit up to put tension between you guys. She's my baby sister, and naturally I'm going to think the best of her..."

I bite my lip.

"Having said that, I also know a desperate woman is capable of anything. Trust me when I say, if she's up to no good she'll have to answer to me."

I nod and exhale a shaky breath. "I hope you're right, Kathryn. I have a bad feeling about this and I just can't shake it." I pat her leg before rising. The chimes on the studio door ring, and Jackson comes in with an ear-splitting grin on his face.

"I got the green light to hit the pow again!" he announces. Kathryn and I look at each other and run to hug him.

"Oh my goodness! That is fantastic news, Jax!" I practically scream. Kathryn follows with a cheer.

After saying our farewells, Jackson and I leave the studio with a skip in our step.

"I'm not going to lie," he says on the drive home. "I'm kind of shitting my pants here, Cat. It's one thing to get the go-ahead to snowboard, another to overcome my fear of another avie taking me under."

I reach out to squeeze his knee as he drives us back to the ranch. I totally understand where he's coming from. Before we met I was traumatized by the snow, as it was a constant reminder of all that I lost, but it was the same thing that patched my broken heart.

"Jax, you need to go back up there and prove to yourself you can do it. You have it in you to give it your all. For too long I lived in fear so much that it paralyzed me, and I wasted so much time dwelling on the past. I know you know this by now, but you will be fine. I'll be by your side every step of the way. Just promise me you'll start slow. No heli jumps until you feel ready."

Jackson nods, but says nothing, not that he needs to. I can tell by the shake in his hands as he death-grips the steering wheel he's scared shitless. We arrive at the ranch with our hands clasped tightly together. As we walk into the foyer, I notice there's a suitcase by the door. My heart skips a beat when I see Stryder sitting on the bottom step of the staircase. He has a gloomy face, sunken eyes, and a full beard. My heart stops when our eyes meet. The urge to run into his arms is great, but his body language freezes me on the spot.

"Jupiter! Welcome home, man!" Jackson greets to Stryder.

Stryder rises, and what happens next shocks the ever living shit out of me. He blindsides Jackson with a punch on the jaw the sound of flesh meeting flesh makes my entire body shake.

"What the fuck, man? What'd you do that for?" Jackson exclaims as he cradles his bruised jaw.

"*You have the gall to ask me that, you fucking piece of shit?!*" Stryder roars, and I jump. "You thought me being across the world was the perfect opportunity to make a move? I just wanted to see if this was true, and lo and behold, you walking through that door holding hands. You two must've had a real good laugh at my expense, huh?"

I take one step forward and raise my hands. "What is going on, Stryder?" I whisper as tears fill my eyes.

"Just don't, Catalina. Don't you fucking dare! I thought you were different, but you're just like everyone else," Stryder spews, hatred evident in his eyes.

"Dude, what the fuck is going on, man? What the hell are you talking about?!" Jackson bellows, heaving with both of his fists balled.

"Wow. It amazes me how stupid you must really think I am. *The kiss, Jackson!* I'm talking about the motherfucking kiss at Hellbenders, you sack of shit."

It's right then and there I realize my suspicions about Olivia were spot-on. She must've reported back to Stryder we were at Hellbenders, but we've never kissed.

"Clearly your qualm is with me, Stryder," I state, as I wipe away my tears with the back of my hand.

"Damn straight it is. Save me your tears, Catalina. It's too late for regrets, *sweetheart*," he patronizes, his voice laced with disdain. "I was in fucking Australia counting the days until I could be back here with you, and I have to admit I never saw this shit coming, especially from you. I'm disappointed, Catalina. I really am."

I step forward in an attempt to look deeper into his eyes, but all I see are hurt and anger. It takes a lot of effort not to take his words to heart. I know we say things in passion, in the heat of the moment and the majority of the time we don't mean them, but Stryder is under an illusion I somehow caused him great hurt.

"You think I cheated on you," I deadpan.

"I don't think, Catalina. *I know.*"

"Then show me your proof, Stryder Martynus. Let me tell you, I have done no such thing, and I never will!"

Stryder shoves his hand into the front pocket of his jeans and retrieves his cell phone. After several angry taps, he dumps it into my hands. "Look."

The images are very grainy. It was obviously taken at a considerable distance, and the zoom feature distorted them a bit. It's a picture of Jackson and me dancing. It does look like he is kissing me, but that is just the angle. Jackson never kissed me on the lips, and for Stryder to even consider I'd be capable of cheating breaks my heart.

With determined steps, I walk to where Jackson is standing by the staircase. Shaking my head, I give him Stryder's phone. "Look at this shit."

Jackson glances at the picture and laughs so hard he almost drops the phone. In the blink of an eye Stryder tackles Jackson and violently presses his forearm against his neck, pinning him against the wall.

"No!" I scream.

"What, Catalina? Are you worried I'm going to break your lover's face into pieces?" he growls, looking at me square in the eye. He turns his head and focuses on Jackson. "You think it's funny to steal the love of my life from me, huh? Do you think it's hysterical for me to be across the world and have to deal with this kind of shit? It's bad enough I had to put up with your sister's bullshit, but you, brother? That title no longer suits you. *You mean nothing to me! You are dead to me!*"

Jackson blinks rapidly, panicked. "Dude, no! I'd never do this to you!" He looks in my direction. "Don't take offense, Catalina. You're cute and all, but I don't like you in that way. Let us explain, man," he says to Stryder. "It's not what you think, but you have to let go of me!"

Stryder's breathing is heavy, and my hands cradle my belly in anxiety. "Stryder! Let him go!"

With reluctance evident in his movements, he cuts Jackson loose. Both men are breathing heavily, and I can see hurt reflected in their eyes as they stare at each other in silence. Jackson eventually breaks the stare-down, and walks towards me. Pulling his cell phone out, he taps his screen a few times. Sam Smith's cover of Whitney Houston's "How Will I Know" begins to play. Stryder crosses his arms across his chest in irritation.

"Come on, Catalina. This is the only way he'll believe us over that fucked-up picture," Jackson urges, grabbing my hands and standing in frame.

"It's supposed to be a surprise, Jax!" I whine, but I straighten my torso and begin to sway my hips.

"Suck it up, buttercup," Jackson breathes. "Now stop thinking and start moving."

As the song plays, I close my eyes and lose myself in the sultry melody, and as Jackson lifts my arms and hugs my body from behind, I open them for the briefest of seconds. Stryder's eyes meet mine, and they instantly wet with tears. The corner of his mouth curves up in a smile. Jackson turns me around and moves to grab my leg. He stretches it and positions it over his thigh, his movements professional, and far from seductive, despite the sensual nature of the dance. We continue dancing until the song ends. Jackson immediately lets go of me, and stalks towards Stryder with determined steps.

"See, you big goof? We were dancing. That's what those pictures are. We were dancing a rumba at Hellbenders, and if you look closer at the picture, you'll see Gregg and Kathryn are in it too, you jackass."

Stryder looks at us with apologetic eyes. "God, I don't know what to say."

"Well, motherfucker, you can start with 'I'm sorry I was a stupid asshole who misinterpreted a picture', and then you can follow by extending a deep apology to the woman who has been pining for you since the moment you left and who begged me to teach her how to dance because loves you with every breath she takes. Yeah, I'd start there," Jackson says evenly, his hands rested on his hips.

Stryder places a hand over his mouth, embarrassment evident on his beautiful face. I stand by the wall with my hands clasped over my belly waiting for him to say something. Every second is agony and the silence in the room makes the blood rush through my ears sound like a freight train.

Jackson, the most impatient of us, breaks the silence. "Well, stop standing there and talk to her." He gently shoves Stryder in my direction, but stops and hugs him hard. "Dude, I love her like I love Kathryn... like I love you. I'd never do anything stupid to break your trust, let alone your heart. Now go!"

Stryder hugs Jackson, and pats his back several times, like close friends do. I love Jackson more than ever because he was able to put Stryder's hateful words aside, to understand they were coming from a painful and misconceived place. "I'm sorry, Jax. I didn't mean to-"

"Save it. The one you need to apologize to is standing right over there, Jup. Now if you'll excuse me, I'm going to put an icepack on my jaw."

Jackson leaves the room, and Stryder walks towards me with his shoulders slumped and his eyes on the floor. He stops a few feet away, and then removes one of his hands from his pocket and combs his fingers through his hair.

"I'm sorry, Cat," he whispers, and raises his eyes to look at me. "I-God, I-"

I close the gap between us and wrap my arms around his waist. He reciprocates, and we stand in absolute silence hugging each other. The sobs I'd been holding back come out full force. Having someone as strong and as loving as Stryder doubt my love and fidelity is heartbreaking, but then again, he was under the influence of a conniving bitch. I know in my heart this was Olivia's handiwork; there's no doubt in my mind about that.

"You dance beautifully, Catalina," Stryder breathes into my hair, reaching for my cheek with one hand. "I guess I ruined your surprise. I'm sorry, baby. I totally messed up here."

I peer up at him, and caress the scruff covering his super-tanned skin. His hazel eyes scream sincerity and regret, and his voice cracks on his last words. I hate that Olivia has put our relationship to the ultimate test, but it gives me the courage to say the words I feel in my heart.

"When I said I love you, Stryder, I meant it. I don't cheat, because I don't share well with others, and it is best you understand that. The moment I said I love you I vowed to love you and forsake all others. I'd never betray your kindness and trust... *never*." Stryder blinks twice, processing my words, and by the third blink two fat tears roll down his cheeks.

"I'm sorry, baby. The possibility of losing you blinded me from the truth. I was consumed by rage, and I hate that I allowed a stupid picture weigh more than our love. I'm an idiot, Catalina. I know what I said was inexcusable, and if you tell me to fuck off I totally will. I deserve it, but you need to know I love you. I cannot breathe when you're not around, and I become a pigheaded prick when our love is at stake. I love you."

"I love you too, Stryder. I'm not going to allow Olivia to break us apart. We belong together, and I'm not going to let a fucking picture get in the way of our happiness. We both deserve it. I forgive you because I know where you're coming from. You didn't know what Jax and I were up to. I shouldn't have kept it a secret, but I wanted to impress and surprise you. It's easy to lose focus when you have a manipulative bitch preying on your weakness to get what she wants. I'm sorry, Stryder, but she's going to get an earful from me."

Stryder cups my face, and smiles apologetically. He lowers his lips to meet mine. At first, his kiss is delicate, unsure, but when I open my mouth and allow my tongue to slip past his lips, the embers that were simmering between us turn into a roaring fire. We kiss like we're harboring the last oxygen on the face of the planet, and in a quick move Stryder lifts me onto his waist. I'm lost in our kiss, but I know we're on the move because my body bounces against his, his hard erection rubbing against my core with each step. He kicks the door to our room shut, and then lays me on top of the white comforter. His body is over mine like a blanket; his lips kissing my jaw line and neck.

"God, I've missed my sexy Raven Girl so damn much," he mumbles in between kisses.

The last time I saw Stryder with scruff was during the press tour, and I absolutely love the effect it has on my over-stimulated skin. My hands tangle through his unkempt hair, rejoicing at his gruff appearance. He's incredibly sexy, looking all caveman and shit. I wholeheartedly approve.

"Mmm. Shut up, and make love to me."

Stryder gives a strangled groan. He breaks our kiss and takes off his t-shirt tugging it from the neckline, over his head, and then kicks off his shoes. I giggle at his eagerness and watch in awe when I see his tanned muscles ripple with each of his movements. There's no denying my body has missed his. The fluttering in my belly increases every time our eyes connect.

I unclasp the buttons of my blouse with trembling fingers. My entire body is humming with anticipation, and when Stryder stands at the foot of the bed in nothing but his distressed low rider jeans, I almost come right then and there. With a devilish grin on his face, he tucks his fingers underneath the waistband of my leggings and yanks them off in one swift move, panties included.

My hands unclasp the buttons of his jeans and tug the denim past his hips. I gulp when I see his cock thick and ready for me with a small drop of dew glistening on the tip. The urge to feel him deep inside me becomes a primal need. I wrap my legs around his waist and dig my heels into his firm ass cheeks, pulling him forward. Stryder chuckles but makes no protest. His hand touches my core, causing him to let out those raspy, sexy sounds from the back of his throat.

"You're more than ready for me," he whispers, licking his fingertips, which are already slick with my wetness.

His body is perfectly aligned with mine and he gazes into my eyes for approval. Not one for words, I wiggle my wetness against his cock which is more than a green light for Stryder to sink into me in one tantalizingly slow move. Inch by inch I feel him; a deep sigh of satisfaction escapes me. He reaches for my legs to tighten them around his waist, and then he lies on top of my body, his head seeking refuge in the crook of my neck. His firm hands squeeze my ass cheeks, and deep inside me I feel the twitches of his cock.

"My true North," he breathes. "I'm finally home."

My body buckles at his words; my need for him becoming too much. I tilt my hips, bringing him to a steady pump. With each thrust, I whimper in delight, and I reach for his overly-long locks, pulling at them gently.

"I'm so happy you're home," I croak.

We make love like it's the first time. Our hands battle, unsure where to grab or what to hold on to, and we kiss feverishly, then let go to catch our breaths as we climb the mountain towards ecstasy. Having

Stryder tangled over my body, falling apart in my arms is something I'll never tire of. He is a passionate man with a huge heart, and while he's flawed I love every single aspect of him; both good and bad.

Basking in the afterglow of our reunion, his eyes meet mine. There's always an edge in the way he looks at me, mysterious and intense, that keeps me on my toes, but today it's different. His eyes are soft and dewy, making him look downright vulnerable. He smiles with a tenderness that takes my breath away.

"Welcome home, Stud," I whisper, returning his smile.

"I missed you so damn much."

His hands reach for mine; our fingers lace with each other's, and then he raises our joined hands to kiss them. I'm melting at his affections and enthralled by the intensity in his eyes as he does it.

"You looked *really* sexy dancing with Jackson. Of all the things I imagined you'd be capable of doing, dancing was the furthest from my mind."

My cheeks warm, and instinctively I close my eyes, feeling shy. Stryder chuckles deeply and lays his head over the swell of my breasts, letting out a contented sigh. "You liked it?" I squeak.

"Mmm-hmm. Very, *very* much. I can't wait to see how you dance with me... Who do I have to thank besides Jax? Which reminds me- I was a complete asshole to him. I need to apologize." He looks at me with apologetic eyes. "I'm sorry, baby. I was so upset I couldn't think straight."

I let go of one of his hands to stroke his hair. "Kathryn and Gregg. I've spent the last month at their studio taking lessons with Jax as my partner," I reply with a grin. "I think Jackson would appreciate the talk. He's been keeping my mind occupied so I wasn't moping all over the place. You don't need to apologize to me, babe. It must've been hell thinking I was unfaithful. I will have words with Olivia... You can count on that."

"But still... I should've known better, Cat. It was wrong of me to assume what I saw in the picture was real. I feel sorry for Olivia. I really do. It was obviously a desperate act from a desperate woman."

I tap his shoulder and wiggle underneath him, trying to get up from the bed. "It is water under the bridge, babe. I'm going to wash up and head downstairs. I'm starving."

Stryder grumbles, but he eventually rolls off. He lies on his back with his elbows propped beneath him and states, "You've lost weight, Catalina. Dancing does the body good."

I look down at myself and smile. "I suppose. Dancing has *some* benefits besides impressing this sexy guy I know..."

Stryder gets up from the bed, and hugs me tight. "This sexy guy you speak of... Is he worth your time?"

I giggle in his arms. "Indeed. He's a dancer, or so I'm told. I have to see if he's a better dancer than my partner."

Stryder takes a firm hold of my hips, and swivels them against his own- very reminiscent of a samba routine Kathryn was teaching me earlier this week.

"I think your partner is great, but maybe you need a new partner. Someone who knows your body better than anyone else," he breathes.

"Let's move this samba into the shower, shall we?" I quip, placing my hand over his shoulder and swaying my hips; dancing around him and elongating my arms with my fingertips fanned and pointing towards the ceiling.

Stryder pulls me towards him, grabbing my waist possessively. His eyes are full of heat, and his erection is back, standing tall and proud. "Rumba? Samba? Remind me to buy Kathryn flowers."

The intensity behind his words makes me laugh, and we literally dance our way into the bathroom. Once inside the shower enclosure, our sensual dancing morphs into a very naughty, non-ballroom type of dancing that would certainly get us banned from any dance floor on the planet. What can I say? He's impressed. Mission accomplished. It's so nice to have him home.

CHAPTER SEVENTEEN

Catalina

I clear the kitchen after preparing us a plentiful dinner. Stryder and Jackson are in Jackson's office talking about the misunderstanding that almost severed their brotherhood. The more I think about Olivia's ploy, the more it has me all kinds of pissed off.

Stryder was right in saying Olivia's actions were coming from a desperate woman, but never in a thousand years had I imagined she'd use her own brother–her flesh and blood–as bait. I understand why she's hung up on Stryder. I mean, who wouldn't be? Seeing Stryder happy with someone who isn't her must be a bitter pill to swallow. I'm just hoping the guys can work things out, and in the future when we look back at this moment we can share a good laugh.

After putting the last dish away in the cupboard, I wait for Stryder upstairs. I peruse my work email on my phone and groan when I see the massive amounts of emails in there. Scrolling by hundreds of messages, I hone in on one from Marcia. She wants to know when I'm going to start working on the follow-up piece for Jackson, and would like an update as she needs to decide which issue it will be featured in.

I type a quick response explaining he was recently cleared to commence training on the slopes again, and that these things obviously take time. Spring has started to appear in Wyoming, so it's safe to assume we'll be traveling abroad with Team Reese for his training. After wrapping up my email, I send a quick text to Faith. I feel so guilty I've neglected her ever since Jackson and Stryder arrived into my life. I know she's probably wrapped up with her wedding planning, and with her insane schedule at the hospital on top of that, I'm sure she's in dire need of some girl time. I need to return to the city for a few days at least to handle mail and check up on my loft. It's insane to think I up and left everything to chase after a story, and ended up finding love all in the same trip.

<CP: Hey, booger. Sorry I've been MIA. How are you?>

It takes a few moments for her to reply.

<FM: Well, fuck me sideways, Catalina! How've you been, girlie? I gather things are going strong with Mr. Tall, Dark and fucking Hot!>

<CP: *smiling emoticon* I guess you could say that. Life's been crazy. How's the wedding planning? P.S. I miss you!>

<FM: Yeah... about that... We're taking this party overseas. Bali. Mom is driving me up the wall with the planning. You'd think SHE'S the one getting married. Ugh. At this point, I just want to elope. Meh.>

<CP: Bali? It's going to be so romantic. Fresh flowers, tons of humidity, and ancient temples? What's not to like! Hell, I'm jumping for joy over here!>

<FM: Good! We're optioning a couple of dates so expect your Save the Date to be in the mail soon. I still have you as a +1. Dad is taking care of everything so you need not worry.>

<CP: We'll be there. I hope this isn't awkward.>

<FM: Awkward schmawkward! Everyone knows, and Mom thinks he's hawt. *winking emoticon* I sneaked a picture of you both when you were at the hospital.>

<CP: Oh God...>

<FM: LOL. I have to go. I'm being hailed on the pager. I'll be texting you options for MOH dresses and stuff. Don't ignore me. *blows kisses emoticon* Love you!>

<CP: Okay. No peeking underneath the blue gowns, Miss Ma'am. TTYL. <3>

I toss the phone aside, groaning loudly and covering my face with my hands. It's no secret the Mackenzies have been championing for me to have a second chance at love, but damn, it worries me a little to have them see me in the arms of a man who isn't their son. No matter where my future with Stryder takes me, my heart will always love Blake. He will always have a special place in my heart, and so will his loving family.

Stryder walks in with his hands in his front pockets and a concerned look on his face. I pick up my phone and rest it on the nightstand. "How'd it go?"

"He's fine. If anything, he's majorly pissed at Olivia– foaming at the mouth angry. I said what I had to say, and a man knows when to apologize when he's fucked up majorly." He takes a seat on the edge of the bed. "What's the matter?"

"What do you mean?"

"Well, I heard you huffing and puffing when I was coming up the stairs. What's wrong?"

I huff again and smile. "I made the stupid mistake of picking up my phone. Work wants to know when I'll be drafting the new piece on Jackson, and then there's Faith's wedding coming up... I'm just a little overwhelmed."

Stryder smiles, and then stands. "Work can wait. Jackson says the team will be training in Chile in three weeks. They've been getting early snowfall, which is great for his plans. He asked me to tag along so it will be like Whistler... us three hitting the slopes again. It's going to be great, Cat. Don't stress over it."

"I know I shouldn't, but I worry about Jackson and the pressure the world is putting on his shoulders. I don't think my heart could take another scare like Kicking Horse. I just can't," I whisper, my eyes watering up.

Stryder crawls into bed and sits beside me, cradling my face with his hands.

"Hey, hey, hey. It's okay. If anything, Kicking Horse was an eye-opener for him and the team. I understand you're worried, Catalina, but you can't allow this worry to determine each of your steps. You can't live your life holding your breath and expecting the worst at every turn. If bad things happen, we'll deal with them then, okay?"

"Okay, Stud. It's been a wild ride, both good and bad since I met you two. I don't want to lose what we've worked so hard to build. Friendship and love take time to blossom, and some people aren't so lucky to experience both in their lifetimes like we have." My fingers absentmindedly play with the fuzzy lining of the Sherpa comforter, and as we sit in silence my mind races with thoughts of our upcoming travels, namely our little getaway.

"What's going on in that pretty head of yours, Cat?" Stryder asks with a wide grin. I lift my head, and he says, "Spill."

"So... Now that you're back and all, I was wondering when we'll go away? You know, like we-"

Stryder interrupts me by placing his index finger over my lips. "With the bullshit with Olivia I cancelled everything. That was another reason why I was downstairs with Jackson I made a couple of calls, though. We leave tomorrow, and don't ask me where because I'm not saying. You'll know when we get there."

My heart beats a steady rhythm against my ribcage, nervous and excited. There's only one person who I've gone away with in my lifetime, and the possibilities of a vacation with Stryder have me all kinds of nervous, but also incredibly happy.

"What do I pack? You have to at least tell me if I need to pack for hot or cold weather..."

He leans in to kiss the tip of my nose. "Hot, so whatever you have here won't work." I raise my eyebrow and say nothing further. His hand reaches for the lamp on the bedside table, and turns it off. "Let's get some sleep. I'm still on Aussie time, and this jet-lag is starting to kick my ass."

I nod and curl up beside him. My mind and heart are buzzing with excitement, and while his breathing evens out minutes after his head touched the pillow, I stay up for the majority of the night wondering what will happen next.

"Good morning, Catalina."

Stryder's throaty voice fills my ears as the light of the morning sun filters into the room. Having spent the majority of the night awake and lost in my own thoughts, I'm feeling less than cordial this morning.

"Go away, Stryder. Just five more minutes, please," I groan in protest.

His soft chuckles reverberate against my body, and in true grumpy-ass fashion I grab my pillow and cover my face with it. He laughs again and spreads over me, kissing my bare shoulder. I don't protest much when his mouth latches on one of my exposed nipples while his gruff hands fondle my breasts. The feel of his twitching erection over my throbbing core has me tossing the pillow aside instantly amenable to the wakeup call. My protests become urgent pleas as we make love into the early hours of the morning.

Awake and invigorated I settle into my morning routine, and once showered and dressed, Stryder surprises me with a large mug of steaming coffee. I sip on it contentedly, while his strong arms hold me in front of the vanity mirror. There's something mesmerizing about his hazel eyes connecting with my dark ones in the mirror as he rests his head on my shoulder. I don't know what the definition of 'perfect couple' is, and it would be silly of me to think Stryder and I are perfect because we sure as hell aren't, but looking at our reflection tells me our imperfections are ideal for each other.

I like to think the way our lives are is simply perfect. My heart flutters in my chest, and all of a sudden I'm so overwhelmed with contentment and hope for the future that I have to put my coffee on the counter so I can hug the man of my dreams. His smile radiates an infectious happiness, and he opens his mouth as if to speak, but then closes it and shakes his head...

"What time are we leaving?" I ask.

"In half an hour. Let's get something to eat. Do you have all that you need?"

Picking up my mug, I nod, and we leave the room and head downstairs, Stryder carrying our carry-on bags. Jackson is putting breakfast on the counter with a Cheshire cat grin.

"Are you guys ready for your love-fest getaway?

"Yes... even though I have no clue where we're going." I reply in mock annoyance.

Jackson looks at Stryder with a knowing smile. "Niiiiiiiice, Jup." Redirecting his attention to me, he says, "Eat up, girl. Get those calories in while you can."

A laugh escapes me, and Stryder snickers and takes a bite from his buttered toast. Jackson looks at us and wiggles his eyebrows.

"Like I said, eat up."

Done with breakfast, I clear the table and tidy up the kitchen. Stryder walks out the door with our bags, and as I'm about to follow him, Jackson stops me. His eyes are slightly misted, yet he's smiling.

"Cat," he says, clearing his throat. "All this time I've never said thank you for sticking around for the past two months. You've been supportive and stayed with me during the worst time of my life."

"Shh, Jax. You know I'd do that and more for you. I wouldn't trade this time for anything."

"I know, but still... All this time both of you have been chasing after me, and keeping me in check and shit, but I'm going to miss you a lot. I hope you guys have a motherfucking blast. Promise me that, Pardo."

I nod and pull him in for a fierce hug. "Will you be okay, Jax?" He nods on my shoulder. "Good. If you need anything, know we're only a phone call away."

"Yes, mother," he quips, and we both laugh again.

Stryder walks in with a broad smile. To think less than a day ago he was under the illusion Jackson and I were having an affair, thanks to his ex-fiancé. I'm thrilled that even though she tried to mess with us, in the end she didn't get her way. If anything, my friendship with Jackson is stronger than ever, and my relationship with Stryder is in such a wonderful place. As the saying goes, "*Only time will tell*." I'm so happy time and actions eventually revealed the truth.

"Are you driving, Jax?" Stryder asks. When Jackson nods, he throws the truck keys at him, and the three of us leave the ranch for the airport, enjoying the cloudless, sunny spring morning.

On the way to the airport, David Bowie's "Modern Love" blares in the truck. While the boys snap their fingers and lip sync, I belt the song out from the back seat, and the boys look at me in the review mirror in awe.

It's a short drive to the airport, and the closer we get the more excited I feel. Stryder hasn't revealed our destination, but I'm positive I won't be in the dark for long. It's not like he can blindfold me through the airport... But the joke is on me when Jackson drives through a private gate. On the tarmac is a sleek cream-colored jet; "Bombardier Global 8000," stamped on its tail. A crew of four is standing beside the impressive jet waiting to greet us. From afar I recognize Marc, the flight attendant who was assigned to our press tour.

I cross my arms against my chest and slump back in my seat frustrated that I still don't know our destination. My petulancy doesn't escape the guys; they break out in laughter in the front seat. Jackson parks by the private plane, and cuts the engine. Stryder hops down to open my door with a small bow and a devilish grin that has me raising my eyebrows with curiosity. As I'm taking a step down from the truck I observe Jackson in an animated conversation with the flight crew, pointing every so often in our general direction. As we approach I hear him talking.

"They are precious cargo. As soon as you land, I want an update, yes?"

The flight crew nods, and the pilot shakes Jackson's hand. Both the pilot and co-pilot, as well as another flight attendant jog up the steps of the plane while Marc waits for us. Our eyes connect and he waves; I return the gesture.

"All right, guys, I hope you have a safe trip, and enjoy yourselves," Jackson says, as he hugs us both. "Promise?"

"Sure thing, Jax," Stryder replies, and pats Jackson on the shoulder. "You'll be okay?"

"Yeah, man. I'll be hitting the training center with Rob. He has an aggressive training plan that will kick my ass for three weeks before we go to Chile. I'll be lucky if I ever walk again once he's done with me," Jackson giggles, releasing us. He holds my face with his gruff hands, and looks into my eyes determinedly. "Have fun, Pardo. Remember, there's nothing a board and a wave can't cure," he hints with a wink and kisses my cheek. "Be good." He releases me and steps back, whispering something into Stryder's ear.

"Are you ready to board, Catalina?" Marc asks with a smile.

I nod at him, and then turn around to wave goodbye to Jackson. Stryder touches the small of my back with his warm hand and guides me up the small staircase. As soon as we enter the cabin, the captain and co-pilot greet us in the galley and shake our hands while Marc raises the ladder and closes the aircraft door.

The interior of the private plane is stark white with ultra-modern seats, and natural light pours into the cabin through the oval windows making it appear airy and spacious. I feel like a pauper sitting inside a millionaire's private plane.

Stryder takes a seat on one of the leather chairs and urges me to sit in the one facing his. He takes my hand and squeezes it tight. "I'm not going to tell you where we're going, so you'll have to wait until we arrive. Having said that, I'm so happy you're here with me, Catalina."

I pat his knee and with my free hand. "Stryder, I'm so happy to be going away with you, but I must admit I'm a little nervous about this."

Stryder chuckles and leans forward for a kiss. "Don't be intimidated, baby. I wanted to do something special for you, and Jackson chipped in. Just enjoy it."

Marc swings by with a small tray with two champagne glasses and a bowl of fresh strawberries and raspberries and places them on the small console next to our seats.

"Welcome aboard, Catalina and Stryder. It's so nice to see you again."

We sit on the tarmac for about fifteen minutes before the jet starts moving.

Flight attendants, please prepare for departure. Thank you.

Marc's voice fills the cabin through the PA system speakers.

"Ladies and gentlemen, my name is Marc. On behalf of Captain Williams and the entire flight crew, we welcome you to flight eleven with service to somewhere warm and sunny. Our flight time will be six hours and thirteen minutes. Make sure your seat belt is buckled, and welcome aboard."

After Marc concludes the safety demonstration, I lift both champagne glasses from the console and pass one to Stryder. I don't know if it's the natural sunlight, or a reflection of how he feels, but his hazel eyes look mesmerizingly beautiful. They are on the greener side today and contrast incredibly with his crisp white polo, and today he is freshly shaven. His obsidian hair is longer than when we first met and every so often a couple of strands skim his well-defined cheekbones forcing him to tuck them behind his ear. To say Stryder looks oh-so-manly and unmistakably sexy is a huge understatement.

"You're giving me that look again," he whispers, his voice oozing sensuality and mischief. I smile, somewhat sobered, and I straighten in my seat with my finger tapping the glass. He leans forward and extends his glass of champagne. "Cheers, Raven Girl."

Our glasses clink against each other's, and I reply, "Cheers, Stud."

Flight attendants, please prepare for takeoff.

We both take long sips from our glasses and giggle when the plane jerks forward. Marc swings by and whisks our glasses away, and we exchange smiles before he returns to the galley and sits down on the jump seat by the aircraft door.

The jet starts its accelerated journey down the runway. This is the worst part of taking a flight; the rattling and shaking usually makes me nervous, but today I feel incredibly comfortable. Maybe it's the champagne or the company, but all I feel apart from the light trembling of the cabin is the happiness in my heart. I can't stop smiling at the man before me, and with each furtive glance we exchange, I can't wait to have him somewhere warm and sunny, and all to myself.

Time flies when you're having fun, or so the saying goes. We manage to entertain ourselves with a healthy mix of poker, movies, music, and even a dance. I love how we can be ourselves, acting carefree without a worry in the world, each of us focused on the other. We've had more than our share of champagne, and if this is an indicator of what our vacation will be like then I can confidently say all of my nerves are out the window. After stopping in Miami to refuel we sneak in a nap for the remaining two and a half hours of our flight.

Ladies and gentlemen, we are making our final approach. I'm going to put on the fasten seatbelt sign. Flight attendants, please prepare the cabin for landing.

Marc collects our glasses, and we fasten our seatbelts. Stryder and Marc exchange a smile, and when Marc retreats to the galley and takes a seat, the jet lands several minutes later. It is early evening when we land, and I still don't know where we are. Just as I'm about to ask Stryder where we are, Marc's voice floods the cabin.

"Ladies and gentlemen, welcome to Isla Grande Airport. Local time is 6:23 in the evening and the temperature is eighty five degrees Fahrenheit. For your safety and comfort, please remain seated with your seat belt fastened until the Captain turns off the Fasten Seat Belt sign. On behalf of Captain Williams and the entire flight crew, I'd like to thank you for joining us today and we look forward to seeing you again. Enjoy your time here in Puerto Rico!"

My jaw drops in amazement when I realize where we are. Puerto Rico is where my grandmother was from, and I've always wanted to visit but never found an opportunity. Among the many things Stryder and I have talked about since we started dating was my wish to come here, and now that we're here my eyes mist over at his thoughtfulness. Ignoring the Fasten Seatbelt sign, I unclip the belt and land in his lap, hugging and kissing him.

He touches my face, and his eyes shine brightly in the dim cabin. "Are you happy?" he whispers. "I've been here many times, and I'm eager to show you around."

"I can't wait!" I cry. My chest feels inflated to the point that I'm practically crying.

The jet comes to a complete stop, and after bidding farewell to Marc and the flight crew, we exit the aircraft, and jog down the steps towards a bright red Jeep waiting for us on the tarmac. Stryder puts our bags in the back seat, and we leave the airport listening to salsa on the radio. The humidity has my clothing sticking to my body, but the scent of the ocean is heavenly.

"Where are we headed, Stud?" I ask over the wind lapping through the windows of the Jeep.

"We're headed to Old San Juan to spend the night. There's this little bed and breakfast near the historic sites we'll visit in the morning," Stryder replies without taking his eyes off the road.

Even at night, the city streets are bursting with life. The locals drive past us with their sound systems blaring different types of music, and the young people sing happily at the red lights. The sidewalks are filled with people, and there's festival music echoing through the streets. The flurry of activity reminds me of New York City, except the people have smiles on their faces, and there's a bounce in their steps as they walk by.

Stryder looks at me and smiles. "I've been here twelve times over the past five years, and I have yet to meet an unhappy person. Everyone is so friendly, loving, and welcoming, Catalina."

I nod and smile. The thought of Stryder knowing more about my culture than me is very odd, but Abuela did the best she could to teach me about life and our ancestry in the years I lived with her. She always said the island Puerto Ricans are very different from those living in New York City, and that I'd only understand what she meant the day I visited.

The first thing I notice is the humble smiles of those we encounter on the narrow cobblestone streets of Old San Juan. Music bleeds from the small bars in the colorful colonial-style buildings, and as we walk by the establishments I see people dancing salsa while the onlookers clap their hands to a pattern that is easy to distinguish: clap-clap-clap clap-clap. It's 'en clave' which is the base beat pattern of salsa music. I stop at the entryway of the bar on Calle San Sebastián, and before I know it I'm dragging Stryder inside with me.

I'm mesmerized by the people dancing adjacent to the bar. There are young couples there, their bodies misted with perspiration yet their dancing so seductive it's hard to look away. They all dance with rhythm and cadence like seasoned professionals, and when the song ends some take bows, while others hug and kiss and then retreat to the bar for drinks.

"Baby, let's check into the hotel and we can come back," Stryder whispers into my ear and clutches my hips from behind. He spins me around, and his eyes tell me he's also in the mood to lay a few steps of his own against the tiled dance floor. I nod, and we walk across the street to the bed and breakfast to check-in.

"Bienvenidos, Señor y Señora Martynus," the young lady behind the counter greets us.

As I'm about to correct her, Stryder leans in for a kiss, distracting me completely. As we break away, the clerk gives us our room assignment, and we walk down the narrow corridor towards the elevator. Our room is on the top floor with a balcony facing the busy, crowded streets. The king size bed is placed against the wall closest to the balcony, and thankfully the room is air-conditioned. My hair, which is usually straight, is frizzing up, and the desire to take a cooling shower in the marble-tiled bathroom has become a necessity.

I strip out of my clothes and jump into the shower, wondering what the hell am I going to wear in this hot weather. I wash my hair and come out of the bathroom in a white terrycloth bathrobe to find Stryder sitting on the edge of the bed. Next to him is a beautiful white dress with spaghetti straps, a cream-colored lacy bra and matching thong, and strappy white wedge sandals. I let out a contented sigh and straddle his lap; my lips crashing onto his.

"Do you like the outfit?" Stryder mumbles against my lips.

"Yes, thank you." I breathe, and kiss him again. My hands tangle in his long hair, and we kiss until we're both left breathless. His hands hold me in place, and a part of me is scandalized and shocked we aren't moving things further along in bed. Instead, he breaks our hold.

"Get dressed. We need to have dinner. If we keep this up, we won't be leaving this room until daybreak, and I *really* want to dance with you." I let out a disappointed huff, and Stryder laughs, then rises. "I'm going to shower." And just like that, he undresses in front of me leaving me a frazzled heap of need on the edge of the bed.

The dress is delicate and pretty; after putting on the sexy as sin underwear, I slip it on and look into the mirror, and I'm thrilled with what I see. To put it simply, I look happy; my cheeks are bright pink, and my dark eyes twinkle. My hair is starting to curl up on its own, and normally I would resort to an up-do. This time I blow out my bangs and put some mousse in, and leave it down. With make-up and sandals on, I open the wooden door that leads to the wrought-iron balcony, and look at the streets below. Music continues to pour from the bars below and my hips instinctively sway to and fro. I close my eyes and let the music move me, and I don't open my eyes until I feel a pair of strong hands on my waist.

"You look so sexy dancing like that, Catalina. So fucking sexy," he mutters as he kisses the length of my exposed neck. I practically melt in his hold, and smile wickedly when I feel his need for me pressing against the small of my back. Turning around, I stand in proper dance posture and lift my hands, inviting him to dance with me. Instead, he turns me back around and presses his body hard against mine leaving no space between us. As the salsa beat floods the air in Old San Juan, we are two lovers lost in each other's embrace.

CHAPTER EIGHTEEN

Stryder

My hands take hold of Catalina's waist as we dance to the beat of island salsa which has a heavier baseline than its ballroom counterpart. I love the smile on her face as she tries to dance with me amongst the locals at the quaint-yet-larger-than-life bar. Everyone is here to dance, and it shows. All the dancers showing off their footwork on the small and crowded dance floor are incredible. I'm impressed Catalina hasn't shied away from me or from the crowd.

Local guys have been eyeing up my girl since we walked into the place. Why wouldn't they? She's a gorgeous woman and looks more appealing when she's around the likes of me- a gringo. The difference is *this* gringo knows how to hold his own on the dance floor, even here in the birthplace of salsa. Someone explained to me once that it's not very common to see interracial relationships here, so we definitely stick out. But I've found the quickest way to nip that incongruence is by showing them that this Italian boy is capable of dancing and not the rigid attempts made by my counterparts who come here on vacation.

As soon as we hit the dance floor, we are welcomed with cheers and claps which make Catalina blush the color of red roses. Song after song, we're lost in the music, and I love the fact that Catalina hasn't stopped smiling. Her giggles are like music to my ears, and that gorgeous, uncomplaining body of hers keeping up with mine has me biting my tongue and then some.

The question I've been dying to ask keeps coming up, and to be honest I don't know how it hasn't slipped out already. I want to propose to her, and while I'm completely certain a future with her is all I want, a part of me fears she'll say no because we've known each other less than six months. I brought the ring with me, just in case, and while I haven't planned the proposal out I know asking her, and hearing 'yes' is all that I want and dream of.

After dancing six songs back to back, I am thirsty and so is she. I grab Catalina by the hand, and we walk towards the bar. When the bartender sees us he smiles wide

"For a white boy you can dance, my man," says the older man, pointing his chin at me. "What can I get you?"

"Dos cervezas, por favor," I ask, trying hard to roll my r's.

The bartender looks at Catalina and smiles, "¡A pues bien... baila, y habla español! Te pegaste en la lotería, amiguita." Catalina laughs and shrugs her shoulders, then moves to hug me hard. "¿*Medalla*?"

I nod in agreement, and when he turns his back, Catalina whispers into my ear. "He said you can dance and speak Spanish, so that means I apparently won the lottery with you..."

I laugh loud and hard, and she laughs along with me. "Damn right, babe," I declare with a wink. Catalina shakes her head and mutters something in Spanish under her breath. I kiss her temple hard and hand a twenty to the bartender, but when he hands it back to me I give him a puzzled look.

"Va por la casa, brother," he says, which I understand right off the bat. '*Your drinks are on the house*'. I step closer to the bar-top and shake the man's hand.

"Gracias," I call out, to which he simply smiles and nods. I pick up our bottles of local craft beer, and we sit at a small table outside the bar. We sip our beer in comfortable silence, watching people walk by and exchanging longing looks.

"Having fun?" I ask.

Catalina looks at me, and the fire simmering in her eyes has me looking forward to bedtime. "You never told me you spoke Spanish, Stryder."

I chuckle, and placing the beer on the metal table, I answer, "I know the basics, mostly because Spanish is very similar to Italian. But when *you* speak it, it's usually under your breath and so goddamn fast I can barely catch a word you say."

Catalina lets out a belly laugh, and almost spits out her beer. "*I do not!*"

Sitting on the edge of my seat I reach out for her hand and bring it up to my lips; kissing the soft skin over her knuckles. "Yes, you do. You may not realize it, but you do... especially with Jax."

Catalina laughs harder, and says, "It's because he's so random and the shit that comes out of that boy's mouth is freaking hysterical! Cut me some slack here."

"Ahh, I see. You've also murmured a thing or two while I'm inside you. Don't think I haven't noticed," I deadpan, and take a swig from my beer.

Catalina squirms in her seat, and the cheery smile she's had on all night turns to a lust-filled gaze. Without a word I stand and wrap her dainty hand around my own, and then lead her back to the hotel. We're barely through the door of our suite when I pick her up and wrap her legs around my waist; my hands touch the silkiness of her thighs and squeeze her shapely ass. The way she moves over me, squirming and grabbing my hair, licking and biting my neck has me in a hurry to undress her and get her into bed fast. Instead, I prop her against the wall and let my free hand tilt her chin upwards so she can look at me.

"You mean the world to me, Catalina Pardo. For you I'd do anything, and for your love I'd do whatever it takes to keep you by my side forever." Catalina's breaths come out shaky, and her gorgeous eyes blink rapidly. I look down to her neck, and in the muted lighting of the room I see her pulse beating at the base of her tanned neck. "I love you."

"I love you too, Stryder," she whispers, looking me dead in the eyes.

I have to bite back the four words I'm dying to ask her; I know this isn't the right time so instead I kiss her like a starved man. Our kisses are feverish, and damn they feel so right. I tighten my hold on her and walk us towards the bed, and once there I lay her flat against the covers; her raven-colored hair, tanned skin, and slightly smudged red lips contrast sharply with the stark-white linens. I take a moment to look at her, committing this moment to memory.

How did I get so lucky? As I stand before her beauty I can't help but think how blessed I am to have such an amazing woman in my life. In one swoop she has commanded my heart with just her smile, and her existence inspires me to be a better man. I want things with her

I've never wanted with anyone else before. While I stand dressed in front of her, my soul is naked before hers, and there's nothing more vulnerable or gratifying. Her love has transformed me from a fickle, bitter man to someone who wants to do well in every aspect of my life, and when she smiles, I know without a doubt my life is no life without Catalina Pardo in it. I will do everything I can to give her the life she deserves.

I kneel, and pull her legs towards me, removing the white sandals from her feet. I know what it's like to have sore feet after dancing, so I give her a quick massage to soothe them. Her moans of appreciation have me a little excited, if you know what I mean, and while I want to rip off the clothing I bought for her, I also want to take things slow.

Apart from the sounds of our breathing, the room is serene; maybe it's because we're far from home, or perhaps it's her love that soothes me. Whichever it is, I'm happy.

My lips kiss the tender spot above her ankle, and Catalina squirms with a giggle. I flatten my tongue and lick the same spot for effect, which makes her giggle again. I'm pretty sure I look like a smitten bastard with a cheesy-ass smile on his face. I put her right ankle down and repeat the same with her left.

"Stryder... stop! That tickles!" Catalina pleads between laughs.

"Shh... shh," I try to calm her all while holding back a laugh of my own. Her legs threaten to kick me in the nuts, and I take a step back in precaution to shield my package. I let my fingers roam between her legs and my lips follow exactly where they left off. My heart is beating frantically with the need I have for her, and when I reach the soft spot between her legs, I push the fabric separating us aside. The Neanderthal in me feels proud at the wetness I find there; I don't hesitate to make my presence there known.

Using the pad of my thumb, I rub her hardened clit in small, measured circles, and when she tilts her hips up I lick her wetness like a thirsty man. Everything about Catalina has me tied up in knots; her scent, her taste, and the way her body responds to mine blow me away. Her body knows its mate. The noises she makes when I'm giving her hers renders me stupid and I fight all urges to undress, to sink myself deep into her until there's no way of distinguishing where her body ends and mine begins.

We exchange no words, just sighs and moans of pleasure as I devote myself entirely to her. Her body is the most beautiful in the world, not because it's perfect, but because it is mine to behold. I know it's absurd to do this deep-thinking as I'm sucking her clit, but the truth is if my mind is occupied, then I can control my other impulses.

She's on the brink, and that's where I want her. When my mouth unlatches her little moans of protest make me grin. I want her to come with me inside her, and not after she's had her first. I undress, making sure to grab a condom from my wallet, and as I'm rolling it down my shaft, she shakes her head.

"I hate those. Please don't," Catalina says, with a heavy sigh.

Just by looking into her eyes I can tell she's considering the risk, but she says nothing further. It's up to me to take matters into my own hands. We've had countless encounters, but now that I have plans for us I'd like for things to happen when *she* wants them to happen.

I quickly remove the condom and throw it over my shoulder. Catalina reaches out to me as she tries to sit up, so I kneel on the bed and let her straddle me. My dick is more than happy with the seating arrangement and a hissed sigh leaves my chest when she positions it into her entrance. I love that feeling, when I'm slipping into her wetness, her snug warmth the perfect cocoon for my dick. We are each other's missing puzzle pieces and when put together we make art in the most beautiful way.

I let Catalina ride me, and each of her thrusts has me holding back the urge to let go. She knows how to work me like no woman has before; I don't know if it's the mental and physical connection shared between us, or she knows my body more than I give her credit for. I caress her and squeeze her, those beautiful breasts of hers bouncing in front of me has me in a trance of sorts. Before Catalina, I was the one in control, but ever since she walked into my life we've found this happy medium where neither of us is fully in control of the other.

"I'm so close," she whispers. Her fingernails scratch my shoulders, and her pussy squeezes my dick. I move my hands towards her face, and when our eyes lock I swear I can see into her soul.

"I want to see you when you come, Cat," I breathe. Her mouth turns down into an embarrassed frown as she tries to break free from my hold. "No, Catalina, I want to look into your eyes. Please, baby."

I grip the nape of her neck with one hand, still holding her face with the other. Her movements slow as her fingers squeeze my shoulders painfully, and then the sound that leaves her throat is so violent and deep I'm instantly covered in goose bumps. Through my shaft I can feel the contractions of her pussy followed by a slick wetness all over my dick and dripping down my balls.

Her eyes are locked on mine, and in them I see what I can only describe as love; she bites her lip, and I know she's holding back from making further sounds.

"Don't hold back on my account, baby," I encourage, looking into her eyes. "I want to hear you as much as feel you, and damn it, Cat, your body is screaming at me right now. Let me hear you!"

Catalina's eyes roll back, and, my little temptress sings a goddamn symphony that has me pushing her on her back so I can extend her orgasm as long as I can. I angle my dick to hit that sweet spot inside of her, and her mewls grow in intensity with each thrust.

"Please, oh my God, please, oh, oh," she chants.

I'm cutting it close here, so I bite my lip to distract myself, and I huff in relief when she comes a second time. I wait as long as I possibly can before I break our connection and empty myself all over her belly. She looks at me with a slightly confused expression, and I'll admit a part of me feels bad, but it's a necessary evil. As we both come down from our highs, I pick her up and carry her into the shower with me. There's this awkward silence between us, and I feel the urge to revisit the condom conversation we had almost three months ago. I also need to explain a few things.

"You're very quiet, Catalina. What's on your mind?"

Her eyes meet mine, and she cuts straight to the chase. "You didn't come inside me. Why?"

"We haven't been shining examples of safe sex, and I know how you feel about kids so I'm just playing it safe. That's all."

Her eyes turn soft and a half-smile brightens her features. "Okay, but..."

"But what, Catalina?" I ask.

"I already told you my chances of getting pregnant are extremely low, and yes, we've been risky, but I don't think there's anything to worry about. If it happens, it happens. If it doesn't then there's no harm." As we're standing underneath the showerhead I feel pretty damn happy. I know what she's telling me without saying it. Her mindset is changing, and all the more I need to be careful about spilling my guts here. She's okay with trying, and having that knowledge helps me breathe easier. "Are we good?" she asks, and I nod.

"Yeah! Why would you ask me that?"

"I don't know, I just felt like I threw you off your game there, Stud," she whispers, pointing towards the bed with her chin.

I shake my head and wrap my arms around her, pressing my chest tightly against hers. "Me, off my game? Never!" I declare with a wink.

Morning surprises us after an invigorating night, and after checking out of the bed and breakfast we go sightseeing in Old San Juan. We visit the historic colonial Spanish fort *Castillo San Felipe del Morro*. I tipped the tour guide a hefty sum so they could allow us into a restricted area of the fort called *La Garita del Diablo*- a small sentry box Spanish soldiers used to keep an eye on incoming enemy ships. There's a certain legend I read about online regarding a soldier who abandoned his post to secretly meet with his girlfriend in that sentry box, and naturally when I read about it, I knew I needed to sneak in a kiss, or two with Catalina. After insufferable protestation she eventually allowed me to take a picture of us kissing inside it.

Once our tour of the fortress ends–complete with snapping countless pictures of her throughout the fort, we walk through the streets of Old San Juan, shopping for clothing for the rest of our trip. We take a walk down *Paseo de la Princesa* a waterside walkway, and browse the work of local artisans, even sneak a bite at one of the food kiosks. With full bellies we continue our path towards a colonial door called *La Puerta de San Juan* which leads to *La Catedral de San Juan*- the Cathedral of San Juan.

We walk into the church and while she looks around, I take a seat on one of the pews. Older women are kneeling, praying the rosary like my Nonna used to. I sit in silence, feeling at peace, and while I'm not kneeling, I'm definitely praying for the future I want.

I'm not the most religious of men, but I am a believer and my faith has been restored now that Jackson is back among the living. I deposit my wishes into God's hands, and as I'm about to stand, I see Catalina sitting on the pew beside me with a smile on her face. I don't know why I feel so embarrassed she caught me praying, but I do. With our hands clasped, we light a candle together, and placing my hands over her belly I silently pray for a miracle before we leave the church.

As we walk up the cobblestone steps towards the hotel parking lot, Catalina asks, "What did you pray for?"

I open the Jeep's door, and with a smirk on my face I reply, "For us."

We start the long drive down the north coast of Puerto Rico to one of my favorite places on this island: Rincón. Many of my assignments have brought me to this beach because it is one of the best beaches in the world to surf, and many of my clients have hired me to cover competitions. While tourists love hanging out in San Juan and the surrounding areas, I prefer to hang out with the locals.

Catalina raises her hands in the air, feeling the salt-kissed air breezing through the roof of the Jeep, and every so often she lets out a giggle. On her face there's a smile that has me feeling incredibly happy because I know I helped put it there. I reach over and rest my hand on her knee. She rests one of her hands on top of it, and squeezes. Without saying a word we are communicating how much we mean to each other. I adjust my sunglasses and keep my eyes on the road, and perk up in my seat when I see the exit up ahead.

Not once has she asked me where we're headed. I'm pleasantly surprised and moved that she trusts me enough to lead the way. We ride down a sandy-gravel road right along the shoreline, and stop at a two-story terra-cotta house I rented for the week. It has a wrap-around balcony with a deck on the second story that boasts a view of the Atlantic Ocean with glass windows all around. It's one of my clients' rental properties and I was thrilled it was available.

Catalina's jaw drops in disbelief, and she shields her eyes from the afternoon sun. She looks at me with wide eyes. "We're staying here?" When I nod, she jumps down from the seat and runs towards me. "It's perfect!"

I chuckle, and the property manager greets us at the Jeep. "Señor Martynus, ¡bienvenido!"

I extend my hand to shake his, and he picks up our bags and brings them inside. As soon as we walk in, Catalina gasps. From the outside, the property looks unassuming, but on the inside the furnishings are ultra-modern with every amenity you can think of: stainless steel appliances, a six-burner gas range stove and cupboards stocked with everything we might need. It's air-conditioned, but the ocean breeze blowing through the house will be more than sufficient to keep us cool. There's a water wall–its sound very soothing and reminiscent of the South Pacific, and when the property manager leads us into the master bedroom on the second floor, my breath catches in my chest. A California king size bed sits in the middle of the room with an unobstructed view of the ocean. We look at each other and exchange glances, no doubt making the manager very uncomfortable.

"There's a hot tub and garden pool on the terrace level, Señor Martynus," the man says with a smile. He drops our bags on the bench at the foot of the bed. "If you have any questions, or need any assistance, my phone number is on speed-dial. Just dial '4' on the keypad, okay?"

We both nod and walk Pedro to the door. Once it's closed, we run into each other's arms and kiss.

"Why don't you put your bathing suit on and meet me down here?" I ask. "I'm going to start dinner."

"Do you need my help, Stud?"

"No, I just want you to be comfortable," I say, swatting her ass affectionately. "Go."

Catalina giggles and skips away towards the spiral staircase to the master suite. I busy myself in the kitchen, going through the cabinets and pantry to start dinner. As I'm washing the vegetables, I look out the window and see the ocean, a perfect shade of blue, and the fluffy white foam of the waves as they crash. In the distance, paddle-boarders swim against the blue, while the less adventurous simply lie on the warm sand. The view is a reflection of my life. It couldn't be more precious, or more perfect.

CHAPTER NINETEEN

Catalina

I scramble through our bags in search of the black one-piece swimsuit I bought at one of the shops in Old San Juan. My heart skips in my chest as I revisit the last twenty four hours. This is quickly becoming one of the best times of my life, and it would seem the more time I spend beside Stryder the more I feel like this is how my life should be. His presence in my life has been healing and call me crazy, but I feel my chest could burst at any moment with the intense happiness I feel.

After the long drive, a nice relaxing shower is the perfect way to kick off this first day in Rincón. The shower could easily fit four people and has jets all over the place. After being in there for ten minutes, it's difficult to get out. With much reluctance I abandon the shower and wrap myself in a fluffy white towel. There's music floating in the air. I slip into a flowery pink sundress with my swimsuit underneath, and after brushing my hair and styling it into a French braid, I walk down the stairs barefoot and completely content.

As I walk into the kitchen I see Stryder wearing nothing but his board shorts which hang sexily over his hips. When he hears me approaching, he smiles that panty-melting smile of his, and lays the cooking spoon against the pan on the stove.

"Look at you! This place agrees with you." He beams, his hazel eyes looking greener and brighter than ever. "Just in time."

"I'd say the weather and climate is doing you favors too, Stud," I reply, and wrap my arms around his bare back, hugging him tightly. I love to feel the warmth of his body pressed against mine, and having him with me like this is one of my favorite things in the world.

Stryder chuckles, and looks into my eyes with an intensity that has me blushing. "Are you hungry?"

I smile. "For you? Always." He groans and shakes his head, then kisses me.

"You don't play fair."

"I never claimed I did, Stud. You *should* know me by now."

He laughs a belly laugh, and hugs me again. "I love you, Raven Girl."

"And I you, Stryder."

We sit down and enjoy another delicious Italian meal of sausage and peppers, and move to the terrace where the sun has begun to set. With a glass of crisp Pinot Grigio we make a toast, and sit on the sun bed watching the sunset. Bright splashes of orange, reds, purples, and yellows decorate the sky, and with the sound of the waves crashing below, the never-ending songs of the seagulls flying above, and the salty ocean breeze blowing around us, I'd say this moment has become one of my top ten favorite moments with the man I love.

"Are you happy, Catalina?" Stryder asks, and turns to face me.

"I think you should rephrase that question to 'Is it possible to be this happy?' because right now I'm the happiest I've ever been. Thank you."

Stryder takes a sip of his wine, and rests his glass on the small table in front of us. He extends his powerful hand and guides me to sit on his lap, rubbing circles on my back beneath my shoulder blades.

"No need to thank me, Catalina. It is me who should thank you. You've given me a second chance in life, love, and everything in between. I was a bitter, shallow man when I met you, and you've brought so much color into my life. You've breathed hope into my heart, and you make me dream of a future with you."

I take a long sip of my wine, and turn sideways on his lap. "Meeting you and Jackson was the best thing that has ever happened to me. I love you more than life itself, and I have no regrets about how we met and ended up together. If I had to do it all over again, I wouldn't change a single damn thing."

Stryder takes my glass from my hands and puts it beside his on the table. He brings his hand to my cheek, tilting it down for a kiss. "Me neither, Catalina. I wouldn't change it for the world."

"Where do we go from here, Cat? Where do you see us down the road?" he asks, his eyes searching mine.

I break our gaze and look at the ocean before us, listening to the song of the native Coquí frogs in the distance and feeling the evening breeze against my face. I inhale deeply, and then turn to look into his eyes again. With my heart in my throat I answer.

"I see us together... *forever*."

Stryder inhales sharply, and his entire body relaxes underneath me. "Good. Assignments and life in general couldn't keep me from you, not even if I tried. From the first moment you asked me to stay in your bed I declared myself yours. I *am* yours, Catalina. From the moment I wake up in the morning until I fall asleep at night, and even in my dreams my thoughts are of you."

My eyes well with happy tears.

"I'm yours too, Stryder. Every single part of me is yours to keep."

His lips crash into mine and we kiss like our lives depend on it. Our tongues dance and our hands hold onto each other's for dear life; wanting, claiming, and conquering. He takes hold of my waist and rolls me onto my back against the sun bed. With his body hovering over mine, he pulls my sundress over my head and peels my swimsuit off.

We make love on that very bed, and when I open my eyes for a moment, I see the twinkling stars above. From the corner of my eye, I see a shooting star. I quickly close my eyes, and make my wish.

I want to be Stryder Martynus' wife.

Our week in Puerto Rico flies by too fast. We spend the majority of our days laying on the beach, taking surfing lessons, traveling into the tropical rainforest and even making love under a waterfall like a couple of teenagers. All week long I've been thinking about what I want to do with my life when my forced vacation comes to an end. With each passing second I'm considering the job offer Jackson made me back in Port de Soleil after he won the World Championship to be a permanent press member of his snowboarding team. As we sit in the private jet awaiting take-off, I can't help the tears that wet my cheeks.

"Hey, what's wrong, baby?" Stryder asks.

I wipe the tears away. "I had such a great time that I don't want to leave."

Stryder chuckles and pulls me in for a hug. "We can always come back. Whenever you want. All you have to do is ask."

I nod and hug him back. "There's something I need to tell you."

Stryder pulls back and rests his hands against my knees, looking into my eyes.

"I'm thinking about resigning from *Xsports*. I've been doing a lot of thinking this week, and ever since I covered Jackson's press tour I feel like *Xsports* has become too confining. I'd like to work with Kaelan and be a part of Jackson's full-time staff."

Stryder sits back in his seat and smiles. "Too confining... I think both Kaelan and Jackson would be thrilled to have you on board. Whatever you decide to do, you have my full support, Catalina. Besides, that would mean we could spend more time together. I definitely approve."

"Do you think Jackson was serious about his offer?" I ask, biting the inside of my cheek.

"Of course he was! In fact, let's call him before this bird takes flight," Stryder says as he whips out his cell phone from his pocket. After a couple of taps, the sound of the speakerphone rings in the silence of the cabin.

"It's been a goddamn week, Jupiter! I've been on pins and needles here! How'd it go? Did you–" Jackson's voice floods through the speaker.

"Jax, you're on speakerphone, and Catalina is here," Stryder says, raking a hand through his hair.

"Oh! Hey, Catalina! How was Puerto Rico?"

"It's such a beautiful place, and I can't wait to come back," I reply.

"What's up, lovebirds? Why the impromptu conference call?"

Stryder inches forward in his seat. "How would you feel about Catalina joining your press team on a more permanent basis?"

Jackson's howls make me laugh. "Like that's even a question! I told her I wanted her on my team! Cat? You will always have a spot, and it would make me so fucking happy to have you around all the time, girl. Are you thinking about it? Pray tell."

"Yes, Jackson. I'd love to work with Team Reese... I've done a lot of soul-searching and I feel at home where my two guys are."

"That's because you're family and where one goes the rest follow. When will you start?" Jackson asks.

"I have to give *Xsports* my notice, and after that I can start right away. Thank you, Jax."

"Dude, you have no idea how happy this news makes me. No more stuffy office, no more having to deal with outsiders. Is it Christmas, or is it just me?"

The three of us laugh and after small talk, we say our farewells and end the call. As the jet lifts into the afternoon sky, I look out the window and see the aquamarine ocean glittering below. This moment marks a new chapter in my life where I'm living life to its full potential, and no matter where this journey takes me I know I'll make the absolute best of it.

After nine long hours of travel we finally make it back to Casper in one piece. Kaelan picks us up at the airport as Jackson spent his day training, and is too sore to move a muscle. As we walk through the wide doors of his home, he walks over and wraps me in a tight hug. I look long and hard at his form. He seems leaner, stronger, and his arms and chest look more defined than when I first met him.

"Damn, Jax. We leave for a week and you start looking like a bodybuilder. I'm impressed," Stryder says, and pats his back affectionately. "How are you feeling?"

"I feel great, Jup. Rob and I have been working hard, putting in long hours at the gym and I've been on point with my diet and physical therapy. I've been cleared to hit the pow whenever I want. Which reminds me... We're leaving for Chile in three days."

I watch the boys lost in their conversation, and rest my head on Stryder's shoulder. The bond I've made with these men can never be undone, and I look forward to many adventures with them in the years to come.

"Cat?" Jackson asks, interrupting my inner thoughts.

"I'm sorry. What did you say?"

"I was saying the follow-up piece will be your final story for *Xsports*. I'm so excited to have you here full-time," Jackson says, hugging me fiercely. "What are you going to with your place in the city?"

The question throws me. It's something I haven't given much thought, and while the loft is paid off I know I'll have to decide to keep it or sell it if I intend to work with Jackson here. All of a sudden I feel overwhelmed with decisions I have to make, and sigh in relief when Stryder holds me, pulling me tightly against him.

"She has a lot to consider. Don't you, babe?" Stryder speaks softly, kissing my hairline.

"Yeah," I reply amid yawns. "I'm tired. If you'll excuse me, I'm heading off to bed."

I hug Jackson and kiss Stryder goodnight. As I'm walking up the stairs I hear their voices barely above a whisper.

"Did you ask?"

"No... I wanted to, but I kept thinking I wanted to wait for the perfect opportunity. I had so many chances, and I'm afraid I let them go," Stryder answers, sounding defeated.

"It just wasn't the right moment, Jup. It'll come. Now come on, there's something in the office I want to show you."

As their footsteps retreat, I enter our room and close the door behind me. I'm curious to know what Stryder and Jackson were whispering about downstairs. I have this unsettling feeling that it could be bad news. I shake my negative thoughts and pull back the covers, and lay in bed until the countless hours spent in the Caribbean sunshine and sleepless nights finally catch up with me.

There's a flurry of activity the following morning at Jackson's. Kaelan and Kathy are helping Jackson pack for the weeklong journey to Chile, and Stryder is working from Jackson's office, submitting files to his clients. I steer clear from everyone and work from bed. I open my email and catch up on all things *Xsports*, and type up a message to Marcia regarding the follow-up story on Jackson. Just as I'm about to open a blank document to draft my letter of resignation, someone knocks on the door.

"Come in!"

Kaelan walks in with Jackson and Stryder flanking her, and I sit up straight in bed, wondering what's going on. In her hands Kaelan has a familiar magazine. My hands rise to my mouth as an excited huff of air leaves my body.

"Oh my goodness! It's here!" I squeal. "Show it to me." Kaelan does, and then leaves the room, closing the door behind her.

The boys plop beside me as I gently caress the glossy cover with Jackson's face on it. He's looking at the horizon with snow covering his scruff, and his bright blue eyes are sparkling with determination. Underneath his picture is the title of the article in big, black letters: *chasing Reese*. It's a great picture of Jackson, and I love it even more because it was taken by Stryder.

It took a lot of convincing on my part to allow one of his pictures to be used in the article. Dominick and Marcia wanted to only use Kenny's pictures, but I'm glad I stuck to my guns. I read the article out loud, and we laugh, cry, and marvel at the events that forever changed our lives.

"*There is more to be seen by this remarkable athlete in the years to come. Jackson Reese is* not *the man I've seen portrayed in the media, and I, Catalina Pardo, am proud to call him a friend. It is truly my hope that the world will come to see the amazing human being I've had the privilege of meeting and chasing after for a month. As I've shown you, there is more to Jackson Reese than meets the eye,*" I conclude, and close the magazine, holding it tight against my chest.

"Cat, you are great at what you do. Are you sure you want to walk away from that to chase after me and my shenanigans?" Jackson asks thoughtfully, cracking his knuckles.

Stryder kisses my hair and I cradle into his embrace. "Yes, I've never been more sure, Jackson. I'd like to discover new places and be surrounded by those I love."

"Aw, shit, Catalina. When you put it like that it's hard to question you, isn't it?" Jackson says with a wink, and stands. "All right, I'm going to get back to packing. Mom must be with Kaelan in laundry hell. See you later."

"I hope you liked the article, Jackson," I call as he walks towards the door.

He stops and turns around with the cutest smile on his face. "I love it, Cat. You made me love myself. From the moment I met you I knew you'd be the only one to tell my story. Something tells me this is only the beginning."

Today is the big day, and I'd be a liar if I didn't admit to myself I'm nervous and nauseated with worry. We've been in Chile for two days now, but weather conditions haven't been ideal for Jackson to make his first run. There's been a lot of tension between Jackson and his coach- mainly due to Jackson's fear. Coach Rob has reassured him the scout team has monitored three sites that have little to moderate avalanche activity. I truly believe Jackson is psyching himself out. After having a heart to heart conversation with just the three of us, I can see he is feeling better about his first run.

The wind is blowing fiercely from the south, and the subzero conditions making it seem much colder than it is. I adjust my scarf to cover half of my face as we make our way towards the helicopter. Its loud, powerful rotors blow snow in all directions, and I find myself adjusting my polarized sunglasses to protect my eyes. Jax opens the sliding door of the helicopter and Rob, Jackson, Stryder and I board.

My heart is racing, and I feel the need to hold back my tears for Jackson's sake. He needs to regain his self-confidence, and facing a snow-covered mountain is the only way he'll get it back. I see Jackson give the pilot a thumbs up, and the helicopter slowly flies towards the top of one of the Pucón Mountains. Last time I was in a helicopter I was scared for my life, but this time around I'm more worried about Jackson. It takes us a good fifteen minutes to arrive to the drop-off point. Stryder has decided to chronicle the run alongside Jackson- all the more reason for me to be nervous. Losing one of them would be devastating; losing them both would be catastrophic.

We reach the drop-off point, and I un-strap myself to give them hugs, and tell them how much they mean to me. You never know what will happen so you have to live each moment as if it is your last. As the helicopter door slides open, I look the other way. I'm still afraid of heights and I doubt that will ever change.

Jackson kisses my cheek, and whispers into my ear, "Just say yes."

I look at him, befuddled, as he grabs his board and straps on his survival backpack. In one swift move he steps out of the helicopter and crouches in the snow as he waits for Stryder to join him.

"Hey!" Stryder shouts over the roaring hum of the rotors. "I love you!" he declares, looking at me and patting his chest over his heart.

I pull him close and hug him fiercely. "I love you, Stud. Be safe!" He pats my shoulder with his gloved hands and waves before he steps down from the helicopter.

As Rob closes the sliding door I feel empty, as if part of my heart is missing, and as the chopper rises into the bright afternoon sky, I sit back on the bench with my eyes closed, clutching tightly onto my safety harness and praying for the lives of the two men who mean the world to me. It's not until I hear Jackson's voice through my headset that I open my eyes.

Base, this is Reese. The visibility is perfect and the wind is just right. See you at the rendezvous point.

"Good luck, son," Rob calls on the two-way radio. I look out the window and see Jackson and Stryder stepping onto their boards and securing the bootstraps. They exchange a solemn nod, shake hands, and lean against each other for one last hug. My heart beats frantically in my chest. I'm scared and happy, I'm nervous and anxious. You name it, I'm feeling it. My breathing accelerates as the moment for them to make the jump draws near. I raise my gloved hands from my lap and ball them into fists, rubbing circles against my chest in a feeble attempt to soothe myself. The tears I've been holding back drop from my wide-open eyes.

I look out the window, and time stands still.

As if in slow motion, Jackson jumps down the slope, and small snowballs quickly roll down the path of virgin powder. I scream in elation as I see him traverse the tall mountain with the man of my dreams following close behind. Rob calls Jackson with instructions over the radio, and while I'm not paying attention to the words, I can hear the pride in his voice. The helicopter follows them, and I notice Jackson must be feeling confident because he's doing tricks when he reaches big air as he goes down the mountain.

I'm no longer afraid, nor am I holding my breath. Instead, I'm cheering and whooping for my guys as I crane my head to look out the window- not once losing them from my sight. As they reach the plateau at the foot of the mountain, I see Jackson un-strap his board and lift it over his head in victory, then fall to his knees in prayer. I cry when I see Stryder approaching Jackson. He falls to his knees before he engulfs Jackson in a hug.

As soon as the helicopter lands, I jump out. My boots scrunch against the snow with every step that I take, and when Stryder and Jackson see me they run in my direction, and the three of us crash into each other's arms.

"You did it, Jackson! You did it!" I scream at the top of my lungs.

CHAPTER TWENTY

Jackson

One, two, three...
Easy does it...
Jump!
My heart is about to come out of my mouth as I begin the descent down Pucón. The sound of my board cutting against the virgin pow vibrates loudly; going through my boots and shooting up my spine. My hips swivel side-to-side as they work in perfect synchrony with my extended arms. I can hear Rob over the headset, doing what he's paid to do, but for the briefest of moments I tune him out as I get reacquainted with the love of my life.
Powder.
The peace snowboarding gives me... The perfect opportunity it provides for me to escape from the worries of the world, and the non-stop bullshit that goes on in my head. Even having a near-death experience under my belt helps me realize how much I love and respect what I do. As I shred down this wild line, I feel a push-pull going on inside my head. I'm juggling feelings of extreme euphoria and sobering caution. Having lost Chris and Rem on a day just like this gives me the shivers, and it's all the more reason I need to make this

ride special. Even though they're not here with me in body, they will always be with me in spirit.

Here comes a jump.

One, two, three...

Flip!

The cloudless blue sky trades places with the mountain as my body twists in the air. I close my eyes for the quickest of seconds, enjoying the freedom of being on my board while floating like a feather in the Chilean air. In the recesses of my mind I hear cheers and hollers, though I'm not sure if they are real or figments of my wild imagination. I open my eyes and land perfectly back on the pow, gaining speed and momentum. Each passing second as I ride down this mountain is a piece of me that I gain back. Every rock that I dodge is a reminder that I'm alive and there's a reason for that. These are the moments I live for, and I'll always look back at this day to remember I'm an athlete, but I'm also a man like any other.

Big Air.

I crouch on my board, and as I elevate higher into the air, I stand and raise my arms into the sky. "I'm Free!" I shout, not caring if particles of snow land into my mouth, or if I come across as demented. I'm delivered from my painful losses. I am free to live without guilt or shame, and having this epiphany makes me want to go faster, dig deeper, and conquer this mountain.

I look ahead and see the clearing, and all of my senses return. Rob is still talking to me through the headset and the tell-tale sounds of the helicopter following us bring me back to the moment. I look back to see my best friend and brother chasing right behind me as I, Jackson Reese, find myself once again.

Our boards come to a stop as we reach the bank of snow at the foot of the mountain. I quickly un-strap my board from my boots and raise it high in the air, screaming at the top of my lungs. This is a victory- not an Olympic medal or a world championship quest, but a victory over fear and death. As my shouts turn into cries, I fall to my knees and give thanks to God above. I feel two strong arms hugging me, and I cry even harder because the relief I feel in my heart is beyond any word a dictionary could ever define.

"You did it, Jax! You did it!" Stryder yells over the wind and the helicopter rotors. His hands pat my back as my sobs turn louder. Kneeling into the snow, I cry into Jupiter's arms, unashamed.

The sounds of the rotors cease and I hear frantic footsteps in the snow. I break away from Jupiter's hug and turn to see Catalina running towards us with her arms extended, shouting with happiness.

"Oh my God, Jackson! You did it! You did it!"

Jupiter helps me up, and we meet half-way, my arms wrapping around Catalina's waist and twirling her in the air.

"I did, didn't I?!" I scream in elation. We laugh, and when I release her, her gloved hand wipes away the tears on my cheeks. Catalina's eyes are red and full of tears as well.

"I'm so proud of you, Jackson Reese," she squeaks. There's a moment of silence between us, and I nod and shove Jupiter in her direction. The two lovebirds kiss for the briefest of moments, and with Catalina's hand caressing his cheek, and their noses touching, Jupiter speaks.

"Are you okay, baby?"

Catalina smiles, and kisses the tip of his reddened nose. "Yes, I'm just so happy both of you are safe and sound," she declares, and hugs him again.

Jupiter looks at me and nods, so I unzip my jacket pocket and retrieve the blue box he asked me to hold onto this morning before we left the lodge. My heart is racing in my chest for the guy; I know he's been dying to do this for a while now. Turning around, I remove the cover of the blue box and tap the black velvet box out from it, making sure not to drop it in the snow. I put the blue box back into my pocket and walk towards Jupiter. I pretend to hug them and slip the black velvet box into his pocket, and then step away to document this moment.

"Cat, since I met you my life has changed. My world lacked color and vibrancy until you walked into that cabin the day we first officially met. From the moment I saw you, an old part of me died so a new one could start living. Not a day goes by when I don't think of you, when I don't dream of having something deeper and more profound with you. I hated who I was before I met you, and now I love the man I am when I'm with you.

"Stryder, I don't unders–" Catalina tries to speak, but Jupiter's gloved hand covers her mouth. With a smile on his face, he continues.

"You've given this once hollow man a purpose, and you've awakened thoughts and possibilities of a future I would've never considered on my own. Each moment I spend with you, the more I know it's you, and only you, who I want to spend the rest of my life with."

Catalina's face flushes bright red, and her eyes grow wide. I'm recording this moment, and for a second our eyes connect. When she turns to face Jupiter, he's on bent knee before her. He reaches for both of her hands looking up into her crying eyes.

"I know we live crazy lives, and the careers we have will keep us apart from time to time. And I know we have our whole lives to figure out what we want to do, but right now, right this moment, I don't want to wait any longer. You are all I can think of. You are the sun that warms my soul, and the moon that soothes my heart, and everything in between. I want to be the man you wake up to every day, and the one you hold tight before you fall asleep at night."

As I stand there with my GoPro camera recording, bearing witness to this amazing moment between the two people I love most, I find myself drying tears of my own. Jupiter lets go of one of Catalina's hands to reach into his left pocket, and with a shaky hand he retrieves the velvet box and opens it with his teeth. From where I'm standing I hear Catalina's loud, sharp gasp, and I grin at the shocked look on her face.

"Your dreams are my goals, Catalina. Will you marry me?"

Catalina falls to her knees and kisses Jupiter's hand. Her pretty eyes look into his as she whispers her answer. "Yes!"

Stryder lets out a breath of relief and smiles, and then pulls her tightly against his chest. As she cries, he looks at me and mouths, "Thank you." I give him a thumbs up and keep recording. He pulls back and brings his free hand to his mouth, removing his glove using his teeth. He moves the ring box to the ungloved hand and repeats the process. Catalina removes her gloves too, and as they kneel before each other, Stryder slowly slides a diamond ring on her finger and kisses it reverently.

"I love you, Catalina. You've made me the luckiest man on the face of the Earth," he says, looking intently into her eyes.

With a tearful, yet happy smile, Cat looks at him. "I'm the happiest girl in the whole wide world, Stud. I love you, too. Always."

Standing here watching them kiss for the very first time as an engaged couple, the lyrics to Bruno Mars' "Marry You" begin to float in my head. Still recording, I sing to them making them laugh and hug each other, occasionally flipping the camera view to record myself. I know in the years to come they will look back at this video and laugh, especially as I look into the sky and howl, "Just say I do!"

As they rise against the crunchy snow, I jog over and wrap them into my arms, "I love you, guys. Now make me an uncle."

Stryder and Catalina laugh, and as we stand hugging at the foot of Pucón. I believe I've been given a second chance to see life with a different set of eyes; to live, breathe, and believe there's more to my story to be written. Hope breeds life, and I'm in the best company to do just that.

CHAPTER TWENTY ONE

Catalina

So much has happened in the last several months... The man of my dreams proposed, and I said yes, and I've successfully penned and published my final article with *Xsports Magazine* titled "finding Reese." a follow-up piece about Jackson's triumphant return to professional snowboarding. I now work full-time for Team Reese, and after selling my loft in New York City, Stryder and I bought a beautiful log home in Casper, Wyoming and we will be moving in soon.

I recently received notice from Marcia Reed, my former editor at *Xsports Magazine*, that I've been nominated for a Distinguished Journalism Press Award for my article "chasing Reese." I look forward to attending the ceremony in the city next week with my fiancé, Stryder Martynus, who is also nominated for Photographer of the Year for his surfing coverage in Australia, and the cover image of my best friend and real-life cupid, Jackson Reese.

I've taken a week off from my new job to attend my best friend's wedding in Bali, and as Stryder and I lean against each other naked in the garden bath of our bungalow, I reminisce on how much my life has changed over the past year. I was consumed with grief and regret before I met Stryder, and was living my life half-dead half-alive. Ever since I opened my heart to love I'm a better person. I'm not saying life is easy or that I don't get scared every now and then when Stryder leaves on assignment, or when Jackson jumps from helicopters. But I know we will never be far apart, and where one goes the others follow.

I turn my body to face Stryder, and looking into his beautiful hazel eyes, I know I am home. It doesn't matter where our jobs take us. Home is where he is, and I'll never lose those flutters in my belly when we're together. My wet hands smooth away those long obsidian strands of hair from his cheeks, and I smile under his affectionate gaze. The fire that was there in the beginning of our relationship still burns bright, and when he smiles devilishly, I feel his hardness press against me.

There isn't much time for us to get dressed and ready for the wedding ceremony, so I move away and try to stand up.

"Where do you think you're going, Catalina?" Stryder growls as his hands take possessive hold of my waist. His lips inch down to the bare skin of my shoulder, and his teeth graze against it bringing me to a shiver.

Cupping his jaw with my hands, I look into his eyes. "I'm all for you making love to me until I can't walk, but it would be bad manners for the Maid of Honor to show up late to her best friend's wedding, don't you think?"

Stryder sits forward in the tub and holds my face with his wet hands. The fire and intensity of his stare makes my skin break out with goose bumps and tingles its way down to the depths of my womb. His hand reaches for the star pendant hovering over my breasts, and, bringing it to his lips, he breathes, "I guess I'll have to be fast then, hmm?"

How can I deny him when my body wants him as well? Let's just say we arrive at the beach with flushed cheeks and five minutes to spare. As I approach the tent where Faith is getting ready, Deedee kisses my cheek and hands me a bouquet with long-stemmed Calla lilies, then retreats to leave me alone with Faith. When she stands, my breath catches in my throat. Her mermaid gown hugs every curve of her tall and slender body, and her beautiful blonde hair is curled and falling past her shoulders. Her make-up is soft and bohemian, and the toes on her bare feet are perfectly manicured.

"Oh my goodness, Faith! You look beautiful!"

Faith looks at me and smiles. "The same could be said about you. Especially that bad-girl twinkle in your eyes that tells me you totally got laid before you got here. Am I right?"

What can I say? She knows me all too well. As we leave the tent, I carry her bouquet as I wait for Aedan, her father, to hug his youngest child before she becomes a married woman. It takes everything in me not to cry at their exchange. Now that I'm engaged, I'm wistful thinking I don't have a father to give me away. As I'm walking down the aisle, I see Stryder from the corner of my eye. The glances he is casting my way make my heart do somersaults inside my chest.

As I stand beside Faith and Matthew as they exchange their vows, I look at the chairs lined up on the beach. Stryder rubs his chin, smiling as he witnesses the moment my friends say 'I do'. I can't wait to be married to him, and there's no doubt in my mind we'll be happy no matter what life throws our way. Happy endings are seldom guaranteed, but that doesn't apply to us. I'll make sure of it.

After the ceremony ends, I see Aedan and Deedee in conversation with Stryder, and at one point the three of them cast a smile my way as I pose for wedding photographs with Faith. My eyes mist over when I see Aedan hug Stryder and pat him on the back, I know he is being accepted and thanked for loving me, and giving me a second chance at life and love. That's all they've wished for me since we lost Blake and our baby five years ago.

During the reception, I join the band and sing a cover of KT Tunstall's "1000 Years." As I stand to take a bow with the band, I see Stryder clapping and wiping away tears. Our eyes connect, I walk towards him, and our lips crash against each other's. As everyone starts cheering, I look around to see Faith standing at her table and whooping. Let's just say, I was caught up in the moment, and don't have a single regret about it.

"And the Distinguished Journalism Press Award for outstanding achievement in a biography-based article goes to "chasing Reese," by Catalina Pardo!"

Stryder and Jackson shout, but I can only blink twice, trying to process what I've just heard.

"Baby, that's you!" Stryder cries over the claps and cheers.

"What are you waiting for, Cat? Get your ass up there and claim that award, 'cause if you won't I will!" Jackson laughs as he stands and pulls my chair back.

With shaky steps, I approach the podium, and as I'm awarded the silver quill statuette, I cannot believe my good fortune. The spotlight shines on me, and a sense of affirmation and realization floods my entire body. All my life I've worked so hard, never cut corners, and prayed for the best. Now, as I stand before my colleagues and friends, I'm left speechless. Hard work truly pays off. Later in the evening, Stryder nabs the Photographer of the Year award, and the three of us dance the night away, giving my former colleagues a thing or two to talk about.

"Have you guys set a date?" Jackson asks, as we board the taxi after spending the night at Stryder's apartment in the city.

Stryder looks at Jackson and me, and replies, "Not yet. Hell, Jax, with work and all we haven't been able to have an engagement party. Trust me, if I had my way, we'd be married tomorrow."

Jackson sits back in his seat and remains pensive on the way to the airport, and all the way back home. After an uneventful flight, we land back in Casper in the early evening, and return to our respective homes. This will be the first weekend Stryder and I have been able to spend together since we bought the property. Our jobs have kept us living out of our suitcases for the past year, and it's a breath of fresh air to see the house we've dreamed of slowly convert itself into a proper home.

As Stryder opens the double doors, he drops our bags in the foyer and wraps his arms around me. "Welcome home, Raven Girl," he breathes as he squeezes me tight.

I'm overcome with emotion. Words as simple as those still have the power to make my heart race with happiness. I used to laugh at movies and books when the hero and the heroine uttered words like, "Your love saved me" at the end, and now I scoff at my past self, because it's very true. Stryder's love and Jackson's friendship saved me from living my life in a blur, and taught me to face my fears head on.

With soft tears landing on my cheeks, I whisper, "Welcome home, Stud."

I look at the remarkable man standing before me, and the smile that captivated me the day we met curls his lips. Those beautiful hazel eyes connect with mine, and I can't help but adore the fierce kindness and love behind them, not expecting or demanding, just adoring and full of unshakable hope. I reach for his hair, and my fingers tangle with those obsidian locks that match my own. I exhale a breath of happiness that makes him smile even wider. "I love you. That is all."

His lips crash against mine, his taste mingling with the saltiness of my happy tears. He pulls back for the briefest of seconds to look at me with a determination that has me squirming in place.

"I always promised myself it would only be a matter of time before I made you mine," he says before scooping me into his arms and walking us to our bedroom. Kicking the door shut behind us, he lays me down on the plush bed. With a devilish smirk he says, "I'm a man of my word, and I keep my promises. Let's christen this bed."

With the pale moonlight filtering through the open windows facing the Casper Mountains, we make love- fast and hard, then low and slow the second time around. Our love grows with each passing day, and while I know nothing in life is permanent or perfect, this comes pretty damn close if you ask me.

EPILOGUE

Jackson

I sit on the steps that lead into Hellbenders, waiting anxiously for the guests of honor to arrive. I invited Catalina and Jupiter here using dancing as a pretext. Everyone is waiting inside, and I'm one hundred percent sure neither of them know what's about to happen.

No one wants to see them ride off into the motherfucking sunset more than me, and the more time we spend together the more I know there is someone out there wishing and dreaming of me just like Catalina and Jupiter's dream of each other. There *is* a special girl out there, and she's all I can think of since the day we met. Jupiter says he felt the same way the day he met Catalina, but only time will tell. I'm not in a rush; I have all the time in the world. Jupiter's SUV pulls up to the curb, and with determined steps I open Catalina's door.

"You must be itching to dance there, mister," Catalina giggles when she sees me. I nod like a giddy child, and that makes her laugh even harder. "Okay then. Lead the way, partner."

"A word, Jackson," Jupiter says with a smirk. "Promise me you'll keep those hands to yourself, yes?"

I groan exaggeratedly. "Dude, you want me to dance without touching her? Fine. Just don't laugh when I'm dancing like a fucking penguin. Seriously." Both of them laugh when I start walking like a penguin keeping my hands pressed to my sides and wiggling around them. "Is this what you want, Jup?"

Jupiter laughs and pats my shoulder, and wiping a tear brought on by his laughter, he says, "Just kidding, Jax. Oh my goodness. That was funny, man."

Catalina snakes her arms around our waists and pulls us close to her. "Shall we do this?" With a bounce in our steps we open the mahogany door that leads into the nightclub.

"SURPRISE!" everyone cheers as soon as we walk in. Cat and Jupiter look at me with wide eyes seeking answers.

"It's your engagement party," I declare nonchalantly, and urge them to greet our families waiting at the foot of the steps. "Go!"

They hold hands and happily jog to hug Lizzie, Vincenzo–Jupiter's folks, and Maddie–Jupiter's sister, and her husband. I feel a hand tap my shoulder, and when I turn my head, I see Olivia standing right beside me.

"What the hell are you doing here, Oli? I didn't invite you."

She looks at me with a smug look on her face. "I was in town again, and Kathryn told me the whole family was here. Color me surprised at the fact that you, my brother, didn't invite me. Regardless of how you feel about me, I'm a part of this family, and I, too, deserve to be here."

I lean in closer so that I can whisper into her ear. "It must suck to see the man you fucked over more than once getting engaged and moving on. It must suck that despite your cuntastic ways you never split them apart. I *know* what you did, and to use me for your petty schemes? That's just wrong. Now have some dignity and get the fuck out of here. *Now!*"

Olivia pushes past me and walks towards Catalina and Jupiter. I run after her, but Catalina's eyes connect with mine, stopping me.

"What are you doing here?" Stryder yells over the music. Lizzie places a hand over his chest and pushes him back. And then we all hear a single sharp slap of skin on skin.

"I've had it with you, Olivia Reese! You do not want to see me pissed. Now get the hell out of here, and let us be," Catalina grits at my sister, who is holding onto her red and swollen cheek with the five finger souvenir Catalina just gave her. "I've tried to be understanding, but get it through your thick head. It's over."

Lizzie steps in between them, and Kathy and Kathryn vacate the dance floor to stand by Olivia. I stand there watching with bated breath wondering what will unfold. Our families are tightly knit. These are bonds forged by years of friendship, if not by blood, and this kind of drama has never happened in my family. *Ever.*

"Stop being a brat and go home, Oli," Kathryn says, as she looks at Olivia with pursed lips and her arms crossed against her chest. "If you aren't the center of attention..."

"Olivia Victoria Reese. So help me God. Get out of here before I drag you out myself!" Kathy threatens through gritted teeth. She points towards the exit. "NOW!"

Olivia scampers from the group and jogs up the steps, and then runs out of the nightclub. I chase after her because, after all, she is my sister, and even though she doesn't deserve an ounce of my pity, my heart tightens thinking how humiliating that little scene must have been for her. As I walk out the door of Hellbenders, I stumble on a familiar face- the one I haven't been able to get out of my head for months. My plus one for tonight. I gave up on the idea she'd actually show up.

I gaze at her beautiful blue eyes, and my hand instinctively reaches out to touch the soft, perfect porcelain skin of her face. "You came," I whisper in amazement and disbelief. Her soft giggles make me forget my name and where I am, and why I ran out of Hellbenders in the first place.

"I did," she replies with a smile, bringing out the cute dimples in both of her cheeks.

With a racing mind and a hopeful heart I realize right then and there it's my turn to find love and start a new adventure, and after all that I've been through, why would I deny myself that chance? Acting on pure instinct, I cradle her face with my hands and bring my lips to hers. The connection is soft and tender, and has my heart tied up in fucking knots. As we kiss, I feel her hands wrap around my waist, her fingers exploring the ridges of my abdomen through my dress shirt. The more I kiss her, the more I want to know more of her. With ragged breaths, I reluctantly break our kiss, and looking into her gorgeous eyes, I speak the truth.

"Feel free to slap me now. I couldn't help myself."

"Neither could I, Jax. Neither could I."

To be continued....

SPECIAL EXCERPT

Please enjoy this excerpt from:

WE MET ON A TRAIN

IMY SANTIAGO

▲

RISC BOOKS, NEW YORK

TRIGGER WARNING:

The following **work of fiction** contains crude language and violence, and includes subject matter such as Alcoholism, Domestic Violence, Child Abuse, and Anxiety, Panic and Post-traumatic Stress Disorder. The scene you are about to read **may trigger** certain feelings and urges upon those who have experienced any of the aforementioned. This excerpt is intended for individuals over the age of eighteen. Your discretion is **strongly** advised.

PROLOGUE

Seventeen years ago

"Dottie!" my father roars, as soon as he opens the front door, and slams it shut–almost rattling it off from its hinges.

I throw my notebook aside, not caring about the worksheet my stupid math teacher gave our class for homework. I seriously doubt long division will serve any valuable purpose in life when I finally grow up and leave this hell-hole. I sit up in bed. Even at twelve, I can tell what state my father is in just by the sound of his voice. Nah... This comes as no surprise, because the truth is, we are used to this. As the saying goes, this is the story of my life.

"Dottie!" he roars again, his speech slurred–no doubt because he stopped at a bar after work instead of coming straight home. You'd think a detective with the police force would know how to behave, but no, not Timothy Pryce. No one knows him like we know him, and if mom doesn't respond soon, there will be hell to pay.

My heart is racing in my chest like a jackhammer because my dad is an impatient man. Blame it on his job, or my mom. I don't know, but one thing I know is I've never met a more hateful, terrible, and scary man. I hear his footsteps coming down the hall, and I know I should get off my ass to run and hide. But I can't because I'm frozen in place.

I'm breathing faster, and I'm pretty sure every hair on my body is standing on edge. I reach out for my pencil with a trembling hand; its point is dulled down to nothing. I know that if Dad opens the door, I'm going to say something smart, and then he's going to remove his belt, and hit me repeatedly. It's happened so many times before, and I'm always the first who gets to feel his wrath. I'm learning to defend myself, and this stupid pencil is my only form of defense.

I'm the youngest of four, unplanned and unwanted- or so I've been told many times before. Mom tried some creative ways to get rid of me, but in the end, Darwin's rule of survival of the fittest won. I didn't ask to be born, yet here I am.

Dad's footsteps stop in front of my door, and the round doorknob turns, its characteristic squeak scaring the crap out of me. I release a shaky breath and say a quick prayer. *Dear God, help me now.*

Another set of steps come rapping against the beaten hardwood floor. They belong to my mother, and judging by their slow approach, I can tell Mom doesn't want to be here either.

"There you are, stupid woman." I hear my father's muffled, angry voice through the wooden door.

"Good evening, Tim," my mother greets him, in her characteristic saccharine voice. "I was outside. You called?"

Slap.

"You watch your tone with me, you stupid bitch," I hear Dad tell Mom.

I get up from my bed, ready to open the door to defend my mother. I hear her muted sobs, and I'm positive her hand is already soothing her battered face. But as I stand, a path of wetness stains the front of my pants. I've peed myself again. I tiptoe to the door and place my ear against the wood.

"Why, Tim. Why have you hit me?" Mom cries softly.

"You're a stupid woman who doesn't answer when I call! Now stop acting so fucking injured and get me dinner. I'm hungry and I've had a bad day."

"Yes, Tim. I made you your favorite. Ribeye steak—bloody just how you like it—with mashed potatoes and peas. I even baked brownies," Mom whispers, her voice wavering. She clears her throat and says, "Come, Tim. It's on the hot plate. Would you like a beer, or something else?"

I can't hear anything beyond that. I step back from the door. Once I'm standing by my bed, I open my fist and the pencil I was clutching on falls to the floor. It lands on the eraser end and bounces a few times before it lands flat against the floorboards, clicking the stark quiet of my room. As Mom's and Dad's footsteps trail away down the hallway, I let out a huge sigh of relief.

My hands are shaking. I grab fresh clothes with the intention of taking a shower. As I shut the drawers, my sister Amanda Rose knocks on my door. I can tell because she always knocks three times. Grabbing a towel, I cover the front of my pants, and run to the door. I open it and she slips in, her dark auburn hair shielding one side of her pale, tear-stricken face. Her crisp green eyes are red from crying, and her breaths are short, as if she's holding back sobs.

I drop the towel and hug my sister. I don't care if I reek of piss, or if I get her flowery pajamas dirty. My sister is my world, and even though I'm four years younger, I feel the need to protect and console her.

"Are you okay, Rose?" I whisper into her hair, and at my question, she breaks down. After crying for a bit, I pull back and keep her at arm's length.

She looks down at me. "Jesus. You pissed yourself again?" Rose whispers, and looks me in the eye. "Let's run away, Evan. Just you and me," she rambles breathlessly. "Any place is better than here. Pack a bag and meet me in my room at midnight. We'll go out my window, okay?"

"Okay," I mumble, feeling uneasy. With a shaky nod, Rose leaves my room and closes the door quietly behind her. I grab my clothes, and open the door, practically racing down the narrow hallway to the bathroom. Once there, I take off my clothes, and turn on the faucet in the shower to heat the water. As I wait, I look in the mirror and what I see disappoints me.

The image before me is not what I want to see. My body shows years of abuse, and that's only on the outside. Bruises and welts; starting on my chest and working their way down to the backs of my legs and up my back. I've never deserved any of this, regardless of what my parents think or say. There are times where I sit in the darkness of my closet and pretend I live another life far away from here.

Shaking my head at my reflection, I get into the shower and try to make it fast. If I don't make it to bed on time, that will be another fight, and the truth is, regardless if Mom steps in to help me, I don't want to get hit with that belt again. My skin is still tender after the beating I got two nights ago for not taking out the trash. Turning off the faucet, I dry and dress myself in record time, and brush my teeth before I sprint from the bathroom towards my room.

I climb in bed and turn off the lamp on my nightstand. I listen to my parents' retreating footsteps; their voices echoing down the narrow hallway. And when they rise, I place the headphones of my cassette player over my head. I rewind the worn tape, searching for my one of my favorite songs, Metallica's "Nothing Else Matters," which I've played a lot as of late. As the introductory guitar chords play, my eyelids grow heavy, and if only for the briefest of moments, I find peace and drift to sleep.

Something is shaking me, and when I realize there's sunlight filling the room, I rub my eyes, trying to wake up. It takes me a minute to find my bearings.

"Evan!" my mother cries, her eyes open wide and pleading.

"Mom?" I ask, in between yawns.

"Rose... Where is she?" Mom asks, her voice raised and panicked. "Evan! Answer me!" Mom cries, and that's when I sit up in alarm.

"Rose!" I scream as I jump from the bed, my bare feet racing towards her room. I look everywhere for signs of my sister, but she is gone. I sit by the foot of her window, and bring my knees close to my chest. I cry hard when I realize what's happened. *Rose left. She ran away without me. Now I have to deal with these two monsters all by myself.*

I wipe the tears away with my knuckles, and when I look up, Dad looks down at me, clutching his black, leather belt with one hand, and the other scratching his beard.

"Get up from the floor, Evan," Dad bellows, his anger spreading over me, making my skin crawl. "You are a man, but if you insist on crying like a girl, then I'll give you a few good reasons to keep crying like one."

Splat.

The first blow of the belt against my leg singes my skin. I want to scream and cry, but I say nothing and I most certainly don't move an inch. Silent, fat tears drop from my eyes and roll down my cheeks.

Splat.

The second blow against the skin of my stomach makes me double over in pain, and as soon as I hit the ground, I lose count of all the blows that follow. I also try to tune out Mom's wails as she gets a beating of her own for trying to stop Dad from hitting me.

I never imagined knowing the true meaning of hatred at only twelve, and I, Evan Pryce, truly deeply hate my parents. I hate Rose for abandoning me, and I hate Caleb and Seth, my older twin brothers for going off to college and leaving me here alone with our fucked up parents.

I hate the world.

I *hate* my life.

In the Rhythm of the Dance

A poem by Marian Girling

Lost in the rhythm of the dance
Two lovers move
Hips swaying freely, hands clasped
She follows where her partner leads.

Feet move in synchronicity
Hands flick, grasp, and mime.
Eyes keep contact with each turn
Bodies both in time

Their moves are sinuous and lithe
Moving as one
Enthralled, enticed, engulfed
In the *Rumba*, the dance of **love.**

ACKNOWLEDGEMENTS

finding Reese. took longer than expected to complete as there were many setbacks: life, illness, injury, and even moments of mourning. By the grace of God I pulled through, but I didn't manage this accomplishment on my own.

To my fiancé, Jc, thank you for keeping me grounded and for micromanaging my butt to get the job done. Babe, thank you for those motivational videos and memes you supplied me with when things got unpleasant in my little bubble, and for reminding me each day why I do what I do. I love you, and couldn't ask for someone better in the Producer's chair or as a partner in life.

To my daughter Izzabella Grazia, I'm still trying to make good on my promise to give you a home and room of your own. I know watching Mommy typing away isn't easy; one day you'll understand all the sacrifices Mommy and Daddy have made to give you the life you deserve. Mommy is still trying. I love you with all that I have. Always.

To my readers, I am overjoyed and humbled you have embraced these characters and have given them a home inside your hearts. My most sincere gratitude goes to you. Thank you.

I want to extend my gratitude to Kimberly Ito, my editor at Sakura Editing, who gave me the quickest, harshest crash course lesson in grammar, syntax, tense, and sentence structure with chasing Reese. I vowed to blow you away with finding Reese., and I think I did. I can confidently say my writing style has grown, and it is all thanks to you. You are my secret weapon, Kimberly, and I will always count on you for the toughest, realest feedback. Thanks to you I am a better writer.

My thankfulness goes out to Marisa Shor, my cover designer at Cover Me, Darling, for yet another awesome book cover. Nailed it! You are not only an artiste, but an incredible loving person with the perfect personality to match! I love that one year later our e-mail messages haven't changed, and get more creative and hysterical with each new project. Thank you.

I huge shout out goes out to Cori Pitts, Marian Girling, and Theresa Sederholt for proofreading this book. Thank you for your insightfulness and comments which had me laughing more than once.

A remarkable thank you goes out to Stacey Blake with Champagne Formats for stepping in to format the beautiful final product that is the eBook version of this novel. Thank you for fitting me in at the last minute even though you were booked solid for nine weeks.

To the amazing core of women at Wordsmyth Inc., captained by my PA Marian Girling, and supported fiercely by Ashley Heather, Cori Pitts, Sheena Graham, Felicia Rodríguez, Sunshine Lykos, Iris Taveras, Terri Turner, Lisa Skonecki Jaskie, LJ Knox, Sue Bashford, Pam Lilley, and Ginelle Blanch. Another outpouring of appreciation goes out to Shirley Wilkinson and Courtney Shockey for being mega SAFELIGHT fans. Thank you for accepting me into your hearts, and for braving all social media platforms to support my work, and for alpha, beta, and proofreading finding Reese., and for every mention, "like" and tweet. Your kindness and thoughtfulness brings me to my knees, and I most certainly couldn't have released this book if not for you. Thank you for keeping me grounded, and for reeling me in when I go astray.

To Emily James and Linda Merkel, my Twitter and Author Signing Event allies, thank you for your unwavering support.

To my fellow Indie Authors and Writers on all platforms, especially Theresa Sederholt, Alannah Carbonneau, A.M. Wilson, Autumn Grey, and so many others, I could never repay you for your kindness, and I feel immensely blessed with your friendship. Thank you for being there for me, and for cheering me on.

To my esteemed friends in the blogging community, Sarah Kenslee Erinn (*Hooks & Books*), Chantel Sharp (*Smutty Book Friends*), Sunshine Lykos (*Saucy Books*), Michelle Simm (*One Click Aholics*), Lena Dublin (*Smut and Bonbons*), Dawn Vickers (*Reading The Sheets*), Danita Montes (*Nerdy Chic*), Jessica Cecconi (*JaM Book Blog*), Caryn Watson (*Watz Books & Teasers*), Louise Hunter (*Books all things Paranormal and Romance*), Marian Girling (*A Book Lover's Emporium Book Blog*), Meaghan Royce (*Love Infinity Book Blog*), the Admins at *Writers Can't Shine Without Readers, and Fictional Men's Room for Book Ho's,* among many, *many* others. Thank you for promoting and supporting my dreams unceasingly. I am humbled and honored.

To anyone who has ever thought about writing, but fears the process or feels like they're not good enough... Please know you are capable of achieving anything you put your mind into, and there are people in this community who will support your journey. Just take the leap, have hope, and *never* give up.

Never in a thousand years did I envision writing a book, let alone two, and the SAFELIGHT series is far from over: saving Reese. will be landing sometime before March 2016.

Love you all madly,
-i

P.S. Please feel free to join the SAFELIGHT series discussion group on Facebook.

Trifecta https://www.facebook.com/groups/1483689511891645/

ABOUT THE WRITER

IMY SANTIAGO

I love to read stories about loss, heartache and redemption, so it didn't shock me that I would end up writing stories revolving around those central themes. I write with my heart, using my life experiences and emotions to dictate the tone and path in which my fictional characters embark in my long list of stories. I believe in the power of friendship and to always remain hopeful because life is always full of pleasant surprises. If you were to ask me if I consider myself an author, I would tell you no–I am not. I'm just a girl who loves a good story that makes you ponder life choices and the darkness that envelopes a broken heart. My stories are about loss, friendship, hope, and love. When I'm not writing, I'm enjoying a quiet life with my family on Long Island New York (yes, on–that's how Long Islanders roll).

Connect with me:

W www.imysantiago.com
@SAFELIGHTauthor
@legalimy
ImySantiagolegalimy
@legalimy
@legalimy
@legalimy
tsu @legalimy

SAFELIGHT Playlist:
http:open.spotify.com/user/legali
my/playlist/26L8Q9AUYh36Zmxq
gby2m
Goodreads
http://www.goodreads.com/auth
or/show/8425449.Imy_Santiago
Amazon
amazon.com/author/imysantiago

www.ingramcontent.com/pod-product-compliance
Lightning Source LLC
Chambersburg PA
CBHW022042240626

47154CB00007B/2522